ALACE
SWEETS

I0662873

MariaLisa deMora

Edited by Hot Tree Editing

Cover designed by Debera Kuntz

First Published 2017

ISBN 13: 978-1-946738-08-0

DEDICATION

Revenge really IS sweet. ~ Alace Sweets

To my friends who have odder obsessions than I
do. Thanks for making me look normal.

CONTENTS

ACKNOWLEDGMENTS

I must confess to a lifelong morbid fascination with serial killers.

Most likely, it can be blamed on the era in which I grew up. While other generations fielded their share of murderers, my imagination was supplied a diet of the unbelievablely intense stories of the Manson family, Zodiac killer, Gacy, Bundy, Son of Sam, and the Hillside Strangler.

Sensational reporting meant my developing sense of right versus wrong was bathed in a stew of gloriously gory articles, movies, and documentaries. Pair that with the perplexing adult discussions I often overheard about seemingly normal people who went on to commit atrocious crimes, and you've got the right setting for the making of a hell of a tale.

As she's written into my story, the character Alace doesn't exist. At least, as far as I know. To me, this protagonist presents an opportunity to put together an interesting blend of situational inspiration, allows me to invent symbol-rich scenes that take your breath away, and then enables me to mix those with a dash of strategic gender role subversion. All to create a believable monster. Her very name is a metaphor. I love it.

I appreciate Becky Johnson and her staff at Hot Tree Editing more than they know. As ever, they helped me take a good story and make it better. I also want to say a huge thank you to Debera Kuntz for her cover design. She took the clay of my rough idea and ran with it, executed in a way that far outstripped my meager imaginings, and created a piece of art.

My alpha crew were astonishing and supportive beyond belief. Kelsi, Kori, Megan, Jamey, and Jesse, I want to thank you for NOT running screaming from the manuscript!

To you, faithful friends and new readers alike, I say get ready for a ride you will not soon forget. Welcome to the world of Alace Sweets. When the laws of men fail, the rules of Alace prevail. I truly hope you enjoy her story.

Woofully yours,
~ML

CHAPTER ONE

Two minutes and forty-seven seconds.

That's how long it took to die inside.

Alace knew it was longer. The whole encounter had been so much longer than that. About seventeen lifetimes, that's how it seemed at the time. From the moment she rounded the corner of the alleyway and saw Trev and his posse waiting for her, a line of bodies spread out across the space, their practiced actions so coordinated, she knew she couldn't be their first target. The instant she grasped that this wouldn't be something she could outrun or avoid—and would be finally tossed to the side, landing on the cobblestones like nothing more than a used tissue—seventeen lifetimes seemed about right.

No. The not-quite three minutes—and that's how their defense attorney categorized it, minimizing it as less time than a parking meter put on the clock for a quarter—was all the jury saw. A portion of her attack had been videoed on a phone, the footage whispered about in the hallways and bathrooms of the warehouse where she and her attackers all worked— the only employer left in the tiny New York town where Alace had lived all her life. Shaky footage discovered by a man's wife one night when he was too drunk to discourage her exploration. A discovery shared with the police who pieced together that the blurry face held against the hood of a car, cheek flattened to the metal, white panties gagging her screams, must be the girl claiming rape at the local hospital.

She hadn't named Trev when she went to the ER. *God, no, I've never been stupid.* If she'd named him, there would have been no saving her. She would have been found drowned in the river, another victim of the particular version of depression that seemed to run as a contagion in the little town. A taint acquired through exposure to the small pond bullies cultivated amidst the economic woes of the region.

Alace was just the daughter of the town slut, not even a father's name to claim. It'd be the joke of the century if *she* had named names when asking for the slim care available at the tiny hospital. Blood tests and a pill to make sure their seed didn't stick. That's all she'd been looking for, the gift of reassurance, but none of that came without a price. With the local bleak climate, even her battered body wasn't unique enough to justify a second glance.

Hopelessness breeds violence, and their town had ample evidence that crop was well rooted.

It wasn't until the next girl turned up dead as well as raped that Alace realized exactly what they'd risk covering their tracks. Same age, same desperate confrontation, but a different, *very* permanent outcome because Tansy had talked, and talked, and talked until she wasn't in any shape to talk anymore.

Two minutes and forty-seven seconds.

That's the length of time the jury was required to watch the large screen brought into the courtroom for that command performance.

She sometimes wondered how long Tansy lasted.

Alace didn't look at the projected images. She would have blocked out the sounds with her hands if she could, but the lawyer assigned to prosecute Trev and his hounds had warned her against that kind of avoidance. Said it could look like she was culpable, like she was trying to withdraw from owning the acts committed on her body. His contradictions didn't make sense, but it didn't matter. Frozen on the bench behind the barrier wall, separated from her attackers by only a few feet, forced to breathe their air, Alace sat quietly, but she wouldn't watch. Couldn't, not and stay sane.

She'd kept her eyes on the judge, noting he avoided the screen, too. But, of course, he'd seen it before since just the admittance of the video was a contentious point for the defense. Argued and argued behind closed doors, while the rustling masses stayed seated in the courtroom. Whispers and pointed fingers bringing the strain of humiliation down on Alace. Regardless of his angled chin turning his face away, she knew the man in the robes already had seen it, forced to watch and make a ruling, implacably throwing his weight on the side of the evidence.

The jury had watched. Some showing an apathetic disbelief, some with expressions of disgust, and one woman had worn such a look of avaricious delight on her face Alace had stared at her for long moments, uncertain of what she was seeing.

"Be quiet, bitch." That had been the only phrase grunted loud enough for the cell phone speaker to pick up. Alace heard the words and was transported out of there, landing back in her crawling skin plastered against cold steel. *The taste of her own panties shoved into her throat, heaving against the cloying feel of wet cotton, tasting the acid tang of ammonia, telltale evidence of her terror. Strands of her long hair in her mouth, tangled on her tongue, shoved in and held in place by the gag.* "Be quiet, bitch."

Alace wrestled her way back to reality in time to hear the sound of ripping fabric tear through the air of the courtroom. That would be her shirt, torn along the side seams so they could grapple at her breasts with flesh claws made from hands.

Squeak. Squeak. Squeak. That everyday sound was the suspension of the car as it rocked back and forth, a timeless motion that should have been comforting. Transformed to violence, the sound was obscene.

Sweat-wet flesh slapping together shared space with broken howls and cries. His thighs had been hammering against her haunches as her throat convulsed around a scream. Thick ribbons of bruises had banded her belly and hips for weeks, darkness slowly bleeding to purple and then green, yellow reminders of danger remaining the longest.

A loud scratching noise, sounding like beetle's legs scrambling for purchase in a hot frying pan. Her nails had clawed at the unforgiving metal surface, bending back and ripping her nailbeds to the quick again and again, wrists pinned in place over her head. She fought so hard the pressure of his hand had torn all the skin off her right wrist, leaving a raw band of flesh that had burned and bled. Alace circled the long-healed wound with her palm, covering it protectively, knowing the action was far too little, too late.

Alace had waited, counting down every damned second of the playback from the worst day of her life.

The entire charade inside the courtroom wasn't anything she'd asked for. In fact, when the police had shown at work and demanded to talk to her, she had told them there was nothing to report. One man, a detective, had looked at her with sad eyes. "I know your mother," he had said, and she'd immediately directed her eyes down, not wanting to see the kindly expression morph to disdain on his face. His words didn't make sense, and she dismissed them out of hand, only keeping the parts that fit into her view of the world. "Alace, what those men did was not okay. They hurt you, but they did so much worse to Tansy. We can do this without you, but with you is easier."

He'd had to come back three days in a row before she would say anything other than, "Nothing happened." Still, the sad-eyed detective had eventually worn her down, his murmured kind words and façade of caring too unfamiliar to resist.

In the end, it was all for naught.

"Not guilty." The woman who'd been wild-eyed during the rape playback read the verdict, her voice shaking.

What if? Alace's brain was plagued with the ideas. *What if I'd spoken up first?* She likely would have preceded Tansy on a walk off the train trestle. Would it have been a fair trade, if Tansy lived?

Tansy had a family who loved and mourned her, attending each day of the trial even if the charges for their daughter's death weren't on the docket. Weeping when Trev and his posse had been paraded in and out of the courtroom, the mother with her hand covering the bottom half of her face, capturing and holding her cries as the verdict rang through the room. *I should have done something.*

That night, Alace went to bed for the last time in her little room on the top floor of the hotel in town where she'd lived all her life, literally, having been born there eighteen years ago. The sign on the marquee read Palace Suites. At night, the P was dark, leaving just her name blazoned against the sky.

Alace Sweets.

CHAPTER TWO

Seventeen years later

Alace swam sluggishly up from sleep, feeling a pleasant burning stretch of muscles well used as she shifted on the surface of the too-comfortable bed. The rise was uncharacteristically slow at first, but as her body and brain awakened, the last moments were a rush to full consciousness, her instincts screaming at her to run, hide, get away.

She was a firm believer in listening to gut feelings. Of course she was. Those hunches were the only thing that had kept her alive and free over the years. She'd learned from past mistakes, however, and didn't give those vague misgivings a chance to push her to panic, instead, holding tight to her better sense. That better sense told her first, she needed to know where she was to evaluate the danger, and second, running without a plan nearly always turned out badly.

Distant voices filled the air, at first just a quiet, near-subliminal murmur of sound. She heard a blending of vocal patterns rising and falling close by with a considerately moderated volume, which meant one of those voices knew of their sleeping guest. Not quite as senseless as the sound of rain on a tin roof, but nothing to further raise the freak level of her nerves. So, she focused, listening hard.

Eyes closed, she homed in on one voice. Male, gruff and hard, filled with gravel from whiskey and smokes. *Nate*. She shifted on the mattress, feeling the rough scratch of flannel sheets along every inch of bare skin. *Nate's bed*.

Not the worst thing, having her boss take her home after work so they could fuck. He'd termed it as giving her a chance to finish what she'd started by wearing short shorts and a boob-exposing crop tank to work. She was inclined to just call it fun. Plus, Nate was safe, never once pinging her radar as anything except what he seemed to be: a hardworking business owner in a small town who was lonely. She generally trusted her radar as much as she did her gut.

Working as a waitress in a sleazy strip club meant her wardrobe was limited. She could dress conservatively and starve on the thin slide of tips that barely covered a 15-percent requirement, or don a costume to look as if every customer could have her for the cost of a single drink. Doing the latter meant

Alace could afford to eat regularly, as well as rent her own single bedroom apartment in a decent complex with security. *In this gig, I'm mostly incentivized by eating*. She justified her actions by habit. It might be true, but it didn't mean the role her clothing bought her fit comfortably.

The voices drew closer, and Alace returned her attention to what she could pick out of the conversation. Not much. Her success at eavesdropping seemed limited only to Nate's side of things, but she still heard enough to have her scrambling across the bed to where she remembered her clothing being tossed last night. "Yeah, she's here, but I'm telling you she was here all night long, Ike."

Ike was Irving Duncan, and if he was looking for her, it would be in his official capacity as sheriff. Which meant her time in this town might be done.

At least I already concluded my business. She shrugged into her shirt, fluffing the bottom edge to free it from the curve of her breasts. Slipping the shorts up her legs, she gave a little hop to get them into place over the apple of her ass, buttoning them as she scanned the floor for her socks and footwear. Tugging her last boot over her foot, she eyeballed the windows in Nate's bedroom, picking out the one next to his side of the bed as the most likely escape point. But the sound of a rough palm sliding across the wooden door stopped her in her tracks.

Out of habit, she checked herself quickly, glancing down to verify her clothes were clean, unstained by anything except the drink spilled on her by the drunken bachelor who'd tried multitasking at the wrong time last night. *Good as it's going to get*, she thought, twisting to face the door and schooling her face to a pleasant expression.

Nate's face appeared in the opening, his chin jerking back in surprise at finding her not only awake but dressed and apparently waiting for him. *If you only knew, honey.*

"Pauline, Ike is here. He's got some questions for us." Nate was being generous with his attribution for the questioning. Ike only wanted to talk to her, she knew. Pauline was her long-time cover name, and one she would readily respond to, even in her sleep. Along with about fifteen others. One for nearly every year of her newborn life. That thought took her aback for a moment. Since this gig was winding down to an end, it was nearly time to pick a new, seventeenth alias. *What the hell name starts with Q?* Giving a mental shrug, she thought, *I get out of this, I'll give Regg a call. He'll know.*

"Is everything okay?" She crossed the distance between them and leaned in so Nate could kiss her forehead, something she'd noted he liked doing. She let him wrap an arm around her shoulders, drawing her close to his side before he turned so they faced Ike.

"Nothing to worry about, baby girl." Nate's voice dropped into the lower registers, and she shivered at a sudden memory. That was how he'd sounded just before he buried his face between her legs last night, finding that delicate balance of aggressive licking and kissing, and a fragile tenderness that had been missing from her life for a long time. *I'll miss you, big guy.*

"Hey, Ike." She offered a little wave with the hand not currently tucked into Nate's back pocket. From the outside, it probably looked like they were a longtime couple, only Nate would know that before last night all he'd gotten access to were her forehead and fingers. She'd gently rebuffed all his overtures while keeping the door open for use when it mattered most. *Like last night,* she thought, keeping the smile on her face small. "What's up?"

"Hey, Pauline. Sorry to bother you and Nate." Ike gestured towards the front room, and Nate led her towards the couch there. "I got some bad news, honey." Tipping her head to one side, she settled next to Nate, letting him hold her close. She rested one palm on his thick thigh, allowing her fingers to curve possessively around it. "Alan Trueward, how well did...do you know him?"

Well, hell. They found him already.

She carefully didn't let any of her thoughts show on her face. Stoicism was something she had long practiced, really since her first breath, if she were honest. All through her youth growing up in that tiny town, she'd had to hide everything inside her. All the pain and anger, the fear and loss. Getting out of bed in the morning meant sliding that particular mask into place, and she was so good at it now it was first nature, bypassing that second nature bullshit normal people lived with.

"Decent guy, he takes care of the girls." She purposely let her smile broaden slightly. "He and April—" Alace tipped her head so she was grinning up at Nate. "—are quite the item." Fraternization between employees at the club was frowned on, but Nate hadn't told them to stop, which meant he probably didn't know the reason behind it in the first place. Alace did. Alan was the entire reason she was in town, after all. Regg had sussed him out nearly two years ago, and she'd started laying plans. It's what she did these days.

"Did you see Alan last night?"

Boy did I ever! I saw him on his knees calling out to a god who didn't give one shit that the man was about to die. Just like Alan didn't give one shit about those little girls he liked to rub off on when he was a teacher. Just like that judge didn't give a shit about those little girls, giving Alan a commuted sentence because he "had such future contributions to give to society" and ignored his existing contributions to eleven little girls' nightmares. Eleven future husbands who would have their hands full considering the woman made for them had been so abused. Alace firmly believed that every person had their one true love, and she just as firmly believed that Alan Trueward did not exist in that column for any woman, or man. God couldn't be that cruel.

Yeah, I saw him. Saw him kneel. Saw him fall. Kicked dirt over his blood and shoveled it into the well after him. Saw the blade rise and fall, a glittering promise in every stroke seeing that taking Alan's life was actually giving him peace, too. I promised him he'd never feel those urges again. His voice begging, pleading loudly, "I'm sick. I know. It's a sickness." He was sick, all right. Sick to death. I promised him release, and I always keep my promises.

"No, he wasn't working. Bobby was behind the bar."

Nate gave her a squeeze and interjected, "He was supposed to, baby girl. I had to call Bobby when Alan didn't show." She looked up at Nate, seeing the crinkles in the corners of his eyes that told her he was a smiler. One of the reasons she hated using him like she had. *You're a good guy, Nate. Never stop being such a good guy.* "You got in a little late, didn't know we'd had to switch things up."

She rolled her eyes and looked back at Ike. "Rosalinda was my ride." That would be all she had to say. Rosalinda, who lived in her apartment complex and had been her ride last night, was notoriously late for everything. The joke was she'd be late for her own funeral.

Ike grinned, and on cue, Nate chuckled. All was well in he-man land, since they thought it was cute an attractive girl like Rosalinda got so caught up in making herself pretty for the customers to the point she lost track of time. Alace could tell them a different story. It wasn't getting dolled up that took all of Rosa's attention, it was girding her courage to enter the world of men again. Her last boyfriend had been free with his fists, something Alace had learned and then taken upon herself to discourage the ex's behavior in her particular fashion. *One body they won't find.* Most of her bodies were never found. One, she was fucking exceptional at her calling, and two, she was also fucking lucky and knew it.

Ike cleared his throat, and Nate shifted beside her, pulling her closer, and she knew the bomb was about to drop. She prepared herself to bring forth shock and denial, two emotions expected when a death was pronounced.

"Not many folks know, but Alan is a registered sex offender." Alace's shock wasn't feigned; she wasn't expecting that to come out of Ike's mouth. She let her brow furrow, waiting, hating herself a little when she cringed into Nate's side. "His crime was such that while he was registered, and his employer knew, we decided to keep his past quiet. Given his line of work, it shouldn't have been an issue. However, it seems it caught up with him after all."

Well, yeah. He fucked eleven little girls, tore their childhood to shreds along with their bodies, stealing innocence, ladling it into a bucket he drained like a demon. She'd ripped his dick off, using pliers and a torsion technique she'd taught herself. *At least I waited until he was dead.*

"Did you see anyone out of place in the club last night, or at all? Recently, or not? Someone who either you never saw before or who looked out of place?"

Shaking her head again, Alace asked the stupidest question she could think of. "Do you think he's okay?" *As if I give a fuck.*

"We hope he is." Alace blinked at those words because they meant his body hadn't been located yet. *Hallelujah.* "But his apartment was trashed, the door left unlocked and open. His neighbor called us this morning. That's why we're starting to backtrack to see if we can find the last person who saw him." She blinked again.

She hadn't taken Alan from his apartment. Stupidest move in the book, if you weren't a female ninja or bodybuilder. Never, ever take a mark from a place where they're comfortable or established. They would use things as weapons you'd never consider. She'd made that mistake once, nine years ago when she was called Helene, never again. She'd made a lot of mistakes over the years, which was why she knew herself to be more lucky than smart.

Alace had waited until he'd stopped to gas up his car two nights ago on his way home. While watching him intently over the months she'd been in town, she'd made a study of his predictable habits. Such as how he always pulled around to the side of the building and parked to go in and pay. A cash and carry guy, Alan didn't even have a debit card. The security camera had taken only a quick moment to loop with a static image

16

and left her free to crawl into the back seat of his car to wait. No more than five sweat-filled minutes later, he had climbed in the front seat, and she'd slung her thickest garrote over his head, wedging her folded knee against the back of his seat as she leaned backwards and out of reach.

As people do, he'd gone for the source of pain first, bending his fingernails back to the quick, clawing at the strand of wire choking him unconscious. No shouts, no muss, no fuss. No camera meant it was easy to secure and then shove him to the side before she drove away, taking him to the old farmstead she'd scoped out weeks before. It had once been used as a sheep farm, and she'd amused herself afterwards by talking to a pretend audience of none between huffs of air as she shoveled, then wrestled the heavy cement cover back into place, sealing his circular tomb. "What's that girl? Little Alan's down the well? Oh, no! Whatever shall we do?"

But, if there'd been someone to come along behind her and go through his stuff? That could mean there had been more eyes on him than just hers, which might mean her actions outside the gas station convenience store might not have gone as unremarked as she wanted. She hadn't pegged any other tails on the man, hadn't caught sight of anyone who raised her hackles. *Who could it be? Shit.*

"I was off the night before last." She shook her head, pressing her cheek to Nate's chest. "You think something's happened to him, don't you?"

"Ike don't know anything just yet, baby girl." Nate's arm gave her a squeeze. "He's just asking if you've seen anyone lately who felt off."

Even if she had, there'd be no finger-pointing from her. Any questions asked might circle back around to the ones she didn't want to answer. Her plan was another two weeks in this town, then Pauline would be moving on, leaving no one but Nate sad to see the back of her. Alace always made sure of that.

"I don't remember seeing anyone paying special attention to Alan." She decided to see how much Ike would give her, and asked, "What'd he do that got him in trouble? You said he's a sex offender?"

Her shiver wasn't faked this time. *Sex offender.* Weak words strung together by male adjudicators who wanted an inoffensive way to describe a man's physical acts. Oh, sure, women could and did become sexual predators, but that was far less often than their male counterparts.

Sex offender was how men wanted to see things. How they wanted everyone to agree things should be. In many men's eyes, all sex was consensual, like what she and Nate had done so energetically in his bed last night.

Offense, well you could take offense to nearly anything these days. It could be offensive to speak in ignorance of someone's religion or political stance. Offend by standing facing the wrong direction when someone entered a room. Offend by breathing, sometimes. All that flagrant offense meant the word was diminished. When everything was offensive, nothing truly was.

Sex offender.

Alan was a pedophile, a rapist, a spirit thief who stole children's dreams. "What'd he do?"

Ike surprised her for a second time that day by telling part of the real story. "He hurt a bunch of kids, Pauline. That's why I want to find him. He…" Ike hesitated, then forged ahead when she held his gaze unflinching. "He goes to the clinic and takes medicine. It makes it so he can't hurt girls like that again. He didn't show up yesterday for his prescription. So, it's urgent I find him. You understand I can't—" He swallowed hard, and she saw how tough it had been on him to stay quiet about Alan's crimes. Probably forced on him by someone at a higher level, leaving Ike positioned to be an accomplice if Alan raped another child and he'd known what kind of risk was living next door to good people he'd sworn faithfully to protect. Seeing that, she liked Ike even more, because in his face, she read his emotions and knew in her gut he didn't have a single shit to give if Alan was hurt. His only concern was for any possible victims caught up in the crossfire. "I have to find him, Pauline. You sure there wasn't anyone you remember who watched him strangely or maybe asked about him?"

She was shaking her head before he finished speaking. "No, Ike. Swear. I'd tell you." Okay, that last was a lie, but she hadn't seen anything, so overall it was the truth. *Close enough for hand grenades.*

"Okay." He made a soothing motion with his hand that Nate unconsciously mimicked, his palm smoothing up and down her arm. "I'm sure I'll find him, and there'll be a good reason for everything."

Yeah, he was a sick fuck who needed to die.

CHAPTER THREE

"Seriously?" Alace shook her head as she fished the piece of plastic out of the envelope. She had a phone propped on her shoulder, held in place by the tilt of her head. Regg laughed in her ear, his voice smooth and quiet. "This is the best Q name you can think of?"

Querida Pansy O'Dell. She sighed, loud enough to ensure Regg heard.

"When you already know it's too late, why do you bother arguing, honey?" Reginald Davies spoke softly. "I have everything setup like I do every time. There's a complex enough trail for your prospective employers to follow for seven years." That was their gambit, always. Enough people were bitten by the seven-year itch that it was a safe gamble employers and rental agents wouldn't check past that period of time. Regg had been her paper guy from the beginning, referred by a "friend" of her mother's during a drunken conversation.

Alace had locked away the information and run with it after the trial, taking to her heels the very next day, and taking her mother's sock of emergency money with her. Only a couple of thousand, it hadn't lasted long, but it hadn't needed to. Revenge was a lucrative business, and one she'd investigated long before she left the no-tell hotel that spawned her.

"You know what Querida means, right?" Upending the envelope, she captured the other items with her free hand. Social security card, credit card, bank card, contact list. "Everything's here. We're good."

"*I'm* good, you mean. And of course, everything's there. I mailed it myself." Now Regg sounded huffy, and she grinned, knowing it was a fraud but still determined to soothe his imaginary ego. Regg was one of the most down-to-earth guys she'd never met, and once he'd learned the real reason for her documentation needs, he'd gotten behind her plan a hundred percent.

"You're the best, Regg. Everyone knows that. Thank you, honey." Still grinning, she listened to him laugh, the sound of his humor cut off by the call disconnect.

Querida. No good nickname from that one. *I'll be glad to hear the last of Paulie, though*. She snorted a quiet laugh. *No doubt some dickhead will come up with something asinine*.

Alice had been her first alias, near enough to her own name so she didn't get tripped up, but nearly too close in the end. Then Alice went away, and Betty Alana was born. Betty went by the wayside quickly, she'd only worn that disguise for two months before an opportunity presented itself and Alace had found herself going off-script in a way that was nearly terminal.

She lifted her hand, fingertips rubbing a slow arc along her collarbone, slowing when she crossed the scar where the bullet had exited. *Got the job done, though*. That mark, and this was before she knew what to call them, had friends in low places. Friends who'd seen her with him. Friends who weren't friends, but people he had owed money to, so when he went missing, they'd come looking for her.

Thornton. She remembered his name suddenly, *Cecil Thornton*. He'd been a serial rapist in college, drugging his dates and fucking them however he liked. He'd held one girl down when the drug hadn't worked like it always had. "A bad batch," he'd been heard to complain. As if he had cause for complaint when he was the criminal. The girl had enough composure to go to the cops, but she hadn't gone to the right cops, hitting the campus police up first. They'd bungled everything they possibly could, and Alace found out later both men were members of Thornton's fraternity.

Coulda called it a sorority with how big those pussies were, she thought, and tried to shake off the unwelcome memories. Even as she escaped the thoughts that moment, when she settled into her motel room for the night, they circled back around for her before dawn. Every death held something in wait for her, like the best kind of getaway driver, relentless and persistent in their pursuit.

She leaned heavily on the bar, locking Cecil in place. The mechanism was intended to hold a gate against the flood of water in the canal, but she'd disassembled it to suit her needs. Rolling him from the top of the culvert had been easy, arranging him in place also easy. Getting the bar to lock was less so because he was bigger than she'd expected. Still, got 'er done. *She listened for the sounds that would precede his death, not yet hearing the thunder. Even after the storm built, she knew it could take a few hours for the water to wend itself down from the distant hills, so she had taken the opportunity to get comfy.*

Checking his pupils, she saw they were still dilated, but not as much as before, which meant the drugs she'd given him would be wearing off just enough, just in time. A roofie mix inspired by his chemist friend's concoction. That friend had killed himself once he realized what his efforts had bought for so many. Another death to lay at your feet, Cecil.

Climbing into the canal, she worked the buckle of his belt free, unfastening and tugging down his dress pants.

Friendly little Cecil hadn't gotten anything more than a slap on the wrist from the college. Even when six more girls came forward to say they thought they'd had nonconsensual sex with him, none of the charges saw the light of a courtroom.

By the time accusations had gained the attention of a real cop, far too much had already been swept under the rug. Evidence gone, testimonies distorted, alibis lined up like kids at the swimming pool slide on a hot day, seven girls made to feel their memory was faulty, or they were teases of the worst sort—cock. Don't insult the penis, ladies. That's just not done.

By the time Alace had heard about the story, four of the women had committed suicide. That left three survivors who would sleep better knowing their attacker had left the world, never to bother them again. The brother of one of the dead was her contact. He'd never meet her, of course. Never know the first thing about her. Alace was good at keeping herself secret. He only knew he was purchasing the surveillance and investigative services of someone who wanted justice.

He wasn't buying a death, but he'd get one, and ten would get you twenty he wouldn't spend time crying about it. She wondered idly if Cecil had heard the one about fifteen would get you twenty, snorting as she lifted her head, seeing lightning playing along the edges of the hills.

Alace hated the word vigilante. It sounded so wannabe. She tried to even the scales for people like her. Helping them out if they couldn't take justice into their own hands, like she had. For a moment, the scenery around her wavered as the dream tried to slide sideways and feed her Trev's voice screaming loudly, but Cecil's death yanked them back on course. Thank God.

Cock tease. Worst thing you could do to a man was send him home with aching balls. "No, the worst thing is to kill him and not send him home at all." *Alace's voice always surprised her in this dream, because she sounded entirely crazy.* "I'm not crazy." *Thoughts given voice in her dreams.* "Just kill him already."

Cock tease. Cecil's weapon of choice didn't look too threatening now, pale and limp, coiled in the dark hair of his crotch. "Blue balls." *A rubber band appeared in her fingers, thick and strong, the kind used to hold bundles of envelopes together at the post office where the man's sister worked before she hung herself. Applying the band was the work of moments, and she took a twist around the end of his penis for good measure.* "All tied up and nowhere to fuck."

Out of nowhere, the water came in a rush, surrounding her and pushing her backwards against the gate she'd somehow reassembled, even with Cecil's unresponsive body underneath the bottom rung. Higher the water surged, all the way to her knees while she twisted to try and pull herself out of the torrent. Then to her hips where the flood was frigid against her core, the cold relentless as it penetrated to bare skin. It rose to her breasts, the force of the water causing them to bob and lift, fighting against the support of her bra. To her shoulders and she suddenly realized she hadn't done everything she needed to do. "Not yet," she cried out, water flowing into her open mouth. "Not yet." Weak words garbled against the torrent of liquid threatening to submerge her.

Pressure against her feet lifted her, pushing upwards, and she felt a cold hand wrap around each ankle. Throwing her arms over the top of the gate, she finally wrenched herself free from the wave of water. Balancing there by an act of will, holding tightly to the bones the gate had somehow been constructed from, she stared down into the water. Clear as if it were the Caribbean, she saw Cecil below, a smile on his face as he drowned, saving her.

She lurched up from where she'd gone to sleep lying crossways on the mattress, feet dangling off one side and her head wedged against a pillow on the other. So soft the words barely disturbed the air, she whispered, "At least it was Cecil." Some nights were harder than others because while Cecil didn't have any family left behind, that wasn't true of all of them.

Squinting at the clock on the nightstand, she saw it was nearing six o'clock, which meant she could give herself permission to rise.

Alace's world was governed by a multitude of rules, all self-imposed. Don't eat red meat—that one mostly driven by a short-term job at a slaughterhouse. It wasn't like she was a vegetarian sworn off all meat, just beef.

Don't buy a car less than ten years old. States had different rules for newer cars when it came to licensing them. The few times she'd needed a car in her name, she'd followed her rule, and everything worked out as it should. It wasn't in the owning them where the problem lay, but in the disposing of them afterwards. An older junker could be left unlocked with the signed title in the seat, and finders-keepers, first to man up—*why do we call it man up? Why not woman up?*—and pop the door was the winner of the day.

Don't rent where you have to get utilities set up. Okay, that was less of a rule and more of a no-brainer. One payment, one background check, one thing to cancel.

Don't get close to the mark. Use the gig as you need to, and get tight with their coworkers, their friends, their family even—that one was touchy, though, since family meant you gave a shit about someone in the end, and she just wanted to do her job and move on—but don't ever, never, get close to the mark. She'd only broken that one once, and that was less of a breaking and more of a cause for the rulemaking.

Donovan Knowles. She'd been twenty-five and six years into the game, which meant her name had been Felicia. Alace snorted, rolling her eyes over the number of times she'd heard the phrase, "Bye, Felicia." *Bad choice, Regg*, she'd scolded him. A lot of his name choices were bad, but he did his job so she could do hers. Felicia Eugenie Danforth. All her names went that way, the flip-flopped alphabet alignment Regg's idea, too. The time before Knowles had been Estrella Dawn Clevinger.

That mark had been Cynthia Birch, a woman who took in troubled girls and boys, and then made them fuck each other with common household items, videoing them to not only feed her own perversion but to make a fortune selling the films online. Cynthia's reasoning, when Alace had questioned her, was because her daughter's tuition was so high, and she posited those educational costs had been set by the bureaucracy driven by men. In Cynthia's warped mind, she was getting a dig in against patriarchal society with every upload.

Even three social worker reports hadn't been enough to convict her, a jury of her peers hadn't spent more than thirty minutes debating the fate of the bitch. They'd probably spent most of that time discussing how long they had to wait to make sure everyone knew they'd given it the old college try.

Alace turned her head to one side, collapsing onto her back, trying not to feel the burn of tears at the back of her eyes. Cynthia always did that to her, not that she felt sorry for the bitch, but for the sake of the woman's kid. The girl had cried so hard at the graveside she'd collapsed and her father had to gather her up and cart the kid away like baggage.

Unlike many of her marks, there hadn't been any poetic justice tied up in Cynthia's death. Alace had found no palatable ways to kill her while making a statement about her crimes.

The cops had gotten closer than Alace liked with that one. She hadn't considered it had been only two years since she'd left a note on a body, but those detectives had compared case logs with the Tampa cops who had flagged her kill down there and confirmed the notes were written by the same person. Damn computers made connections where humans wouldn't. *That was all they could prove*, she thought. That time.

Back to Knowles.

She'd tried all the planned ways to enter his circle without getting close to him. Her dossier on him was exhaustive, and Regg's expectation was she could have dug her way in, but none of the planned contacts in his close-ranked friends worked for her. One guy had just gotten engaged, to an unknown girl he'd met the week before on an island trip. Alace snarled at the memory. *Surprise!* The sister got a job transfer at the last minute, winding up across the country in Boston. Alace had toyed with the idea of replacing his assistant at work, but Knowles had developed a reputation for being a straight arrow guy after his legal troubles.

That was how the news accounts put it, their written summaries slanted to minimize damage to his reputation if nothing could be proven. Innocent until proven guilty, except in the court of Alace. So, the whole affair had been generalized as legal troubles for the local whiz kid. Knowles had started his own company at twenty, skipping a masters' program in favor of bringing his ideas to life. They were good ideas, interesting twists on software used every day, and Alace had no doubt that his name would still be a household word within a few years, even without his hands at the helm.

His legal troubles started in high school but didn't catch up to him for nearly ten years. Long past the expiration of any statutes, and an eternity from when he'd expected the axe to fall. Kneeling and looking up at her as he'd bled out, he'd told her it was a relief. According to Knowles, since he was a junior in high school, he'd been living his life in purgatory, waiting.

She wasn't proud of what happened next, considering she wasn't supposed to lose her cool. All of this effort, this work, it was anonymous. She was virtually nameless, and none of these cases were personal to her. She'd dealt with Trev and his henchmen years ago. Doggedly waiting until she was strong enough, she'd managed to wait nearly too long, an unexpected liver disease almost taking Trev before she could. But even if it wasn't personal, Knowles wasn't supposed to feel relief his fate had been decided, oh no. Alace had exploded, rage taking over and the planned slow death by exsanguination had been escalated with an addition of a significant amount of blunt force trauma. *Jesus, the body held a lot of blood.*

Every blow had ripped a little more of her grief free, since while she'd been Donovan's girl, back when she'd been working him as a mark, he had seemed normal. Kind and sweet, so openly patient and good to the point she'd broken one of her rules and called Regg to make sure she had the right Donovan Knowles. Hoping they'd gotten it wrong. They hadn't.

That had to have been why she'd snapped the way she did. His confession meant the info wasn't wrong, which mean he'd fooled even Alace into believing and trusting a monster. Each swing of the bat had driven that knowledge home, etching the rule in stone, sealing it with blood set in a mortar of bone.

Squeezing her eyes shut, Alace took a chest-expanding breath, then another one, using every exhale to envision a bloody hand pushing those memories aside. Donovan and Cynthia and even Cecil were history, not even a blip in her rearview mirror. Alace glanced at her phone, checking the time again. *Time to rise and shine. Time to become Querida.* She snorted. *As if.*

CHAPTER FOUR

Three months

"Jesus, do you think my order's going to be ready this lifetime?" Alace cut her eyes to the left, taking in the bleached blonde's angular eyebrows. The chick flipped her longish extensions and rolled her eyes, making those dark, eye-framing freaks of nature climb even closer to her hairline.

Don't belittle the natives, she chided herself. *Remember the end game.* "Yes." Querida paused a moment, just long enough for the woman to catch the patronizing tone when she finished with, "Ma'am."

"Did you just say that to me?" The blonde started shoving at the shoulder of the man seated next to her, trying to push him out of the bench seat with no luck. "Did you just say that to me?"

Querida plastered a fake-as-fuck smile on her features and turned to face the woman fully, taking the opportunity while the man was staring in disbelief at his date to give the woman a good look at the person behind the mask. Not something many people glimpsed, but for this floozy, Alace would pull back the curtain as much as was required. What Alace needed was for little miss bimbo to take a hike, leaving the man seated in her section with no one to cushion him from Alace's initial play. She repeated the trigger word deliberately, knowing the snowflake would latch onto the ageist insult. "Ma'am?"

It worked. Muttering quietly, blondie asked to be let out to go to the "little girls' room" and the man unfolded, standing and stretching his arms over his head, elongating the frame of what Alace already knew was a six foot and plenty tall piece of man meat she would dearly love to get her hands on. He angled backwards, stretching in more elaborate ways, the hem of his shirt rucking up to give her a glimpse of several inches of firm abs dusted with golden hair that thickened to a trail where it entered the waistband of his deliciously tight jeans. Mouth suddenly dry, Alace sucked her bottom lip into her mouth, releasing it with a pop when he turned to face her, broad grin on his face telling her he had conducted that little performance entirely for her benefit. *Jesus God. I'm gonna die and go to hell.*

He winked, impossibly full lashes drifting to brush his cheek then lifting over eyes so deeply brown they looked black. Eric Ward folded himself back into the booth, long fingers reaching out to lift the menu from where blondie had tucked it behind the napkin holder. Handing it to Alace, he cut a glance up at her, grinned again, and said, "Too much to expect there's time to cancel Donna's order?" Twisting his neck, he looked out the window where the tramp was already climbing into the cab of a pickup, handed into the seat by a thin man wearing a baseball cap. "I'm guessing she discovered a pressing previous engagement in the bathroom."

Alace took a breath and then settled deliberately into her skin. This was what the past three months had been aiming towards. The two jobs she was working, waitressing at the local diner and bartending at the classier of the two bars in town, both had been engineered to put her in Eric's path.

Querida shrugged and grinned, threading the line between flirtatious and smug. "Order should be up in five, sorry, sugar. Too late to cancel." She hesitated and then informed him, "You're my last table."

Eric tipped his head back, eyes doing a down and up sweep. "Is your name really beloved?"

"That or dear, depends on who you talk to, and yeah. My ma had a funny sense of humor." She shrugged again, using the motion to lift her breasts, watching heat hit his eyes as he focused on the shifting flesh behind the bodice of her uniform. "She said it was the drugs."

As she knew it would, that pulled his attention back to her and away from the girls. *Pity, they always like being a man's sole focus.* "Drugs?" As someone who voluntarily stood-in for the local guidance counselor at the high school as a second, unpaid job, she knew he would be sensitive to those kinds of problems and the wreckage left behind.

"For the labor, silly man." A bell dinged behind her, and she twisted, seeing two plates of food on the pass through. "Your order's up. Hope you're hungry."

"I'm your last table, right? That means you're off work now?" Querida turned back to face him, recognizing his intent expression as interest in more than just her tatas. *Good. It's about fucking time.* She nodded as the bell dinged again. "You hungry, beloved?"

Querida kept her gaze locked with his, giving him a glimpse of her very real interest as she nodded. "Starved."

Two hours later, they walked out of the diner, arm in arm, strolling towards where his SUV was parked. Alace couldn't remember the last time she'd felt this close to someone. Probably never. The realization hit her, and she stumbled. Eric wrapped an arm around her waist, letting her find her feet again naturally. Caring came so easily to him. Even the stories she'd teased out of him tonight about the women she'd seen him with were sweet. Not a disparaging word about any of them, even the ditzy blonde Donna who had ditched him.

"You sure it's not out of your way?" She pressed the same question she'd already asked twice. Eric had offered to take her home, and she knew for a fact her small, furnished apartment was the exact opposite direction from his house. "It's no trouble?"

"Beloved." He hadn't stopped calling her that, even when Querida had offered up other diminutives like Rita. "I want to."

The damned truth was he probably did and, given her unbridled interest, likely expected more than she'd be willing to do tonight. This would be a long job, and Alace anticipated spending another eight to ten months in town. That would take her through the job and give her six weeks on the other side for any suspicion to settle out. *Doesn't do to kill and run. Cops always suspect the stranger who immediately decamps.* Capturing Eric's eye was part of the plan, sure, but she needed him well and truly hooked so she could use the relationship to not only kill suspicion when all was said and done, but more importantly— to get close to his father.

The father, Amos Ward, was her mark. Regg followed a lead she'd picked up from a news article and managed to dig up a steamer trunk full of old skeletons about the man. Stories passed down from friend to friend, all circling the Colorado senator who liked abusing interns. Present tense. His body of power so great he felt his usage of their bodies warranted. Bought and sold for a line on a resume. How a man as decent seeming as Eric could spawn from trash like Ward was a conundrum that had kept her up at night. *And isn't life just the damnedest thing?* It was a question for the ages that someone as truly useless as her own mother could birth Alace and someone as deeply twisted as Ward could have given Eric to the world.

"Okay." She smiled up at him, tipping her chin slightly more than was necessary, inviting him in, and watched his eyes dip closed as he accepted her invitation. A soft touch of his lips against hers was followed by a tightening of the arm at her waist, then a second, less tentative brush. Her steps faltered, pulling him to a stop, and he swung her around to face him, lifting one hand to thread his fingers through to the back of her skull. Gripping gently and tipping her head to the side, he came back for more, the touch transforming from a caress to a kiss in the space of a breath.

A spark she didn't expect ignited between them, and before Alace could think, she'd risen to her toes, seeking more contact as he deepened the kiss. *Delicious*. He tasted of chocolate and coffee, dark and sweet. His silken tongue traced the curves of her mouth, his rasping murmurs begging an entrance she could no more deny than refuse her next breath. Once opened to him, he swept in, the touch velvety soft as it stroked along hers, spreading the taste of him throughout her mouth. Lips moving against hers, he explored what she'd given him, and his groan of delight rolled through her as she tangled her tongue with his, giving and taking everything he wanted.

A heartbeat later and he broke away, burying his face against her neck as his arms wrapped her up, holding tight. He breathed deeply and groaned again. "Jesus, you smell as great as you taste, *Beloved*." The accent on her name was unmistakable, shouting to the world that from a single kiss, he intended to have so much more of what he'd just taken.

Alace stood in his embrace, stunned, swallowed whole by the desire thrumming through her veins. She rolled her head, plastering her cheek against his chest, hearing as well as feeling the thudding of his heart as arousal made her wet and aching between her legs. Her erect nipples teased by the touch of fabric were two distracting sources of electric stimulation playing on her nerves, working in perfect time with the demanding throb of her clit. Everything orchestrated to bring her to her knees, and she wanted that. Wanted to be prostrate before Eric, take his cock in her mouth to pay homage to this thing she could never have. Arousal and desire, need and lust were all part of it, but the sense of coming home as she stood there in his arms was overwhelming. *Not for me. Never for me*.

"Querida, say something." Eric's whisper sounded like a plea, and she had a moment to wonder what he wanted, but then as if he were a genie and she'd wished for clarity, he handed everything to her. "Jesus, baby. Tell me that was as good for you as it was me."

"Yeah," she set the word free on a silent exhale, knowing he'd still heard her when his arms tightened.

"Come to my place." A request he didn't expect to be denied, and she didn't want to. God, no. But there was the plan, and then there was this, leaping off the cliff at low tide without knowing the map of how things could go wrong. Jumping off this cliff right now could have her plans wrecked among the rocks, or worse, have her settled into a role that would never bring Ward's justice to his doorstep.

Alace shook her head, forcing the action from a painful place deep inside. "I can't."

"You were here just now, right?" His arms relaxed slightly, and he bent back at the waist, angling his head to look down at her. *He wants this.* "You kissed me just now? Kissed me like that?"

Cock tease, her mind whispered, and she silenced it harshly. "Yeah, Eric. I'm still right here." *Like father, like son.* She wanted that thought gone, rejecting it as all signs pointed to the untruth of the statement. Nothing he'd shown her tonight, or even in her research, would lead her to think him like the elder Ward.

"Then you know how good that was. Come home with me." He gave her a little squeeze and a shake, as if he could rattle loose the inconsistency he sensed. "Best kiss I've ever had, Querida." Leaning down, he brushed his closed lips across her cheekbone, then whispered in front of her ear, "Beloved."

"Best kiss?" The tone of disbelief sounded rank to her own ears, painful as sandpaper across fingertips, scrubbing all identity away for a few short moments. She knew it was good and expected the kiss would make his short list of really good ones. Hell, it rocketed up to her top spot easily. "Ever?"

He nodded, the scruff of his five o'clock shadow just enough to make sure she knew it was a man who held her. Hair tidily trimmed, Eric was someone who faced the world clean shaven, nothing to hide, but now, after spending hours with her, he was more himself than she'd ever seen him. "Baby." Hot breath fanned across her ear as he murmured the endearment, one hand dipping to flatten against her low back, pulling her close. His jeans and her uniform skirt did nothing to hide the rigid erection that lay hot against her belly. "Never had anyone do that to me with a single kiss." Alace smiled, and he must have felt the movement because his lips drifted to her jaw, working down the column of her throat. "I want to know what else you can do to me."

A thin sheen of sweat covered her skin, chasing goose bumps along the bones of her spine. He wanted to know what she could do.

I can kill you fifteen different ways with just my hands and the clothing on your body. I can dispose of you in three locations I've already scouted, all within a five-minute drive. But, you are not my mark.

Ardor cooled, Alace pulled Querida back into place in her mind. Time to set him on his heels. "I can pay for my dinner." Her flat statement had the expected effect and his arms loosened as his head came up.

"What? No. That's not what…" She kept her head angled down and away, avoiding his expression so she wouldn't feel quite as guilty. "Querida, that's not what I mean."

A noncommittal "No?" was the best she could do, because she still wanted him. A longing bleeding through her that was so fierce it hurt to breathe.

"No." Adamant, he rattled her again before letting his arms fall away. "Is that the kind of guy you think I am?"

Chin down, she asked, "Are you?" He made a gruff, anguished noise in his throat and slipped his hands around hers, lifting and holding them against his chest.

"Look at me, Querida." Chin lifting in a rush, she stared into his eyes, daring him to tell her the truth. *Are you your father's son?* "I am not like that. Whatever you're used to from whoever made you feel that way, I'm not him, okay?" He shook his head, fingers tensing around her hands, his tight grip dancing the edges of pain. "I would never think a woman owed me anything for a meal. Your company was more than enough. In fact, I think I owe you. I've never met anyone quite like you, and I just got…carried away." He leaned closer, pressing his lips to the tip of her nose for a moment, in a gesture that was far more endearing than it should have been, then pulled back and whispered a truth that shone in his brilliant eyes. "No lie, though. Best kiss I've ever had."

Gaze still locked with his, she let him see through to the honesty of her words when she admitted, "Me, too."

He smiled, the edges of his mouth curling up, eyes crinkling at the corners, and she got to watch as his gaze warmed, the color of his irises deepening to that of a rich whiskey. "Tomorrow night. Let me take you out."

"I work tomorrow night. At the bar over by the steakhouse." He already knew she was employed there; she'd served him enough stout beers to cement the association.

"Then that bar was just guaranteed a filled stool for the duration of your shift." He stared at her intently, lifting her fingers to press his lips against her curled knuckles. "I'll be there."

Without another word, he turned and guided her to his SUV, opening the door for her as if it were something they'd done every night for years. He waited for her to buckle in, then leaned close and pressed a final soft kiss to her lips before closing the door.

Parked in front of her apartment, he halted her hand as she went to open the door and shook his head. She smiled, but waited, content to let him be the one to hand her out of the vehicle. In front of her door, he paused while she unlocked and opened it. Then he reached out a hand to pull it nearly shut, making a silent statement that he expected to stay on this side of the entrance.

Hand to her cheek, he leaned in and pressed his lips to hers. As it had before, the kiss started as a slow slide and then flared out of control the moment the attraction between them blazed to life. Heads angled back and forth, his mouth slanting over hers again and again until Alace scarcely recognized her own moans. Eric had one hand at her waist, the other threaded through her hair and holding her close. Alace's arms were twined around his neck, pulling him down as she rose on her toes, back arching with the movement, pressing her closer.

Tongues tangling, that dark flavor she was coming to crave flooded her senses, the scent of his spicy aftershave mixing in the air with the smell of arousal, teasing her to take the kiss just a little farther. Each breath pushing past the next marker and into unmapped territory until he pulled back on a rough groan and once again buried his face against her neck, lips working against the skin there. "Jesus, you taste so fucking good."

On a sobbing breath, all she could manage, Alace told him the truth, "You taste dangerous, but it's addictive."

"I'll see you tomorrow, Querida." Nuzzling her neck, he got her to lift her chin so he could capture her lips again momentarily. "Beloved."

"See you tomorrow, Eric." Pulling away, she backed into her apartment and watched as he reached out, knuckles going white as he gripped the doorknob and pulled the door shut. Her inside, him outside. A thud rattled the door, startling her, and she called out, "You okay?"

Voice closer than she expected, Eric responded, "Yeah. Just...can't quite walk yet. You know?"

"Yeah." She turned, leaning her shoulders against the door, angling her head to ask, "You want to come inside?"

"More than my next breath." His answer was immediate, and she was already reaching for the handle when his words stalled her motion. "But, I've got a promise to keep."

"A promise?" He hadn't promised her anything other than he'd show up at the bar tomorrow night.

"Yeah. I promised you I'm one of the good guys."

Alace smiled as she shook her head. "Already proved that, Eric."

"Well, I have it on good authority that you need more convincing." The door creaked, the wood bending under his weight as he pushed off the surface. "Good night, Querida."

"Night, Eric."

"See you tomorrow, Beloved."

Well, shit. That wasn't supposed to happen.

***

Alace sat on the edge of the bathtub, hands smoothing inexpensive lotion over her skin, the soothing scent of vanilla teasing memories out of hiding. This was the same kind of lotion she'd used five years ago.

That was one of the more reassuring things about the life she'd chosen to lead. How things and events cycled around, all of them wobbling out to the horizon at one point to then circle back close enough to touch. For a moment, the phantom calls of a midway barker sounded in her ears. "Round and round she goes, folks. Where she stops, nobody knows." *Sure as fuck not me.*

She cinched the towel tighter and bent at the waist, reaching for the back of her leg, ensuring she covered every inch of skin still soft from the hot shower. The carnival hadn't been the worst job she'd ever worked to do a gig. There'd been so many more terrible things she'd seen over the years, skimming a bit of money off people who came there for that exact reason didn't even register as wrong. Malleable morality.

And that, my friends, is one of my least favorite things about...everything.

Alace wasn't stupid, not by a long shot. Regg had told her once that he reckoned her IQ was even higher than his, a compliment from a card-carrying member of Mensa. She snorted a laugh. *I'm smarter?* He was the one who lived in the world he made, able to keep family and friends no matter his job simply because he wasn't her.

Being smart enough to see the next move clearly, as if it were drawn in neon lights, simply meant she stayed ahead of anyone looking for someone like her. It also meant she had enough leeway in her head to allow for an easement system. The insignificant culling of money from a target on the midway was such a far cry from what she'd done to Cecil, Cynthia, Donovan, Trey, Randall, Nick, Jack, Mike—Alace pulled her memories up abruptly, firmly stopping the recital of names before she ran through them all.

Reaching for the bottle of lotion, she lifted it and then felt her belly drop as it unexpectedly slid through her fingers. Reflexes kicked in and her hand clamped down tightly, too tightly. Even as she stopped the bottle's fall, she caused an eruption of lotion to jet out the top, splattering up the mirror. With a sigh, she set the bottle down and stood, letting the towel drop to the floor. Turning her back to the mirror, she leaned until her shoulders touched the cold surface, hissing at the chill that settled into her skin. Sliding sideways, she used her body to gather as much of the lotion as possible, grinning at the smeared mess left behind. "Always have a backup plan."

Later, mirror properly cleaned and nightgown donned, she settled on the couch with her laptop open on the coffee table. Movie app launched, Alace leaned backwards then froze at a pounding on her door. She'd made no friends in town, other than Eric. Her landlord knew her, her bosses knew her address. That was it. She didn't get close to people without reason, and she hadn't had reason yet. Padding silently towards the door, she looked through the peephole then jerked backwards in surprise.

Opening the door, she only had time to say his name before his mouth was on hers. "Eric." She barely heard the door settle into the frame over the pounding of blood in her ears, the rasp of his breath gusting across her lips. The sweep of lust carried her into his arms, pushing tight, the buttons on his shirt rough against her breasts through the thin fabric of her gown. "God." Dizzy, her senses were teetering on the brink, and it felt as if she couldn't get enough breath, sounds of her forgotten movie playing in the room.

"I went home, swear I did." The words were muttered against the skin of her throat when he broke the kiss, both of them breathing hard, as if they'd run a race. "Tried to stay away. Tried to wait. Kept telling myself tomorrow. Wait for tomorrow. Couldn't get the thought of you outta my head, Querida. Needed another taste, baby." Lips grazed the soft skin behind her ear, sending a shiver up her spine. Rich and low-pitched, the words rasping against any resolve she'd been holding. "Gimme a taste."

She opened for him again, how could she not when he'd asked so sweetly? His tongue plundered the depths of her mouth, sweeping and tracing the tip of her own before stiffening to thrust inside again and again. His hands rested on her hips, fingers curved and locked into her flesh, holding her close. Eric groaned when she wrapped an arm around his shoulders, her other hand slipping up to cup the back of his head, giving herself to the contact, the kiss, the demands he made of her. He'd had to bend low, their height difference highlighted by her bare feet, and when he made to pull away, she rolled far up on her toes, needing just another moment more.

"That enough to hold you?" As breathless as he was, she let her eyes slowly open to see him staring down at her. He was silent for a moment, then shook his head, dipping close to press a gentle kiss on her lips. "Now?" she whispered against his mouth, shivering when he captured her bottom lip between his teeth, tugging gently. *Tease.* He shook his head again but let a lazy smile curve his lips. She loved seeing how it hit his eyes, turning them dark and sweet. *Jesus, just the way he tastes.* Alace steadied herself with a hand on his arm and one on his chest, lifting to her toes a final time so she could pepper the corners of his mouth with kisses. "Now?" He shook his head again, and she grinned. "It's a stubborn need, huh?"

"Yeah, baby. It is." Now that their breathing was back under control, he looked a little chagrined. "I didn't scare you, did I?"

Alace looked into the face of a sweet man, a kind man. A man who may know what his father had done, but probably didn't understand the extent of the depravity. She looked into the face of a man who'd met the woman made for him and knew it. Met his soul mate, feasting on her words and lips until he was drunk with lust and still backed away when she told him to. A man who held that resolve as long as he could. She glanced at the clock, then smiled at him. That resolve lasting nearly five hours before he returned to the source of his addiction. "No, Eric. You didn't scare me."

Soul mate. Something she'd believed in her whole life but never expected to find for herself. Sometimes the people who sourced her funds were soul mate to one of the wounded ones. Those were the jobs that broke her heart. She knew they'd do anything to bring their loves back to life. Forgive any transgression. *Can I have this for myself?* She'd never thought it possible.

"I should go," he murmured, taking a deep breath. In that moment everything rode the blade, the edge along which she lived her life. She could let him go and the next time she saw him, pretend it hadn't happened quite this way. Play at coy, flirt until he wondered if that was all it had been. It's what Regg would tell her to do. Fuck, it's what her gut was telling her to do, and that gut was seldom wrong.

Still. What if she were wrong? He'd be fine, a gentleman, untangling himself from her grip with grace if asked. She'd be fine, eventually. Never the sort to cling, she'd close the door after him as she had once already tonight. Fine was how she'd spent much of her life. Fine was a lie, because it covered up the need.

Covered up the want. Fine floated in the space behind her teeth, waiting for the chance to assert itself once again.

The length of a breath drawn and released, no more, yet it was at least a thousand lifetimes agonizing over the decision made with a single word. One syllable.

"Stay."

"God." He groaned as he crushed her to him, his actions and the sounds he made revealing how much it had cost him to offer, how much he feared being turned away. Alace had the upper hand here, as she always did, knowing so much about Eric Ward.

Thirty-eight and never married, only dated seriously once. That woman dead in a freak golfing accident, struck by lightning on the fourth hole. Par two, bar none. No passing go from where she'd stood. What could have been a ridiculous death, had become one that had weighed on Eric. A good man, he'd studied the stats and extrapolated the dangers. Spreadsheet in hand, he'd set to work, raising enough money to install lightning detectors not only on the public golf course, but leveraging his contacts to force the private course where his Ariana had died to install their own.

He didn't stop there, but worked his way in a wave around the county, badgering business owners who sponsored baseball and football teams to cough up just a little more cash, and installed detectors at their playing fields. A good man who took his grief and turned it to good, making his girl's death a legacy.

Committed to his job, he might be the most dangerous ploy Alace had ever worked. He was a prosecutor, the kind of lawyer she wished had been seated at that table in the long-ago courtroom. With Eric's intelligence and penchant for doing the right thing, the outcome might have been far different. *Not in my cards.* She hadn't nearly that quality a deck at her disposal, and an ignorant teen didn't know she could have asked for a redeal. Regg had taught her a lot, and her studies had sifted more knowledge into her head.

"Baby." His hand slipped down her back and over the curve of her ass, fingers spreading, five separate brands of heat against her skin. He gathered the fabric of her gown, dragging it up, the skate of lace and satin along her skin lighting every nerve ending on fire. Then his hand was on her bare flesh, fingertips skimming up to the elastic of her panties and tucking under, pushing down so he could grip her ass again.

His mouth grazed her shoulder, nose buried in her skin, strap of her gown falling away. Alace turned her head, mouthing her own path along his neck, working at him with lips and teeth, nipping and tasting. He lifted and pulled, taking her off her feet and bringing her up his torso until his erection pressed against her core. Wrapping her legs around him as best she could, she hung onto his neck with a steady grip, arching back to gain more friction as her hips tipped again and again. His fingers dug in as his head dipped, mouth following the edge of exposed skin along the upper curve of her breast, each lap of his tongue feeling like he strung lines of electricity in its wake.

"Jesus, Querida." His head came up, and he peered down at her. "What's wrong?" Shit. Her flinch at the cover name shouldn't have been enough to bring him out of the spell they were both under, but somehow he had known.

"What do you want, Eric?" This was her thing, something she never veered from. Explicit statement of expectations and a clarity of awareness. Critical for her, and the reason she'd never fucked a man or woman who was drunk, or stoned, or unsure. She couldn't ever wonder if she was that person, the one they cringed at the memory of. "Tell me what you want."

Some of her fucks tried to play it off, dancing around their desires in a way that meant they didn't know their own needs. Some of them turned all hard attitude in this moment, thinking she wanted to be told what to do. *Not it at all, poor schmucks.* Eric did exactly what she'd asked. He told her what he wanted, what he hoped for, and—thank God—it lined up perfectly with her own wishes.

"I want to go to bed with you, baby. Wanna love on you until I can't breathe, until you don't know your own name." She stared at him, those dark eyes seeming to see everything inside her at once. Taking it in, accepting all of her, feeding back the need he found there. "I want you to make me come, hard. Want you to want that. Beloved, I want you to tell me what you want, too."

Alace nodded, tightening her legs along his sides as she hitched herself up to put her mouth next to his ear. "Bedroom is the second door on the left. Take me to bed, Eric. I wanna fuck."

"I can do that," he murmured, lips moving against her shoulder again as he turned and walked to where they both wanted to be. "Oh, yeah, baby. That I can do." Her laughter followed them up the hall.

Next morning was a revelation. She'd woken alongside partners in the past, but never anyone like Eric. He cuddled, dangerously close, holding her against his side in his sleep as if they'd been doing this for eons. She tried to ease out from under his arm, and he grumbled an oath, curving his hand around her belly and dragging her halfway under him.

Alace smiled, reaching down to peel his fingers off her waist. "Eric," her tone aimed for softly scolding, "let me go."

Single words that altered the path of the universe seemed to be their thing, because he rocked her world with five letters. "Never." Alace froze, her fingers gone numb, the idea of someone wanting to spend so much of their life with her unfamiliar to the point of terrifying. *He doesn't know what he said*, she thought, looking for stable ground. Probably thought she was his long-lost girlfriend. Then he ripped that shield away from her as fast as a thought. "Stay here, Beloved." Nuzzling into her hair, he found her neck and brushed a slow, tender kiss against her vulnerable nape. "Stay with me, Querida."

Alace stared across the room at her dresser. She'd been inside other people's bedrooms before. Hell, Nate's room had been a revelation, providing her a window into the sentimentality of the man she'd have never guessed at after only seeing him at work. A wooden tray on his tall dresser had held ticket stubs from movies, receipts from dinners out, and two silver dollars he'd picked up from places unknown.

People who lived within their own lives had things like that. They had things they cared about, people they cared about, and things to anchor memories with those people. They had pictures of kids, brothers and sisters, parents and friends. Their homes reflected those lives.

As hers reflected how she chose to live. The top of her dresser was clear, a clean sweep of wood from edge to edge. Nothing there to give her away, and the very barrenness so telling.

Last night had been a wonder. Never before had she experienced closeness with another human on that level. She and Eric had been in sync, each move a choreographed dance spinning them to heights she hadn't dreamed existed. Fingers, mouth...hell, his entire body had played with hers, teasing and tempting until they'd exploded. The first time he'd pushed inside her, she'd looked up and realized he was holding his breath. So perfect the moment, the clarity of connection, their joining had been as effortless as a clock's pendulum, swinging back and forth in perfect time for the overall construct.

Alace had taken her time with him afterwards, too. Easing them into a casually sensual petting that gave her opportunity to savor the delights spread out on the sheets next to her. Eric hadn't complained, what man would, when a woman willingly wanted to worship his body? But once she was done and he finished for a second time, he'd turned the tables on her. A gentle massage had given way to a final round of fucking so fierce she knew there were bruises on her hips, branded there by the force used to pull her back onto his cock. He'd grunted and strained, ordering her to touch herself, instinctively knowing she needed more and not wanting to finish before her.

"Fucking tight, baby. So tight and hot. Wanna feel you come on me, baby. Come again. Get yourself there, Beloved." Slamming into her with such force she had a hand wedged against the headboard, propelling herself backwards, willingly impaling herself on his cock. "Come on, baby, play a bit, wanna feel you."

Alace reached back, fingers sliding through the slickness between her legs, parting her fingers to either side of his cock where it entered her. "Jesus, hot." He groaned, their rhythm stuttering for a moment at her touch. Then he caught up, plunging inside at a faster pace. "So good." She felt his cock pulse inside her, felt the jerk of it against her fingers. "Get yourself there."

That gruff order was enough, and she moved to conduct business as ordered, working her clit side to side with rapid passes of her fingertips.

Her orgasm was on her no more than a minute later, sweeping her along in front of the wave of sensation, tossing her belly down on the mattress. He followed her down, grunting and thrusting harder, losing himself in his own pursuit of the wave still swirling around her. Covering her like a blanket, braced on an elbow, he gripped her chin and turned her into his kiss. She took him in, tangling her tongue with his as it swept and thrust. Then it was his lips pressed tight to hers, breaths mingling as he plunged deep, holding in place while his hips jerked, harsh grunts making their way down her throat, warming her belly knowing it was her who took him there.

Now it was the morning, and she'd banked on him not being here when she woke. But he was, and from the feel of the growing heat behind her, Eric wasn't done with her yet.

Alace hovered for a moment, suspended between the delight that awaited her on one side, and a reality she knew would be happy to carry them both to the shore. They'd arrive tattered and battered from the torrent, but alive. For once, the final decision wasn't hers. There was an unfamiliar ringtone in the room, coming from the floor where his jeans were discarded. *Saved by the bell.*

"Shit. Hold that thought, Querida." His arms tightened for a moment, then released, heat from his palm chasing across her bare skin as he caressed her hip and ass. Then even the memory of that was gone, chill flooding the space left behind as he stood. Alace shivered, turned to her back and scooted up in bed, angling a pillow behind her as she leaned over the edge of the bed and scooped up her nightgown. "Hello?"

When she straightened, he was looking at her with a dark frown, phone held to his ear. That look registered as an extreme displeasure, and she froze in place, gut unsure if it was with her, or whatever he heard on the phone. *Please, not me.*

Her fear must have shown on her face because his expression subtly softened, and he smiled at her, the look in his eyes gentle. His lips moved, mouthing the word, "Beautiful." Then his dark eyes cut away, angling down to look at the floor. His sideward focus allowed her to look her fill. Handsome in every sense of the word, Eric Ward's face held a classic ruggedness that drew her in. Not in a lumberjack way, his ruggedness had as much to do with the strength of his jaw as it did the line of his brow.

His body was one a sculptor would kill to have as a muse. Defined everywhere, but with enough softness to feel real. A man who worked out because he liked it, not as a job. A thin mat of hair across his chest, enough to trail her fingers through, narrowed as it traced his centerline. A map she'd willingly followed last night, leading her to the treasure at the end. *X marks the spot.* Runner's thighs had spread at her insistent push, making room between his knees for her body, giving her mouth free rein as she pleased. *Pleased him, too.*

His whiskey-brown eyes flared wide, and he snarled one word. She had another moment of ringing clarity of how it seemed single words would be how they'd break each other in the end. Then she was hanging on every word, Alace in full control, because the word he'd uttered was, "Father."

Silence for a moment, then Eric's breath blew out, the sound angry and tense, echoing the strained lines of his neck and shoulders. "No, I hear every word. I am just not going to toe the line this time." He still wasn't looking at her, as if dismissing her from sight meant she wouldn't have to witness whatever rebellion he was staging.

Another angry breath, but this one held a tone of capitulation. "Okay." His eyes flicked side to side, then lifted and his gaze landed on her face. Belligerence swelled in the clench of his jaw. *Oh, shit.* "I'm bringing someone." A pause, his gaze never leaving her. Alace stayed still, frozen like a doe hearing the snap of a branch behind her, seeking out evidence with every available sense to sort out friend from foe. "No, it's not someone you know." He shook his head, lips curving down in a mime's parody of a humorless grimace. "Just put me down as a plus one, Father. If you're going to force my attendance, I will bring whom I choose."

She blinked. His head tipped to the side in a question she'd never dare answer. *Shit.*

"Yes. Have her text me the address." Eric's head tipped the other direction, and he took a step towards the bed, gaze sweeping her clothed and covered body like a physical touch, heat raking her in its wake. "I cannot say the same." His chin lifted and he barked a sharp laugh, the edges fraying painfully. "I'm pleased to know I fulfill that expectation, at least." Without another word, he disconnected the call and dropped the phone, abandoning it on the floor and crawling up the bed on his knees.

"Don't know why you got dressed," he muttered, hands diving under the covers to locate the hem of her nightgown. He tugged, lifting, and her arms went up, allowing him to strip her. He was still unclothed, and she watched as his cock hardened, surging from soft to hard, arching upwards with jerks and pulses. "I have ideas for so many things we can do naked."

Alace allowed him to pull her down, prone on the mattress, pillows swept to the side as he hovered over her. "I'm out of condoms," she lied, needing to slow things down. Alace was not sure what to do with this Eric. An early morning lover, a nighttime cuddlier, and a man who openly disliked his father. None of those were things her research had prepared her for.

He groaned and pressed his forehead between her breasts, one hand lifting to cup a mound, thumb gliding softly across her hardening nipple. "I don't have any with me." He turned his head, capturing her nipple between his lips, feeding it into his mouth. "Guess I'll have to improvise."

She frowned, not certain she liked the sound of that. Improvising was the downfall of planning, and not something she found appealing. "Improvise?"

He shifted, sliding down the bed, lifting to straddle her for a moment, kissing her belly as he slid between her legs. "Yeah." He dipped his head, nosing at her mound, the tip of his tongue darting out to lap at her once, twice. She gasped and arched into the touch, whispering his name as he told her, "Improvise."

CHAPTER FIVE

Alace stared at her reflection in the mirror, smoothing the frown from her brows with the pad of one thumb. Not her favorite thing, dressing up, but something she could manage when the situation demanded. Dress carefully chosen with Querida's identity in mind, it was stylish and fit well, but wouldn't stand out as being a quality out of reach on a waitress' budget. Palms to her hips, she gave the stretchy jersey a tug, settling it into place. Black with a high neckline, it dipped low in the back and had just enough swing to the skirt to make some dance moves slightly daring.

Her glance at the clock revealed she had another twenty minutes before Eric should arrive. Alace made the rounds of her apartment, checking the windows and back door, ensuring they were secure. *Better safe than sorry*. Glancing over her shoulder towards the rest of the house she knew to be empty, she opened her closet and pulled down a shoebox from the top shelf. Lifting the lid, she quickly verified the contents were undisturbed, then carried it over to place on the dresser.

Within the box were the anchors of her life. Her personal reminders of the upcoming job. *This* was how she chose to accessorize her décor. *This is who I am*. A folder, an envelope, two filled holsters, two filled sheathes, a tiny earwig, and a plastic bag with two even tinier circles of technology. *Everything a girl needs to have a good time*. She scowled, not certain why that thought stung.

Tonight, Eric was taking her to a fundraiser benefiting his stepmother's favorite charity. Something to do with childhood cancer, no doubt. That was great for building support of a political candidate, and Alace knew it was no coincidence that tonight's dinner and silent auction preceded the next election cycle by only a couple of months.

Stepmother, since a year to the day of the second round of accusations, his mother had filed for divorce, citing irreconcilable differences. She remarried several years later, about the time Eric hit his stride in law school, and for the past seven years, he had vacationed every spring at her home in Malibu. Whatever differences there were, she'd kept her mouth shut. Not one whisper of her first husband's scandals ever darkened her door. Colorado wasn't that far, but once she got out, she was history as far as Ward's life and campaign were concerned.

Alace contemplated the shoebox of goodies again. The fundraiser was at the Ward estate, but it would be highly unlikely security would allow attendees into the family portion of the house. Eric no longer lived there, so asking to see his etchings wouldn't get her anywhere a bug would do her good. The devices were quality, so they weren't cheap, which meant she couldn't afford to waste them on an uncertain location. Chewing her lip, she decided on the earwig.

A sophisticated piece of technology, she hadn't asked Regg where he'd located it, simply accepted it as a critically useful tool in her arsenal. It could work as a transponder, relaying everything in earshot to an accomplice, if she had one. It could work as a receiver, amplifying all detectable conversation and boosting the indistinct to audible. Or it could be connected to an innocent-looking app on her phone, one that didn't actually record steps—she snorted—but conversations for later playback.

Retrieving the case, she picked up the earwig between finger and thumb and pinched, waiting for the screen on her phone to light up. Once everything was connected, she tucked it into her right ear canal, having already noted Eric liked having her on his right arm. That would put the nearly undetectable device on the opposite side from him, and if everything went as planned, he'd be the only one paying attention to her tonight. Blending was one of the things she did best, and it would be Eric who was on display as supporting his father, not her.

Ducking into the bathroom after putting the box back in its place, Alace studied herself in the mirror. Regg had tried more than once to get her to alter appearances, and at times, when no other way seemed open to her, she'd done so. Coloring her hair or wearing a wig, pretending a need for glasses, plumping her lips with collagen, all temporary measures intended to turn aside surface interest. This time, the face that stared back at her was her own, and she found herself inordinately glad the countenance Eric had seen was real.

Shaking her head at her own musings, Alace moved to the living room and had just gathered her clutch when Eric knocked. She took in a single steadying breath and then reached for the handle, slipping the expected smile into place. *Showtime.*

***

Alace stuck close to Eric's side, not because she was uncomfortable in the elite fundraiser setting, but as any woman would who was slightly shy, but supportive of her date. She aimed for a delicate point somewhere between poised and polite when she greeted people as he introduced her. Eric's hand was draped casually but possessively across her hip, and gave her a squeeze every time she leaned against him. Keeping up a constant stream of information, his preparation for each encounter made her grin. Clearly wanting her to feel comfortable, he gave her a running background on everyone who approached. "That's his second wife. I don't remember her name, but the kids don't like her."

She'd seen the why of that statement when the woman simpered at Eric, reaching across Alace's body to boldly rest her hand against his chest while her husband looked around for a server and his next drink. When the couple had finally moved away after what seemed like a round of endless small talk, Alace tipped her head back and informed him, "I don't like her, either."

His easy laughter at her quip captured her full attention, and she watched his throat work with the sound of his amusement. When he met her gaze, he was still smiling, those lips remaining curved even as he bent to brush his lips across hers. The contact buzzed like lightning along Alace's veins, reminding her in intimate places of exactly how well they fit together.

A quick glance around as he straightened confirmed what she already knew. "Everyone's watching you."

He leaned close, lips to her ear as he whispered, "Because I'm watching you."

Pulling back, she glanced around again, then up at his face. Chin dipped to his throat, his eyes were trained steadily on her face. "Why?" A carnal look, dark and intimate, broke across his features and he had just opened his mouth when a voice from behind her caused it to snap shut. Eric's eyes darted up, gaze fixed at some moving point over her shoulder, his brows drawing together into a scowl.

"Father." His greeting was curt, brusque even, causing a sense of dread to crawl up her spine. There was no hiding her shiver from him, not when his arm had curved around her shoulder, pinning her in place.

"Eric." Loud to the point of brazen, a man standing just out of her view spoke. Then a large hand, dark hair bristling from the backs of its fingers, reached around her and clamped tightly on Eric's bicep. She stared across the width of Eric's chest as those fingers flexed, wrinkling the fabric as they dug deep. Alace's neck twisted, angling her chin to the side, and she looked up into Ward's face. His attention was on Eric, which was good. Rage suffused every cell in her body, and if he'd looked at her, there was no doubt he would have recognized what she represented. Death, looking up at him from suddenly wobbly kitten heels. As it was, having his sole focus on his son gave her the time she needed to drag Querida back into place, settling the mask firmly over her intent. "Glad to see you made it, son."

The rigidity of Eric's body was unmistakable. He didn't want to be sharing air with his father, much less have the man's hand on him. Alace shuffled to the side slightly, and then let her ankle roll, stumbling. Eric moved with her, holding her upright, which dislodged the grip Ward had on him. It also had the unfortunate effect of directing Ward's attention to her, but by then, she was ready.

"Your date, son." A click of his tongue, as one would to a favored dog, made her stomach do a slow roll. "I approve." Shoving his paw in her direction, he let it hang a moment before stretching another inch, making it clear if she snubbed him, it would be evident to everyone around. A waitress cum bartender wouldn't do that, and she couldn't afford to have anyone looking at her any closer than they already would be. Swallowing hard, furiously reminding herself she'd touched slimier things, she let him wrap his hand around hers. Up and down once, twice, and then she was tugging herself free, leaving no question in his mind that if he tried to retain his hold, she'd be the one making it apparent to his guests. Ward's eyes narrowed as he looked her up and down, then effectively dismissed her, lifting his gaze back to Eric's. "Haven't seen enough of you this season, Eric. We'll be putting together the campaign schedule soon. Should I just have Julie let you know when I need you?"

Eric's voice was as tight as his muscles, even pitched low for privacy. "You seem to have selective memory. I'm pretty certain we've already had this conversation, and I felt I made myself clear." Alace let her arm creep around his waist, holding tightly, giving him what she hoped was a clear signal of support. "I'm not going to be campaigning for you this go around."

"I'll let Julie work the details out." Ward dismissed Eric's argument breezily, as if it weren't worth the breath taken to voice. "Dinner starts in fifteen. Don't be late." Clipped instructions that illustrated how out of touch Ward was. "Your table is next to mine."

Ward turned, effusively greeting someone half a room away, and Alace took in a steadying breath as he moved in that direction, taking the mushroom cloud of anxiety with him. Meeting him in person had been worse than she'd imagined. Clearly Ward was entirely convinced of his own superiority in everything, and over everybody. That was why he felt invincible when it came to the women who dared speak against him, steamrollering them as effectively as he'd parted this crowd on the way to his next target. *Give an egomaniacal person the taste of power and it becomes addictive. Feed them a steady dose and that need turns into a surety of privilege*.

"Are you all right?" Eric's mouth was so close the air around her ear trembled with his question, gusts of hot breath caressing her skin. "You stumbled."

"Who's Julie?" She straightened and turned, looking up, wondering how to play this. As he had since the beginning, Eric somehow saw past what she held as a disguise and into the center of her.

"You did that on purpose." His tone wasn't scolding but marveling. Tone quivering with laughter, he continued, "You did! Look at the way you're blushing. Why?"

"You didn't like him touching you." She shrugged, dipping her chin so he couldn't see her eyes. "It's an old waitress trick. Less offensive than stepping away, and people are more likely to believe a stumble than an apology."

For the second time since they'd arrived at the party, Eric threw back his head and laughed, the bold sound ringing through the tux- and gem-bedecked crowd around them. Crows and magpies, looking for a feast or treasure. "Priceless." Bending close again, Eric managed to create a feeling of intimacy even though she knew there were a hundred inquisitive couples nearby. "I'd rather not stay for dinner. How about you? Mouth set on veal cutlet and cheesecake?"

"Won't he be angry if you leave?" Not that she'd expected to get much of anything tonight, with such an impromptu setup, but she'd spent the evening much too far away from Ward to capture anything of interest. Adjoining tables, however, might give her a different angle. "Are you sure?"

"Very sure, Beloved." Still cocooned in the cushion of space he'd created around them, Eric shifted so she was curled to his side. "I find I'm a selfish bastard tonight. I thought I'd like showing you off, but now I'd rather have you to myself."

"And dinner? You're still going to feed me, right?" He was set on leaving, and hesitating wouldn't gain her anything. Giving way with grace, she reminded him, "I distinctly remember there was the promise of food."

Chuckling, he took her words at face value, turning them towards the exit. "That's something you'll learn about me. I always keep my promises."

"So do I," Alace muttered, trailing behind him, clasped hands connecting them as he wove through the groups of chattering magpies, clustered around the power in an effort to find shiny things. "So do I."

***

"Jesus, baby. You're going to fucking kill me." Panted in her ear, Eric's words made her muscles tighten around him. "Fuck, baby." This was something she'd noticed about him, noticed and liked. The fact he got a dirty mouth in bed seemed to draw her closer to the edge. "Mm-hmm. Oh, do that again, baby. So hot, the way you feel under me. Gimme more. *Fuck*."

Breathing hard, Alace did as demanded, letting him ride her hips as they angled to meet every thrust. Giving him her mouth, she took every stroke, sucking hard when he groaned. When he rose over her, she kept her arms wrapped around his shoulders tightly for a moment, cool air snaking along her sweaty back as he lifted her from the bed. Collapsing back, her hands went over her head to wedge against the headboard, breasts offered as her back arched, and he bent his neck, mouth seeking. She brought one hand to her breast, cupping and directing the nipple to his mouth. Gasping aloud as he gripped with his teeth, she held tightly before Eric took her into his mouth on a voracious suck.

"God, Eric. The things you do to me." Her words were panted, much as his had been. "Hard, God so hard. I love you inside me." He rocked into her fiercely, hips rolling to grind deeper, and his growl was barely muffled by her flesh. "So close, honey." He collapsed to his elbows, releasing her with a slide of his mouth up her chest. One hand shoved under her shoulders, up her back to wind into her hair. He gripped, angling her head for a kiss, and she gave herself to him. "Please." The word felt wrong, tasting like ashes on her tongue, and she froze for a microsecond. She'd never begged for anything, not since that day. Shoving the memories down, deep, past the bottom of the hole inside her, she buried them in a way that meant she never wanted them to see the light of day. "Honey."

Fool to think that instant of hesitation would go unremarked. Eric slowed, hips moving on a thrust now instead of pistoning. "Baby?" He pushed up, angling so he could see her face. "Querida? Are you okay?" *He's such a good guy.* "Did I hurt you, baby?" She shook her head, lifting her hips, asking without words that he let her put this moment behind them. "Baby?" He ignored her unspoken demand and slowed further, each movement now a slow glide that kept the fire stoked, but allowed it to pull back from the raging blaze of before. "Is everything okay?"

What do you say to the man inside you when at that very moment you're remembering being violated? Nothing, that's what you say, because in no way did any man worth anything want to be thought of in the same nanosecond of emotion as a rapist. She couldn't even apologize, or he'd demand to know what she thought he'd done wrong. Misdirection and lies. Her only defense was an offense.

"Did you hear that?" *Fuck, I was so close, too.* "I thought I heard the door. Just for a second, and then it was gone." She smiled and rocked her hips, catching him in the cradle that seemed made for him. "I'm not used to your place."

"Alarm is set, baby." He smiled at her, threading his fingers through the hair at her temple, soothing her fears. "It's just you and me here. No one to see."

"Just us to hear you. Be quiet, bitch." That's what the recording had caught. What her ears remembered? So much more. Between one breath and another, she was caught, thrown back years and years to the terrified girl she'd been.

Trev had a grimy hand gripping her throat, choking the fight out of her. Mouth to her ear, he spoke, not even lowering his voice, unconcerned about witnesses. "Ain't no one gonna hear you scream, Allie." Off to the side, his cousin Steve crowed with laughter. "Well, we'll hear you scream." He gripped harder, and Alace saw stars sparking along the edges of her vision, blackness creeping in tight spirals. "But we don't fuckin' care. Make all the goddamned noise you want, bitch."

That was the first of the seventeen lifetimes it took for the attack to end. Men and boys, so many of them, hands reaching out to twist and pull. "My fuck. Y'all get to watch this first time. Wanna bet me there'll be blood?" There'd been plenty when he was done. Trev had pulled out and waved his dick at the circle of onlookers. He'd crowed then, proving the blood link between him and Steve. "Bitch let me tear her V-card up!"

He kept his palm on her back, holding her in place against the hood of the sedan he'd selected for use, hand around her throat as he casually measured the height against his hips, looking for a comfortable ride. Bent double, Alace couldn't have run, even if waves of pain hadn't still been ripping her in half. Her tights were cinched tightly around her knees. Hobbled by hosiery, *she thought, and her laughter sounded suspiciously like weeping.*

"Lookie at this," he preened, wiping his bloody cock up and down her thighs, painting the skin red with her own blood. "Bitch is still bleeding. Tore her up." He shifted behind her and prodded with the tip of his cock. "Least she'll be wetter for seconds." Pushing inside her, he proved his point with a vicious thrust as she writhed to get away. "Fuck, yeah. She's ready now, boys."

Steve was the second lifetime, and he'd yanked the gag from her mouth, fingers hooking around either side of her cheeks. He'd used that hold to pull her back against every plunge, forcing her body to fuck him as if willing.

"Baby, come back to me." Crooning, this voice didn't belong in her nightmare, and Alace thrashed, trying to escape the iron hold of the arms around her. "Shhhh, sweetie. Be still, honey. I won't hurt you. Won't let anybody hurt you anymore." The voice seemed to know the gravity of those words, cementing them into place with the bonds of a vow. A promise he'd keep forever if she'd let him. "I won't ever let anyone hurt you again."

She heard her own voice now, babbling, rising on a cry that exposed her truths. Things she hadn't willingly confronted for seventeen years, scraped raw by a carelessly uttered word that had thrust her into the past. Her words, spoken on air where ears could hear. "I'm Alace. Still Alace. Alace Sweets. They can't take that from me. I'm still Alace."

Her name returned to her on a soft whisper, meant for her ears alone. Reassuring her that she'd been heard, even if, in the end, she didn't want to be. Eric told her, "That's right, baby. You're Alace. Always my Alace." With that, she surrendered, letting herself dive underneath the dark tide of exhaustion, tired from seventeen lifetimes of fighting.

***

As ever, when she woke it was as if she'd been struck, wide awake in an instant. Her gut seemed to be lying. It said she was safe; however, she knew waking in an unfamiliar bed was anything but safe. Ears straining, she sought confirmation she was alone, and the absence of heat or sounds nearby let her pull in a quick breath of air.

Pushing out from under the soft blanket that had been thrown over her, she crept to the door and pulled it open an inch, then two, letting enough light into the room to recognize Eric's bedroom. Sheet and comforter still puddled on the floor where he'd tossed them before stretching out on top of her, the blanket looked to have been taken from a nearby chair. A glance at the window showed faint light, probably false dawn, given the lateness of the hour when they'd kissed their way upstairs.

Shoes and clutch would be on the main floor, but her dress—she crouched and scooped it from the floor, tugging it over her head, not bothering to look for her underwear. Out the door and down the hallway, she stayed close to the wall, listening intently. *There*. Light and sound from a downstairs room, off the hallway that angled away from the stairs she needed. Hand on the rail, she eased downward tread by tread, nerves singing at every creak of wood under her bare feet.

Her shoes were by the entryway table, but the top was bare, her bag nowhere to be seen. Alace angled her face towards that partially open door, getting close before forcing herself to stillness. A shadow passed between the light and doorway, and then back again. Eric's voice raised for a word, and then hushed, as if he'd silenced himself. The single word overheard lifted every hair on her body as if charged with lightning. "Raped."

Pressing her back to the wall beside the door, Alace listened, at first able to pick out only a few scattered words and phrases, stacking them alongside the others in her head as she wove them together. A noise, the groan of an upholstered chair. Eric had evidently taken a seat facing the door, aimed her direction, his voice grew clearer, filling in the gaps.

"No, Todd." Todd Worthson was his best friend, an official judge at the courthouse, his place behind the bench where Eric stood in front of it. "Her name's not Querida. I don't care what her ID says. It's Alace. Alace Sweets." Breath thick in her throat, Alace stood on numb legs, listening to everything falling apart at once. "And she's got this listening device. Like a hearing aid, but smaller than anything I've ever seen. Smaller than anything I've seen from Father's security force, that's for sure." She'd removed the earwig on the way to Eric's house, tucking it away in the case stored in her clutch. Where her tiny wallet was. Where her phone was. "Her phone's locked, no surprise. Hell, I keep my phone locked all the time. But, it wiped itself after only two password fails. Who does that? I screw up my password all the time, most people do. Two tries and then a reset? Something's so wrong here I don't know what to do." He paused, no doubt to listen to Todd. "We were in bed earlier and it was going well. Really well. It's been off the charts every single time, man. But she freaked out. Bad. Shaking and crying, curled up in a tiny ball. She flinched when I tried to touch her." Another pause. "Yeah, I figured that out on my own. A flashback. PTSD or something. She was crying so hard, sobbing." Alace put her hands over her ears for a moment, then in the silence between her ears heard the lawyer telling her it looked weak. *Hell with looking weak. It was pathetic.* Folding her hands into fists, arms rigid at her sides, she listened to Eric's voice calling out the death knell of their fledgling whatever it could have been. "She was raped. Sounded so young, too young. The things she said, how she described everything. All I could do was hold her. But then she said a name, and it wasn't Querida Pansy O'Dell. It was Alace. Alace Sweets. I need your help, man. I need to know everything I can about her."

Enough. Alace moved through the house to the garage door, flipping up a card taped inside the alarm panel to see the code written there. *Found it in one.* The discovery gave her no pleasure, but it made her exit significantly easier. The car keys hanging on their orderly pegs made his pursuit likely, but they were easily gathered up and stuffed into a decorative vase on the kitchen table. He'd find them, just not right away. Out the door, into the street, the kitten heels not the most comfortable running shoes she'd ever worn, but they'd do.

Twenty minutes later, she was exiting her apartment, backpack in hand. The only condemning things left behind were the items Eric retained possession of. Pulling away from the curb, Alace didn't bother to look back. There wasn't anything here for her. Never had been.

CHAPTER SIX

"No." Alace tipped her head back, squeezing her eyes shut. "Sorry, Regg. I just...use the name I gave you. Okay?"

"Honey, you are not a Rita." She heard sounds in the background, children shouting and the unmistakable yell of "Cannonball" that preceded a loud splash. A far cry from the distant droning of semis as they growled their way up a remote hill. "Let me give you what I've already got ready to go."

"Regg." If he wouldn't stop arguing, she'd hang up. Hesitant to even call him and admit how she'd fucked up, she'd already determined a secondary paperwork source. Maybe it was time. No partnerships lasted forever. He had been the first one to tell her that truth, more than a decade ago. *Is this it for us?*

"Tell me what happened." That was his ask. If she gave in, he'd stop arguing about the name, shredding whatever identity he'd already concocted in favor of what she wanted. Rita Quinn Perry. A mix of common and unique, followed by something that sounded like family. "Alace, I know you had to bug out, but why?"

He had been the first call she'd made, the only call that counted for anything. Telling him the identity had been compromised and discarded, she'd hung up and then waited the agreed-upon five days before contacting him again. In between, she'd run a relay of calls to her landlord and employers, not wanting to leave them wondering. When you could, it was always best not to ghost. An unexpected absence just caused memories to get long and twisted. And the possibility of cops being involved, which was the last thing she needed.

"Alace, I'm in your corner, you know that. Hell, we've fought each other's battles enough. You know I'm on your side."

He was, and she knew it. More than him spouting words just now, it was built into the partnership they'd crafted through the years. Through the gigs. He'd pulled her bacon out of the fire more than once, and she'd come through for him in different ways.

"You remember that time in Worchester when I needed an exit and there wasn't anything around?" No taxis, no public transport, not even any cars to boost or hijack, she had been stranded in the middle of an urban desert with no egress. "His brothers were about a half a block behind me."

Regg picked up the thread of the story, his rich voice building the scene in her head. "Yeah, you were desperate. The mark had jacked your knee, and then you had company while you were finishing up." He paused, and she heard a rising shriek in the background followed by a silencing splash. *Someone got tossed in the drink.* "What was his name?"

"Joseph Montgomery. The county judge. He had killed four sex workers when they threatened to talk about his proclivities." The name slipped off her tongue like glass shards, cutting powerfully and burning. "That we knew of."

"It was more, honey. I know." Regg's voice turned soothing, and Alace let it wash over her. Montgomery was a near failure. Not only had he gotten the drop on her, but it was one of the first times she'd questioned their information. Once she got inserted, he hadn't fit the profile. *Except he did.* "You called me out of breath from running and asked, 'Get me a ride?' and what did I do?"

"You got me a ride." She never knew how he managed it, but when she turned the next corner, there'd been an SUV waiting with an open door. Alace had tumbled in and the driver had taken off, momentum of the vehicle slamming the door closed. She'd volunteered an address, and he'd driven without speaking for minutes, eyes hidden behind glasses, hat tugged far down his head.

"I got you a ride because you needed it, and we're partners. I have your back. So now, tell me what you need today. I'll turn over any rock I have to if I can get you what you need." She listened as Regg took a long, even breath. Not a sigh, but something to bolster him through this. "You had to bug out. Why?"

She'd followed a rehearsed routine about a sudden illness in the family, so sorry. No, there wasn't a good number to reach her, sorry again. The forwarding post office box was safe enough, and drew less attention than telling them she didn't need those final checks. Florida would send to Ohio, which would send to Wyoming, and finally, all mail would be routed to a shredder in Texas. By the time they realized she never cashed those checks, she'd be less than a blip on their radar.

But now Regg was demanding the real story. Maybe he deserved it; he'd never steered her wrong before. *I can just bounce it off him, see what he thinks. It'll be okay.* She decided this on the fly, leaning back against the door of her car, twisting to put her feet on the opposite seat.

"You know how Lena is your one?" Lena was Regg's wife and soul mate, coming into his life about three years after Alace first met Regg. He'd gone from being the braggart king ,of one-night stands to a settled example of domesticity within a single conversation. Regg had talked about making every adjustment needed without quarrel, ensuring that Lena knew without a doubt how treasured she was. He'd once told Alace that the instant he heard Lena's voice from behind him, he'd known. Without even having to lay eyes on her, he'd known she was his one.

"Yeah?" The gruffness in Regg's voice told her he already knew what story she'd be spinning tonight. Realized, and might already regret the asking. Gravel and glass in the word, since he knew if she were calling him for a new gig, then the story she had wasn't about to have a happy ever after ending. Happy for a moment didn't cut it for a man who held the stars in his hands every night.

"Met mine." She hated to be the one to shatter his illusions, the idea that the meeting was the hardest part. "He's an unattainable goal for me. N'er the twain shall meet kind of divide. Held it in my hands, Regg. What you have with Lena." Alace felt her throat closing, trying to cut off the sounds, as if that would keep the truth from being true. "Held it in my hands, and lost it because of who I am." Her face was chilled. Alace lifted a hand, fingertips skating across the river of salt rolling down her cheeks. "I can't change who I am. Can't change who I've become." She swallowed, tasting bitter regret on her tongue. "What I've become."

Softly, gently, Regg asked her, "He couldn't see past that to the you I know?"

Alace flexed her ankles, first one then the other, toes wiggling just out of sight inside her shoes, any imperfections hidden from view. "He's a *good* man." She didn't know why she felt the need to defend Eric, but it was critical, no, *necessary* that Regg knew this was her decision. "A *really* good man, Regg. The kind of man who comes along once in a lifetime. I couldn't ask him to take me on."

"Will you circle back to him, love?" His voice was still so soft and sweet, taking such care of her emotions, his very gentleness making things boil over.

"No." Her shout rattled the windows on the car, shook the springs in the seat underneath her. "No, Regg. I can't. I can't. He knows my name." She forgot caution, forgot her decision to never share this detail. Forgot the danger that might follow the knowledge, because in knowing her name, Eric could learn Regg's name, too, and Regg could always decide to mitigate his own threats. She held no illusions of anonymousness. In a world where access to millions of records was governed only by the click of a mouse and money to open doors, Eric could learn everything about her if he dug long enough. Regg's abrupt inhale cut through her tears, his carefully controlled exhale made her sit upright from her slouch, eyes scanning the interior of the car as if Regg had the ability to teleport himself from a backyard pool party to where she sat in a highway rest area. "I can't go back. It wouldn't be safe for me. For us."

In the silence following, she scoured her recent memory, searching for her mouth saying Eric's name and coming up blank. *I didn't tell him who.* Eyes closed, she took a quiet breath. *Thank God.*

Regg broke the long quiet that hung between them, pushing and asking for whatever guarantees she'd be willing to give. She found it in herself to reassure him, but only barely, because she suddenly hated him with a fierceness that stripped her already frayed nerves bare. Her oldest friend the target of an unexpected, consuming rage that burned like poison. He had everything: his soul mate, a child, friends, and family. *A backyard pool, for God's sake.*

And she had...nothing.

"He's a good man?" The question might have been one a father would ask a beloved daughter, seeing her face shining with joy over an outstretched hand, adorned for the first time by a platinum promise. "This man. He's good?"

Alace released a breath she hadn't known was caught in her throat, sobbing as she told the truth. "Yes, a very good man." She waited, hoping Regg would leave it there, and for once in their very long association, he gave her what she wanted.

"And Ward? What about him?" No surprise Regg would wonder. Alace had never left an investigated and flagged mark alive. She'd already decided Ward wouldn't be the first.

"He goes more places than home. I'll keep my ears open for his itinerary and catch him out one week, see if I can't get him alone. Not now." She shrugged, hoping the motion would translate into her play at being nonchalant. "But not too far down the road, either. I don't want our work to go to waste, and we both know how cold the tail gets when it's not wagged."

"Fair enough." Regg's voice turned business-brisk, and the sounds of the pool party faded as he moved through his home to his office. "It'll take me a few days to get Rita put together. Are you sure you won't use what I've already got?" Beeping, then she heard the sound of a metal panel closing. Regg had disarmed his alarm. She noted this, no reason to, but all information was always good to have. *He keeps his office alarmed even when home.* "Did you pick a gig yet?"

"I've got cash I can use for a few days while you get Rita lined out. No worries there." Her second stop had been three towns over from where Eric lived, a long-term locker in a 24-hour gym that held a duffle with her emergency stash. Cash, her real identity, and the phone she was using right now. She'd paused for two minutes and canceled her membership on her way out the door. Her third had been an Internet café, tapping into the private cloud server where Regg uploaded potential marks to scan available targets, knowing she'd need to give Regg a direction. "The coach in Alabama. He's hurt enough people, Regg. I know I've put this one off before, but it's time."

A high school coach who had a torturous method of incentivizing his players to win. Two of his players had committed suicide in the past year, vague notes of self-loathing goodbyes not really pointing fingers. The father of one of the boys finally had recognized the signs, too late. As a teen, he'd lived through the nightmare himself, and surprise-surprise, *his* predatory coach had been the father of the current one. Glad she'd had earbuds, Alace had listened to the man's messages three times this morning, swimming through the sobbing waves of agony from a father who only now saw how he could have saved his son.

"Sounds good, Alace. I'm on it," Regg said. "One Rita Quinn Perry, brand-new resident of Alabama, coming up."

With a smile, Alace tried a joke to see if she could pull it off. "Did you say Quim? Regg, do not make a mistake setting up this ID. You call me a pussy and you and I will have words."

His shout of laughter was so unexpected she found herself joining in, still giggling when he hung up with a growled rendition of an old, repeated threat she knew he'd never deliver on. "You piss me off and I'll make you four foot tall and older than dirt."

CHAPTER SEVEN

One year, three months

Rita glanced up from her desk, gaze flickering past Coach Olsen's dark door to the clock on the wall of the outside office. It showed two thirty on the last Friday of the school year. Normally a day everyone looked forwards to, she knew the profound lack of sound from the hallways out front wasn't surprising given what had happened, the buzz and hum of students respectfully muted.

Today had been Coach's memorial, and it had taken all of Rita's self-control to force herself to sit through the farce she knew it to be. It had been torturous, listening to the lies. The administration didn't have any proof of what the man was—a monster—and they had three thousand days of service they felt compelled to pay homage to. It was definitely unfortunate they didn't have the benefit of her insight. If they had? She shivered. *They'd have burned him in effigy.*

It had been a short two weeks since she'd caught him in his kitchen, casually cleaning the dildo he'd last used on a basketball player. Olsen had first tried to bluff her, picking up the phone at one point to dial 9-1—but he'd paused there, his fingertip never quite making contact with that last number. "Sure, I broke into your house." She'd shaken her head at him even as she agreed with him. "But, you betrayed the trust of every child in your care."

After they'd bantered back and forth for those initial few minutes, Rita had stunned Olsen, literally, pulling a Taser out and triggering it, watching as the barbs flew across the room to attach to his chest. She held the trigger down until she smelled scorched fabric and burning hair, the shining strands of metal tethered to the device seeming to hold Olsen in place. Only when he toppled backwards, head thudding gracelessly against the floor as his body landed in a crumpled pile, had she'd finally released the trigger.

Stunned as he was, securing him to the chair was easy. She'd laid it behind him, rolled his body into position and taped him into place. One end of a strap over the newel post at the foot of the stairs and the other around the back of the chair, and voila, she'd had a working pulley. *Come along*, she'd thought as she inched him upright.

When he regained his senses, she'd needed just one thing from him. For him to admit his guilt. Needed that cleansing clarity that came with knowing she had the right guy. Forget she'd seen the kid limping out to his car not an hour ago, forget she'd had to sit and listen to the kid scream through her earbuds, the listening device in the hallway picking up every sound that echoed down from the master bedroom. She'd still needed Olsen to own up, take responsibility for his actions in a way that meant he understood what was coming.

"You tortured them." Circling the room, baseball bat in hand, she tapped the tip against the legs of each dining room chair she passed. Solid thumps of aluminum racketing through the room, sounding out a Morse code Olsen would never decrypt. "Tortured them for your own amusement and pleasure." This was met by a grunted denial, the sticky strip of tape holding its place across his mouth with tenacity.

For some of them, she thought the worst thing nature did was give them an impaired self-awareness. She hated seeing the blind terror when one of the monsters didn't have it in them to see their guilt. Hope he's not one of those. *She circled the table again, the end of the bat tapping her way like a blind mouse in the nursery rhyme. See how they run. It didn't turn out so well for the mice in that story. She quelled an unexpected surge of fear boiling up her throat and forced it down, using it to feed her adrenaline and turning it into courage.*

"Come on, Olsen. You can't tell me you tripped and fell on at least fifteen of your players. No jury in town would believe that." The idea he'd be called in front of his peers did it, that was the slough of humanity that allowed him to tip, collapsing like an overbalanced iceberg, the change exposing a diseased underbelly he'd kept hidden for so long.

It had been almost a kindness to help him find purity, to cleanse him in the most elemental of ways. Of course, in the end the flames weren't what had killed him.

No, that was me. Rita finished typing the e-mail that would resign her position. Another year out of her life, and it was time to move on. She sighed, leaning sideways to tug on the handle of the communal snack drawer. She dumped her handful of candy bars in on top of the packages of popcorn, knowing they wouldn't last long. Chocolate seemed to draw stressed-out teens like flies.

A sound from outside caught her attention, and she straightened, turning to stare out the window into the parking lot. A tall man was just unfolding himself from the driver seat of a dusty SUV. Dark blond hair shone in the sun as he lifted his arms over his head, twisting this way and that as he stretched out the kinks of road travel. He closed the vehicle door with a slap, the movement bringing his head in line with the windows. She knew he couldn't see her, couldn't have recognized her from whatever dark silhouette was visible, but he went still, staring at the window where she was standing with such intensity common sense no longer mattered.

Two minutes later, she was out the cafeteria door and on the walkway leading to the elementary school, glad she'd listened to her gut this morning and parked in the much less convenient lot down the hill. "Regg," she breathed into the phone, fear making her unreasonably certain Eric could hear her over the wind and shouts of children on the playground. That he could sense her pounding heart like in the dark poem and seek her out, following the beat that could lead them both into darkness. Hers might be an unreasonable fear, but it held a tight grip on her throat nonetheless. "I'm bugging out. Can you take care of the closing aspects of the gig? I'll be home in ten, and then I'll be wind."

"Alace," Regg's voice seemed to come from a great distance, making its way to her through tunnels and dim rooms filled with all the things that terrified her. "Are you okay, love?"

"No," she said, choosing honesty for her oldest friend. "I may never be okay again."

Without giving him a chance to respond, she disconnected, tossing the phone to the passenger seat as she wedged herself into Rita's car. It had surprised her when the technology for a hybrid had been old enough to meet the ten-year criteria, but it was the kind of car Rita would drive, so hybrid it was. Didn't mean it was comfortable, just cheap to drive.

Reversing out of the space, she twisted the wheel as she faced front and froze in place. Eric had seen her, or had sensed her somehow—*fucking, fucking heart*—and was standing at the end of the sidewalk. Not fifty feet away and Alace gave herself two beats, then a third, to take him in. Time hadn't touched him, not that so much had passed, but she knew she felt and looked much older these days, her heart—*fucking, fucking heart*—yearning for what it couldn't have. Eric looked as delicious as ever, and even more so when she caught the quirk of his lips, one corner of his mouth curling up.

Shoving the gearshift into first, she gave herself another beat, then tore her eyes away and drove off the lot and into traffic on the local highway. Not before she'd seen his lips move again, this time to frame one word. One fucking word always seemed to be their thing, dammit. "Beloved."

***

Parking three blocks away from her house seemed the smallest of countermeasures, and as she walked through as many shadows as she could find, the alley behind her rental still seemed spotlighted, open and vulnerable. She paused and worked the house like she would one she intended to enter by force, trying to see everything at once, not knowing what detail would be critical. Nothing moving inside, no shadows where there shouldn't be. No doors or windows ajar, and the back gate still had the can leaning on it where the garbage men had left it. The front of the house offered no additional information. There were no cars, SUV or not, parked at the curb. No mysterious tall, broad, and so fucking sexy it hurt to breathe man standing on the porch, and from the side window she could see the alarm panel blinking amber. Armed but not alerted.

Alace took her first real breath since she'd looked out the window at the school, tossed the confusion about Eric knowing where she worked, but apparently not where she lived, into a box in her head, and pushed it against a wall to look at later.

Inside and upstairs, she pulled the folder from the small safe in the master bedroom closet and shoved it into her backpack. Dangling the pack by a strap, she surveyed the room for a moment. It hit her, suddenly, how much she'd changed over the past fifteen months, and Alace bent double with the force of the blow, finding her breath so much harder to catch than it should be.

From that position, she lifted her head, intending to study the mirror over the dresser. The dresser captured her attention instead.

A dresser that held a single picture frame, one the office assistant kids had given her. It was of her, wet and bedraggled, fake scowling as she climbed back onto the narrow seat of a dunking booth. Two boys were posing in front of the water-filled chamber of horror—that's what she'd called it in her head— laughing and hamming it up for the camera. That had been the day before she'd found Coach's stash of kiddie porn, one day before she'd known without a doubt her gut was right. One day before the burden of knowing weighed so heavily on her it felt like an ever-growing brick lodged in her chest.

Her eyes shifted, and she looked at the mirror. Tucked in along the edges were notes and photos, mementos of her brief tenure here. Kids in the office, kids in the hallway, it had been bizarre at first, when after only a couple of months of working at the school, they'd seemed to adopt her. She couldn't go a day without one of the kids coming in to park a cheek on her desk and shoot the shit. Her coworker Marsha—and that was a name nearly as bad as Felicia when it came to pop culture jokes—told her once that Alace, or Rita, just seemed to "get it" in a way that grownups never did.

Alace straightened, hands to her knees pushing, levering herself upright with brute force. She'd taken one step towards the dresser, not sure if she wanted to bring everything with her or discard it when a knocking at the front door stopped her in her tracks.

Sidling to the window, she peered out through the available cracks in the blinds to see that fucking SUV at the curb. *Shit*. Not a single one of her nightmares about being caught ever started with it being the man she loved who brought her in. Alace grimaced. She might not shy from introspection about her job, her reasoning about what she did, but since leaving his house, she had tried desperately to not think about what he might have meant to her. And now here he was, stalking her at the job that allowed her to get close to this gig's mark, and shouting down the house in an effort to get her to answer the door. *Well, maybe more a polite knocking than a shouting down.*

Then she found out she was wrong. Still, him being there and doing what he was doing gave her something she hadn't known she needed. Her name in his mouth, not spoken to a friend, but directed at her, telling her he knew who she was.

"Alace, I know you're in there." Pitched to carry through the door, his voice was still softly sweet. "Alace?" The briefest of pauses, followed by three solid raps of his knuckles against the door. "Can you let me in?" *Can and would are on two entirely different ends of the spectrum. Would and should nearly as far apart.* "Baby?"

Alace was halfway down the stairs when she heard that last word, nearly stumbling with the power it held over her. Trembling knees forced her ass to a tread, and she sat and waited, hoping it would come again, dreading it at the same time. *Please, say it just once more.*

The door rattled in the frame, and she watched as his shadow moved away. She was so caught up in the sound of his voice, the call of her name from his mouth, the tenderness of that single "baby" that she almost didn't notice him heading around the corner of the house and not down the walk towards his vehicle. Her gut kicked in, however, and she closed her eyes, running her entrance to the house back through her head. Door opening with the key, closing behind her, alarm panel opened, and code entered to disarm. Not a single memory of her locking the fucking, fucking door.

She timed her closing of the front door to his opening of the rear one, giving the Colorado-plated SUV a fond glance, remembering one night when he'd intended to just kiss her once. Parked at the curb in front of her house, there'd been no passersby to remark on the steamy nature of the windows when they'd finally exited the vehicle.

In her car, she took a moment to sit with bowed head, hair curtaining her face as she swallowed hard. Then with a deep breath, she sat straight. She drove two towns over and used an app on her phone to book a room in what was loosely termed a bed and breakfast. In reality, it was a woman hard up for money, using a rental loophole to lease out her spare room for cash.

Car parked in a nearby sale lot, Alace sat cross-legged on the sagging mattress and logged into Regg's servers. Opening the folder she needed, she entered the thirty-six character passphrase then tapped keys in an unlogged sequence. Anyone who got that far *and* knew her passphrase would still fuck up that part of it, and a longer than ten-second pause before entering the blind code would wipe the contents of the folder. Layers upon layers of reassuring security intended to keep things from happening like they had today. *"Baby."* Alace blinked slowly, letting the sound roll around inside her head for a moment before she put it back in that fucking, fucking box and shoved it aside.

She took a breath and then opened the first document in the list. Time to find out her next gig.

CHAPTER EIGHT

Thirteen months

In those moments between sleeping and awakening—those isolated instances of time that could stretch out forever or snap back, tight and short like a rubber band—that's where Alace was caught when she heard the truck's engine, the sound growing louder as the vehicle approached. In those moments, she could be anyone she wanted to be. Right there where the tail end of dreams lingered and imagination soared. In those moments, she was young and beautiful, she was older and surrounded by family, she was rich and powerful, and she was living a hardscrabble life. She was everything.

Two breaths beyond those moments and her life dropped back into place in her head, the mass of reality suffocating. Without opening her eyes, she sucked in a hard breath of the already hot air, and blew it back out on a huff, scrubbing the inside of her mouth with her tongue, trying to erase the results of sleeping hard in the open air of northern New Mexico after drinking herself sick last night.

She lifted her hands and opened one eye in a narrow slit to try and see how crusted they might be from the evening's activities, thankfully finding her palms and fingers, even her nails were blameless and clean.

The truck engine rumbled closer and closer, and she let the weight of her head roll it to one side, that single, slightly-opened eye struggling to focus. Greens and browns swam into view. She sighed.

Ranger Rick.

She didn't actually know the man's name, but he'd made it a point to check on her every fucking morning for the past two weeks. From months in the park with no notice paid to her presence to a daily welfare assessment, it struck her as odd. Odd was never good. At first, she'd thought he was looking to make bank for the park on fines if she didn't have her permits in place. Or make bank on bribes to keep those fines from hitting the official books. Or he'd be after a different kind of currency to pay those fines. *Oldest profession in the world, if not an honorable one.* Those thoughts fell by the wayside quickly when all he ever asked after was her well-being. He seemed to simply care about the people under his protection, which—

given his position—was every visitor who set foot inside the entire fucking national park.

I can't deal with him today, she thought, and closed her eye. Grunting, she struggled with her sleeping bag, rolling to her stomach while keeping it straight under and around her. Sliding the off-side zipper down a little more than halfway, she arranged it to cover her ass while letting her bare leg lay uncovered. She'd found the quickest way to get rid of Ranger Rick was to flash a little skin, and it didn't matter if she had her shorts on underneath or not. If she made him think she was naked, he wouldn't come close.

Him coming close was a risk she wasn't willing to take. Even one with an erratic schedule, a forestry employee this active would be missed, and Alace had that long list of rules which included things she wouldn't do. Dealing with the kind of attention that would come from someone like him going missing was high on that list. *Don't shit where you eat*. That's what her mother had taught her long ago, showing by her actions that when it did happen, you turned and skedaddled as quickly as you could. It was the only way to avoid dealing with consequences.

Propping up on her elbows, she gave a quick look at her cleavage, intending to verify there was enough showing to make him uncomfortable. That's when she saw the red stains on her shirt. With a grimace, she flopped to her belly, crossing her arms in front of her and resting her forehead on them. Now that she was aware of it, she felt the fabric sticking all along her chest and belly. She huffed out another breath, this one sounding different even to her ears.

Last night had been the worst one in a long time.

The knife rising to glitter in the light that bled in from outside. A dark spray of shining liquid across the walls and ceiling. Experiencing a terrifying shimmy of the handle trying to escape her grip as it wedged between bones when she thrust deep. Even the smell was embedded in her memories, fear and anger vying with the bright copper scent of aortic blood. Alace shivered.

"If you're cold, you should get a better bag." The man's voice was closer than she expected, and Alace jerked her head up, glaring at him through squinted eyes.

"Hey, Ranger Rick," she said, settling her cheek onto her crossed arms. "How's it hanging?"

"Ma'am, I think the better question is how are you doing?" Warm brown eyes stared at her in concern, and for an instant, Alace wondered if she had anything on her face to worry about. "You're not usually asleep this far into the day."

Glancing around, she gauged the time by the sun's position, coming up with midafternoon. He wasn't wrong. Normally she was up with the sun, making coffee and breakfast before the campers rolled out of their tents. A quick perusal of her site showed everything in order. Her food bag was hanging about a hundred feet into the woods, her backpack dangled from a hook in the rafters of this little picnic table shelter, and she and her sleeping bag were on top of the table. Easier to avoid critters of all sorts by sleeping up here.

"Recovery day." Total bullshit and a blatant lie. She hadn't hiked enough to warrant a recovery day, hadn't expended enough energy on anything, really. *Except for last night*. She sighed. "Girl can always use a little more beauty sleep."

"All right, Thistle," he said, using the trail name she'd provided the first day. "As long as you're okay, I'll be on my way."

"Right as rain." A little extra pep in her voice was the encouragement he needed, and she watched as he strolled back to his truck. One minute and a lifted hand later, he was gone, dust from his slow passage barely stirring off the roadbed.

Thistle. She yawned wide, jaw cracking, and worked her way onto her back. *Need to get Regg to use that one next*. Sutton had worked for this gig, a noncommittal, non-regional, gender-neutral, fucking nondenominational name. She lifted a hand and sank roughened fingertips far into her eye sockets, letting the ache build along with the flaring lights before releasing. The sudden lack of pressure helped to relieve her headache somewhat. She'd never done something like that before. Gotten drunk after a gig.

There was a buzz from something that felt like a stone wedged against her ass, rumbling against the cement tabletop through the light padding of her bag. Fumbling under the sleeping bag, she dug into her pocket and pulled out her phone. A phone that shouldn't be in her pocket and on, but in a waterproof bag tucked inside her backpack. *Fucking, fucking phone*.

Fourteen missed calls. *What the fuck?* Propping up on an elbow, she stared at the numbers. Regg's number showed, which wasn't expected even though he knew she was close. Alace had told him on their last check-in that she'd isolated the information she needed and simply had to find the opportune moment. Or create it, as she had last night. The reservation cop stopping to help a stranded motorist, a nail-punctured flat tire on the junker she'd bought for two hundred bucks cash had proved just enough of a lure. After she'd knocked him out, the stocky Native American man had been heavier than she'd expected, but she'd managed to lever him up and over the back bumper of his vehicle.

Leaving the junker was easy. The original owner's name still on the title meant she had no tie to the car. It had been hours before the cop's radio had crackled to life, the dispatcher calling his name with such a tired lack of interest Alace knew he often went off the grid.

Off the grid, and into the woods. She hadn't been present for his last kill, no. If she were, she would have stopped it, letting the little fourteen-year-old runaway go free if she'd had the chance. Alace had seen the aftermath up close and personal, though, when she'd toured his cabin last night. She'd found the child still strung up like a deer, ponytail tied to the waistband of her pants with a frayed shoestring, working as a harness to keep her head bent backwards and out of the way, letting the last of the girl's blood drain into the bucket that fucking res cop had set so tidily beneath her.

Alace had ID'd the kid from a Tennessee junior high school lunch ticket she found in a backpack. The sum total of the backpack's contents had been the ID and a red sweatshirt. The backpack had been stacked along the wall, last in a line of twelve. Before everything was said and done, Alace had spent part of the day scouring the woods, finding his burial sites for most of the kids represented in that line.

By the time he came to, groggy from the blow to the head mixed with a nose full of the chloroform he kept in a duffle by the door, she had everything ready. Admission of guilt took no time at all. Officer Waterdrum had no hesitation about telling her what he'd done. His term for the kids, calling them disposable children, turned her stomach. *"A kindness."* He'd claimed his end was more merciful than what awaited most runaways.

The damned thing was...Alace didn't entirely disagree with him. At seventeen, if offered the choice between going peacefully to sleep and not waking up, or being gang raped by men and boys she would have to look in the eye for months afterward—twenty-

twenty hindsight. Alace knew she would have picked death.

Regg would say she was still trying to pick that path.

Why does it always have to be kids? she thought, still staring down at her phone. That was the real reason for the drinking. She hadn't been able to get the girl's face out of her head. Wide-open eyes, staring at nothing but the floor, but her gorgeous red hair tied into a fucking ponytail and kept out of the gore surrounding her.

Regg's number was on the screen, but there was another one, too. An area code she recognized, and a number she knew, but it wasn't in her contacts on this phone. Hadn't been a contact for more than two years.

Thumb to the screen, she flipped to recent outgoing calls. One. One in the past week. Three in history before that, in the thirteen months since getting this phone and becoming Sutton, she'd only called Regg. Then, last night, apparently wasted and without any sense of self-preservation, she'd called fucking, fucking Eric. Tapping the three dots that led to more information, she stared at the screen. Sixty-two minutes.

Alace collapsed backwards onto the table. Unblinking, she stared up into the sun Ranger Rick had so helpfully announced was high in the sky. *Jesus, what did I tell him?* Eyes shut tightly, searching her memories, she found a trailing edge of a single word, then followed that bare thread to the softer resonance of Eric's voice saying her name, "Alace." Once she had that, the rest came easier, and she began to piece things together, word by word, sentence by sentence, until she was sure she had nearly the entire hour of conversation.

"Alace, baby. Tell me where you are." Eric's plea was soft, cajoling, sweet as syrup, and she wanted to lap it up, let him rest on her tongue for a long time.

"You always tasted so good. How did you do that?" Slurring so badly it was like the sounds were foreign in her own head, so it was a wonder he was able to make any sense out of her words. "Addictive. Minute I tasted you, whoosh, man, I was gone. 'F you could bottle that shit, you'd make a mint."

"Baby, where are you?"

"Can't tell ya. 'Gainst the rules. I live by the rules." She cupped the phone to her face, trying to get closer to Eric. "Can't tell ya."

"Okay, if you can't tell me where you are, then tell me you're okay. Are you safe, baby?" His voice dropped an octave, the rough gravel in his tone pulling a shiver from her bones. "Please be okay, baby."

"'S okay. I'm always okay." Outside the cabin, she'd laid back on the hood of the reservation police car, eyes on the stars wheeling overhead. "Best lie I know. I'm fine."

"You're not fine. You're drunk." Eric wasn't laughing, which surprised her. "Who's there with you, baby?"

Rolling her head to stare at the open cabin door, she sighed. "Red's here for now. She don't gotta worry about the big bad wolf anymore." Alace turned onto her side, curling up, tucking her knees close to her chest as she faced away from the cabin. "None of us do. I played Granny's part tonight."

"Didn't Red Riding Hood's granny get eaten?" He sounded nearly frantic now, words coming faster than she could make sense of them at the time. "Baby, don't get eaten. Don't get caught. Tell me where you are. I can help you get out of this. I know people. I have friends. I can make it all go away."

"Depends on the fairy tale." Alace stared at the unmoving darkness behind the opening she knew led into a scene from hell. She remembered the blood splattering, flung far and wide by her frenzied attack on his still breathing body. "In my story, Granny's the one who kills the wolf."

"I like your version, baby. That's a good one. The best. Tell me where you are."

The empty bottle mocked her from its position on the top stone step. One of three that lead upwards into the cop's lair. "No stairway to heaven, that's for sure." She rolled to her back, eyes once again on the cold, unblinking stars. "No heaven for the likes of me." Pushing to a seated position, she leaned back on an

arm as the world swung around her. "Whoa. Dizzy."
She waited it out, Eric's voice a pleasant anchor to
reality, even if she couldn't make out the words.
Propping the phone to her ear with a shoulder, she dug
out a scrap of paper from her pocket. "I gotta go now,
Eric, before someone comes. I shouldn't have called."

"No, baby. Stay on the phone with me. It's just you
and me, yeah?" He stumbled for a moment, his words
for once not coming smoothly. "I just...I've missed you,
Alace. I saw you in Mobile."

"I saw you, too." She unrolled the paper, smoothing
it flat against her leg. "I kept your number." Scrawled
along the paper, angled across the evenly spaced lines
in a way it couldn't be contained was Eric's phone
number. He'd given it to her the first night they'd
talked, the first night they'd kissed. Given it to her
before he came back, when he didn't yet know what
they might have been.

"I'm glad. So glad, baby. Keep it. I'll always pick up
for you."

They'd talked about nothing from there forwards,
just words to fill the void, and Alace had let him lead
the conversation. He'd pulled her in, lulling her with
soft renditions of his everyday life. A life she'd never
had. She'd gone from being Alace to what she was
today. The fourth or fifth time he'd tried to get her to
tell him where she was she'd slipped, dropping the
tiniest of comments about camping. Eric hadn't
pounced, not right away. He'd waited, which was
unfortunate for him since it meant she'd had nearly an

hour of sobering up under her belt. So when he pushed, asking about a series of state parks she at least hadn't blurted out anything. However, her very silence was telling for him, and she'd known it.

"Baby, I can help. I promise. I've been piecing things together, and I know why you do what you do." Sweet and soft, his words ran through her veins like liquid cocaine, sending her heart into overdrive. *She hadn't responded, and he pushed again. "You're not the bad guy, Alace. I know that. Baby." He paused, and she wondered if he was wavering on how to push her next. She was wrong. "We don't have to talk about that. Just be safe. Always be safe, yeah?"*

She'd hung up after that. Hung up and then sat crying for an hour. It was all the time she could allow herself. She'd had a hell of a lot of work to do, and still had to be back here before sunrise.

I didn't tell him where I was. She held tight to that knowledge. Him not knowing meant she could let the rest of the gig play out. He might guess, but he couldn't know, not from what she'd said. So she'd wait and see who the cops looked at, since she thought the wolf in cop's clothing had an accomplice, but hadn't been able to get a name out of the man last night. Got a lot of other stuff out of him. She glanced at her backpack, the bottom section where her bag would normally go already packed full with bricks of cash. Seemed selling parts of little girls was a lucrative biz, who knew? *Fetish out there for everything.* She yawned, then had a thought that made her shiver, skin crawling with goose bumps. *At least he hadn't killed them inside first.* Small wonder, that. He'd only killed their shells, not their souls.

***

Ugh. She hiked the backpack higher on her shoulders, trying to relieve the pain where the straps were cutting into her muscles. It was far too heavy to be comfortable, and she'd known she was pushing it before she set off from the campsite. If she could make it to town, she'd scavenge a box from behind the local liquor store then beg some tape from a clerk. The address she'd memorized years ago was great for things like this. It would forward to another address, then that location would put the box inside a new box, and that would be sent on its way another two times before it ended its journey in Regg's hands.

Time consuming to set up, and Regg argued against the maintenance of the process every time she used it. But, and here was where it became worth it, packages sent this way were virtually untraceable. Regg would get the box and deal with the contents in a way that split the take sixty/forty.

She'd already decided half of her money would go to help support a runaway shelter on the east coast. If kids like Red had a place to go that was safe and confidential, they might not end up in the hands of men like Waterdrum. Escaping from abusive homes, or abusive relationships, or sometimes just from their own reactions to the shit life threw at people, if they had a better option to escape to, it could make the

MariaLisa deMora

difference between life and death. She shook her head, trying to dislodge visions of the girl hanging from the bar, feet spread wide, head tipped back at an unnatural angle.

One of her marks—a self-castrated priest who made people forget it wasn't just the pricks men had in their pants that could do deadly damage—had a parrot. That parrot had screamed at her every time she walked into the man's house. Screamed and screamed, sounding like someone in agony. After a few times, the parrot had begun to alternate caterwauling and shouted words. It had taken Alace nearly a week of daily visits to sort out the words, since the minute the parrot—its name was Walter—began talking, the priest would give it a gnaw bone to keep it busy. *Keep it quiet*, she thought. *Put this in your mouth, little boy.*

On the last visit to the priest's house, made so by her actions later the same night, Walter had greeted her when she walked in, strutting his stuff by pacing back and forth across the wooden floor of the foyer. Not in his cage, not on his perch, it seemed the bird had escaped captivity just in time to welcome the cleaning lady. She'd crouched and offered a cupped hand, smiling when the parrot's soft, heated feet had gripped her fingers, claws slipping harmlessly into the spaces between. "Hi, Walter," she'd said, and braced for the screams.

What she'd gotten had been so much worse.

"Please, Father." A stuttering little-boy's voice came out of the bird's throat, his beak held wide as he forced the unnatural sounds. "I don't wanna die. I don't wanna die. Die in here. I'll die in here. Please. Father die, don't make me die." She lifted the bird, reaching to stroke the back of his gray head, fingertips slowly ruffling and scratching down to the skin, wanting in a small corner of her active brain to soothe the animal. Walter tipped his head forwards for a moment, then shook and looked at her out of one yellow eye. "Don't hurt me, Father. Please. I'm good. Good boys don't go in the closet." Goose bumps shivered into life on her arms when the bird spoke next, his tone and cadence an imitation of the priest's speech. "Good boys don't tell their Father no. Good boys do what they're told." Walter whipped his head side to side, shrieking in the little-boy's voice, "No, Father. Please, Father. Please. Die. Die. Please. Don't."

There was a closet in the priest's study she'd been told to steer clear of. The reason given about how it held the filing cabinet with the parishioners' personal information. The priest's instructions to the temp agency had been very specific. Light dusting and vacuuming only in the study, all locked doors to be respected.

Walter looked at her again, then twisted his neck so his head lay along his back, upside down. He was back to wailing like a banshee, wave after wave of raw sound that now held a bleeding edge of little boy. The priest came bustling into the foyer, hands out to take Walter from her, scolding him in a mockery of an old man's voice. "What's this? Tut, tut, Walter. Bad bird." His words seemed to trigger the bird and again he screamed, "Don't hurt me, Father. Please. I'm good. No dark for me. Please."

Alace met the man's eyes as she handed over the bird, and they shared a moment. The kind of meeting of the minds she'd come to believe was a mutual understanding. He saw how she'd sorted out his secrets. Recognized what she was, his face collapsing in on itself in resignation. She knew he needed to die. He knew death stalked him, walking through his house wielding a dustrag. Somehow, just from looking in her face, he knew.

Alace was expecting the call from the temp agency early the next morning, the young receptionist telling her the job was canceled. Not that she'd put it in so many words. No, it wouldn't be professional to spread rumors about clients. But, while Alace was waiting for a reassignment, the girl on the phone let drop that it seemed the priest had offed himself during the night. Listening to that, Alace had smirked at herself in the bathroom mirror of the one-bedroom apartment she was renting. He'd done more than kill himself. He'd killed himself by first ingesting nearly an entire spool of unedited videotape, then by braiding a rope out of his several cinctures and stepping off a chair.

His still seemed one of the more fitting ends she'd orchestrated. The cincture was supposed to symbolize the virtues of chastity and exercising of self-constraint in sexual matters. Ending his life was the only way to truly gird that man's loins. While man's medicine might have taken away his body's ability to get it up to rape little boys, they'd left him his fingers and teeth. That's what was all captured on the video she'd shoved down his gullet, as well as on the piles of other videos in the massive filing cabinet taking up half the space in the closet. The other half contained a tiny staircase that led to a hallway terminating in a tinier room under the baptismal.

Walter. The motion he'd made with his neck reminded her of how Red's neck had been stretched back. Like she'd had extra joints, flexible in death as she'd never have been while breathing. Alace's stomach rolled, quietly threatening. A soft crunching edged into her consciousness, and Alace glanced over her shoulder to see a vehicle approaching at a crawl, barely fast enough to stir dust on this dry-as-a-bone gravel road. The hood was all she could really see, and it was painted a familiar shade of green. *Ranger Rick.* Alace rolled her eyes, stopped and turned to face the oncoming vehicle, feet planted wide. *I do not have time for this shit.*

The SUV pulled even with her as the passenger window silently lowered, "Hey, Thistle. Need a ride?"

She'd opened her mouth to explain half the fun in hiking was the part where you actually walked places when he moved. Held close to his leg, the black rectangle in his hand caught her attention, and with an instinctive reaction, she was already turning away, preparing to sprint at a slant into the woods when he lifted and triggered the Taser. Alace's body went rigid, and the sky swapped places with the trees edging the road. There was a burst of brilliance, disorienting her. It was followed by a hollow ringing in her ears and splitting pain in her head. She felt the biting angles of sharp-edged gravel grind into the skin of her elbows and skull, her back and shoulders protected by the backpack.

Ranger Rick's face appeared above her, and he grunted, tugging on the silver wires that connected them. "Damn. Caught the strap." Alace's chest was on fire, burning like she'd been stung by a hundred wasps. She felt her skin lift, then his arm moved and made a sharp motion that correlated to a pinching pain in her shoulder. Her arm hurt like someone had dipped it in kerosene and set it afire. She'd seen a pack of street kids do that to a cat once. Down in Miami. She'd been a homeless person for that gig, the ending of which saw her taking a four-hour shower and still feeling as if she'd never be clean. The cat had yowled like she wanted to, but trying to suck in air was beyond her right now. The weight on her chest shouted heart attack, while the electrocuted parts kept her lips stitched firmly shut. The cat had run away, hoping to leave the agony from its tormentors behind, never knowing there'd be no escape. Some pain follows you all your life.

"Thistle, I'm going to put you in my car now. I want you to be quiet, or I'll have to hit you again." Her brain must have short-circuited and lost a few minutes, because she found herself lying in the gravel at the back of the SUV, not alongside the road. *Why?* Her brain was screaming the question, but all she could hear over his panting breaths from the exertion of moving her were odd grunting sounds. A moment passed and the world spun, shifting so the roofline of the SUV bisected the sky which had gone upside down, tops of the trees inserting themselves into the top of her vision, her brain too scrambled to interpret the images.

Gloom descended, and she felt her body being moved, then something touched her face, and true darkness enveloped her.

When she came to, she was just as confused. It took a moment for her vision to resolve into an up-close view of carpeting that covered a vehicle's seatbacks. Dark gray and nubby, if the seats were laid down, they'd form a solid floor big enough to stretch out across, instead of the tiny space between the last row of seats and the back doors. Alace jerked her wrists, but the material used to bind her bit in, tearing her skin. *Zip tie, fuck.* She tried to sit up, but her legs were bent, and when she attempted to straighten them the restraints on her wrists tightened painfully. *Hogtied.*

Quiet crunching from under the vehicle, the soft pings against metal telling her they were still on a gravel road. That didn't mean anything. Nearly all the roads around the park were dirt or gravel, and once you crossed the line onto the reservation, it was the same. Her excesses from the previous night weren't far enough from present, not yet. Even with the hike, the alcohol had not quite sweated out of her system, and she found the heaviness of her eyelids threatening to pull her back under. Alace shook her head, bumping the back door with a soft thud. That noise interrupted the sounds that had been so muted and innocuous she hadn't even noticed them until they were gone.

He'd been talking to himself. Ranger Rick didn't like quiet, it seemed. She lay still and waited, flexing her fingers to try and stave off the worsening pinprick sensations. Out here, the normal radio stations didn't reach, and the DNR wasn't the kind of organization to spend money on satellite music for their rangers. Alace lay as still as possible, holding her body against the lurch and sway of the vehicle's chassis. After a moment, Ranger Rick began again, and with his first words, her blood ran chill in her veins.

"Waterdrum was always too sloppy. I told him a thousand times, bury them on the res. Did he listen? No. I told him. More than once. Man had an argument for everything. No weak blood on tribal land, not for whites, trash belonged with trash. A thousand reasons and what did they get him? Dead. That's what they got him. Dead."

Jesus, fuck. Ranger Rick had been working with Waterdrum. He was the blind partner. *Jesus, how did I not see that?* Ranger Rick had been so far off her radar, she hadn't even bothered to find out his real name. She had no intel on him, no info, nothing to help her through this current situation. *Jesus.* Waterdrum didn't have anything on her kind of slop, it seemed.

Slippery slop if it meant her radar hadn't even pinged weird on this dude. Hell, she'd stood still and let him drive up to her while rolling her eyes, because he was just a nuisance. *A nuisance who got the drop on me, and a hell of an annoyance who knows his way around a zip tie.*

The angle of the floor under her tilted as the nose of the vehicle slanted down, and she rocked forwards against the seatback. A moment later she heard water, then splashing against the tires as they rolled through a creek. Alace took in a careful breath. If there was a pothole in the middle of—the vehicle lurched as first the front then the rear wheel churned through the deeper water of a dip. *He's taking me back to Waterdrum's cabin.* A place she'd walked away from only hours before, stopping midstream in this creek to try and wash the worst of the blood from her hands and face. The logical idea was that he knew she'd been the one to kill his partner. It wasn't much of a leap to assume he would want to deal out damage in return. The engine revved, wheels slipping and losing purchase on the riverbed, then gaining traction.

Gingerly, she tested her bonds again. No give at all, but her wrists were skin to skin, which meant he'd only used a single tie there. The ties felt thin. If she could manage to get her hands in front of her, that would be easily broken. She'd need to solve the hogtie situation first. With a few moments work, she knew she could accomplish it, but there were tools and supplies stacked around her. That had been what the thump came from earlier. Not her head hitting the door, but hitting a bag that knocked against the door. If she tried to turn to her back and worm her wrists around her ass, she might as well ring the dinner bell. Shivering, she thrust away the idea of Ranger Rick lifting a sliver of raw meat to his lips. *Stop it*. This wasn't the worst situation she'd ever found herself in, not by a long shot. And at least now she was older and better trained. Not overly confident, but still, experience had to count for something, right?

"Woman worth her salt."

She heard the words clear as a bell. Then the car was crashing around her, body and head pelted with fast-moving debris. Alace hunched her shoulders, eyes closing just before her face impacted the leg of the seat in front of her. Agony burst into life under the skin of her nose and forehead, and she blinked slowly, every reaction blunted by the pain. Ranger Rick was cursing, his voice echoing over the sound of a hissing radiator and crunching metal, the grinding shriek of whatever had impacted them dragging along the side of the vehicle. Gravel pelted off the inside of the wheel wells as the SUV slid sideways, tilting enough to launch a new onslaught of projectiles to bounce off her body before settling back onto all four wheels.

Alace gathered herself enough to take advantage of the overpowering noise, pulling her wrists up at the same time she forced her feet down and out. She needed three hard yanks like that to break the tie securing wrists to ankles and knew her arms were bleeding when she was finally successful.

The engine revved loudly, then started knocking, the metal in the motor hammering hard enough to shake the vehicle. Ranger Rick's voice was a shout now, and the SUV gave a lurch forwards, then slid sideways again, the sound of water all around. Sudden silence from the engine left the man's wordless yelling louder than ever, and Alace twisted around to find no handles on the inside of the doors behind her. She jerked one foot up while pushing one down, nearly smacking herself in the face with a knee as her ankles were suddenly freed. *Hands,* she thought, turning to her back as a cascade of noises chimed her movement, bottles, and camp stove fuel tanks rattling and jostling for space against each other. Alace's arm chilled immediately, and she looked to see water seeping under the doors. The sound of the water was close, running swiftly, and she knew if they'd been swept off the graveled crossing, the water could be deep enough to partially submerge the vehicle. She wiggled, bringing her knees up to her chest, pointing her toes as much as she could in the hiking boots as she shoved her arms down, spreading her elbows as wide as possible.

The vehicle moved again, and as it shifted side to side, her heart jolted, pumping triple time as she heard Ranger Rick, still cursing, coughing as he made his way towards her. Just as her arms maneuvered free of her boots and she brought her elbows down to either side fast, breaking the tie, his head popped over the seat, blood coating half his face. Silent, lips moving soundlessly, his eyes were squinted tight. What she could see of them were bloodshot and weeping. As the smell of bear spray made its way to where she lay, Alace squinted her eyes, mouth sealed tight as he lunged over the seat, his hand swiping the air within a foot of her face.

She rolled, shoving her face into the scant inches of water at the back of the SUV. Back and forth, she scrubbed against the saturated carpeting as the stinging set in. It felt like her sinuses were on fire, as if she'd snorted ghost pepper juice for the fun of it on a dare. The skin of her face grew taut, already swelling from the capsaicin used to make the bear spray effective against a thousand-pound bear. The canister must have ruptured in the wreck.

Sudden, brutal pressure across her chest had her gasping in a lungful of water. She surfaced coughing and choking, eyes running with tears and refusing to open. Disoriented for the umpteenth time today, she felt something pulling at her shoulders, then a hard bar scraped across her low back before she dropped what felt like two-feet onto a bouncy surface. Flailing with her hands, she caught fabric and yanked, tearing whatever it was she'd grabbed. More pulling at her shoulders, another stomach-churning drop, this one farther down, then she was moving horizontally before dropping again, finally onto a solid surface. Rocks and sticks poked the backs of her arms, scratching streaks across the backside of her legs as she was dragged, still gagging from the strength of the bear spray.

It took Alace a moment to register she'd stopped moving, that the rocks imprinting on her ass were stationary and not a fresh discovery with already raw flesh. Eyes closed, she lurched, trying to sit up, yanked backwards by the backpack strap still fastened across her chest. Fingers to the clasp, she released it, rocking forward to get her legs underneath her in an effort to get up and away.

A thick-sounding shout, as if Ranger Rick's throat was filled with phlegm, then hard fingers latched onto her arm. Forward momentum halted, Alace stumbled and lost the precarious hold she had on her balance. Falling backwards, she flung out her arm, hearing Ranger Rick curse as her elbow caught some part of his anatomy. She still couldn't open her eyes, tears streaming down her face, and even in the clutch of panic, her brain compared how he sounded to the way her nose was flowing, and she thought he must have gotten a worse dose of the spray than she had.

An arm, thick as an Amazon anaconda, wrapped around her throat, and Alace pried her eyes open finally, the barest sliver, shocked when she realized it was still broad daylight. Somehow between being hit with the Taser, waking up to find herself kidnapped, involved in an accident that included the possibility of drowning instead of being killed by a serial killer—it seemed absurd for it to not be the deepest part of night. Breath choked off, Alace barely had time to rip at his arm in an effort to free herself and think *the fainting game*, and then she was gone for what had to be a very long time.

When she came to next, the stench of blood on the air gave away her location.

Waterdrum's cabin.

It shouldn't have been a surprise since she'd figured out that was where Ranger Rick was headed when he wrecked his Park Service SUV. Still, it caught her off-guard. She hadn't intended to ever return, and didn't want to see the scene again, knowing it would play with her memories of Red's slaughter. Swollen eyes fighting every opening blink, she forced herself to look around. Trussed up again, the same kind of ties probably, given the bright pain of her wrists, she'd been tossed to the side, wedged against the bottom of a wall like windblown trash.

Same cabin, same room, same smells—very different scenery.

Hanging from the suspension bar was Waterdrum. Alace stared in disbelief, fighting her stomach's immediate revulsion, gagging at how his corpse had been butchered. *Oh my God, oh my God.* It wasn't the evidence of the multiple killing blows she'd landed in her frenzy to make him pay for the children he'd killed that had her writhing against her bonds, no, what was twisting her insides was the sight of him gutted. *Jesus.* Entrails laid in several tidy piles in plastic bins, it looked as if the heart and liver had been separated from the intestines and other offal. *What...why?* Ribs gaping wide, bones outstretched as if they were welcoming someone in for a grisly hug, her mind imposed the image of an innocent Red on his body, and she shuddered, glad he hadn't gotten that far before she stopped him.

Where the fuck is Ranger Rick?

Alace found no answers from Waterdrum. His hands had been removed, and even trying to not see details, she noted there were entire pieces of him carved off. If she'd been looking at a prime cut diagram, she'd label them as rump, flank, and shoulder. Alace swallowed hard, her throat working furiously to force down bitter bile, eyes burning with the effort. She'd left him lying on the floor, fleeing the cabin after she'd regained enough sobriety to realize her mistakes, but someone—likely Ranger Rick—had strung him up. She strained against her bonds again. *Fuck.*

A sound from outside forced itself onto her awareness, the soft whoomph of a heavy object being placed on a padded surface, a bass grunt signaling effort. Alace allowed her lids to droop almost closed, filtering light with her lashes to see who was coming in through the door. Pausing just outside the opening, Ranger Rick stamped his feet twice on the porch, courteously clearing his boots of debris before walking into the dead man's cabin. He had on a pair of chest-high waders and a plastic rain jacket, open to show bright yellow suspenders. Without even glancing her direction, he moved through the room and into the back where she knew the kitchen was. He returned a moment later with a large knife, jacket now fastened tight around his neck. One gloved hand on the body, he studiously spun it in a slow circle, paying careful attention as he paused here and there, finally settling it with the corpse facing away.

Alace watched with disbelief as he prodded Waterdrum's back, hips to waist, poking hard with a stiffened thumb, grunting when he seemed to identify whatever he'd been feeling for. He set the knife to a section of flesh low on Waterdrum's back, skin already removed in a strip. Wiggling the knife's tip into the muscles alongside the dip showing the man's spine, he drew it down towards Waterdrum's neck.

The steel sliced through the soft flesh, and Alace couldn't look away, sickly fascinated with the skill and speed with which it was used. Hissing undertones of sound accompanied four long cuts, the swiftness telling her everything she didn't want to know about Rick's experience and expertise with the flashing blade he wielded. Pink-tinged bone shone through the open space, silver fascia covering the different muscles. All the things intended by God to be hidden, exposed for her to see.

Rick worked his fingers into the cut he'd made, parting and easing it open wider and wider until at last, he grasped the exposed wad of meat with his fingers, one hand steadying the carcass while he ripped the length of backstrap from the body.

Still not looking at her, he began murmuring, and as his words became audible. It chilled her to realize that of the pair, Waterdrum may have been the sane one.

"Every man's worth something. Gotta find out what that is, sort the good from the bad. Wheat from chaff. Find the balance between the light and dark." He lifted a hand to wipe sweat from his forehead, painting a broad swath of red across his skin. "Wheat from chaff."

The efficient separation of flesh from the human carcass produced a noise unlike anything Alace had ever heard.

A memory crawled along the edges of her mind. *Anything would be better than this.* Closing her eyes for a moment, she concentrated, trying to bring it into focus.

She'd lived in Florida a long time ago. The gig had her staying in a camper park near a resort. One of the things almost all the residents had in common was the sheer quantity of offspring they produced. Towards the end of the day, those children would run the park in packs separated by age, older of the kids searching out hidden places to light their stolen smokes and the younger moving in waves from trailer to trailer at the whim of the current ringleader. Those groups only flocked together when the ice cream truck would make an appearance, the bright music luring them close.

She'd happened to be outside one night when the ice-cream truck came. Sitting on an open tailgate, legs swinging through hot, humid air, the only breeze was stirred by her movement. There had been three kids left at the end of a line that had snaked for a half an hour towards the window set in the side of the truck, disappointed when the driver announced he'd run out of drumsticks, the local favorite. In recompense, he'd given those kids frozen ice pops for half price.

She remembered, wishing for once she could forget.

The sound their mouths made as they slurped the fruit-flavored ice on a stick had been obscene. Obscene to the point the man she'd been sitting next to had blushed bright red. The kids were determined though, not willing to let a single drop of their rapidly turning-to-slush treats escape. Slurping and swallowing with a loud suck, the kids had walked past and into the gathering night, careful—as all Florida kids were—to watch for the dangerous shine of eyes in the dips separating the camper lots.

She opened her eyes. That sound didn't hold a candle to what Rick was doing to Waterdrum's body. He paused and stepped back. Leaning to one side, he grabbed something balanced on the edge of a bucket, and his arms began making steady, measured movements. The harsh scraping sound of a knife blade on sharpening stone filled the air, and she breathed deeper for a moment, relieved he'd stopped even as the sour at the back of her throat filled her nose with burning fumes.

"Wheat from chaff." Rick—at some point she'd unconsciously abandoned the helpful-sounding Ranger—spoke quietly as he approached the body again, aiming himself at the other edge of Waterdrum's spine. His knife flashed again, the blade making ticking noises against rib bones, bringing to mind picket fences and sticks, small bodies flying as they ran along, their plaything of choice easily discarded if the homeowner was discontent at the plunking along his fence. "Man's gotta be good for something, needs to stand for something. Still—" Rick grunted, elbow jerking as the knife sawed through a bone. "—looking for yours, Waterdrum. I told you." Another grunt, then a section of ribs sagged free, and he leaned over to place it in a container. "Wheat from chaff."

He's occupied. Find a way out. Alace closed her eyes for a moment, focusing on her bonds for the second time that day. Ankles and wrists restrained separately this time, she tested the bounds of movement allowed, finding more than before. It made sense; he'd been impacted by the spray more than her, and with the SUV in the middle of the creek, he would have only had the contents of his pockets. She moved cautiously to check circulation, cheek pressed to the floor, and awareness of her body let the stench from the blood-soaked boards drive into her brain like a spike. Pushing that away, she wiggled her fingers and toes, relieved to find them stiff but not tingling. *All I have to do is break free again.* The ties would make noise as they gave way, so she'd have to wait until he left the cabin once more.

Rick had removed the other rib section while she'd been busy inside her head and laid it in the same container. He straightened and studied the body for a moment, slowly twirling it left then right. With a jerk, he twisted to face her, and Alace rejected her body's demand for more air, movement, anything—keeping her breathing steady and shallow, eyes closed so only the barest of shadows could be seen through her lashes. After a moment, there was the sound of steps moving away, and the scrape of the container's bottom against the sticky floor told her he'd been satisfied with her performance.

Lids lifting a miniscule amount, she followed the dark outline of his body as he moved to the door and through it, forcing herself to wait for an eternity of five seconds before she began working her way free. Fifteen seconds more and she was kneeling on the floor, angling to see out the door. Waterdrum's vehicle was still parked in front of the cabin where she'd left it, and Rick was stacking the container in the open back, adding it to the myriad of boxes already placed inside.

She had taken a single step towards the front door when Rick lifted his head, and she froze, thinking he had somehow heard her movement. A moment later, she realized he'd caught the grinding noise of an engine in the distance. Having walked out from the cabin just hours ago—*Is it still the same day?* She dismissed the thought as unimportant—she knew there were no buildings nearby. The road continued past the cabin only to make a wide loop through the trees, probably used by semis when winter hay was trucked in for the venison herds. A vehicle this close meant either Rick had called for reinforcements, or he was about to be interrupted by someone unexpected.

From his aggressive stance, she suspected the latter.

Creeping along the wall, Alace secured a position near the single window at the front of the cabin where she could keep an eye both on Rick and the approach to the cabin. A dark SUV drove into view, crawling up the rough road, front end rocking as the suspension took a beating navigating over the rocks exposed by recent erosion. Dust was thick along the side panels, and the front plate on the vehicle was familiar, a neighboring state to the north. The whole damn vehicle was familiar.

Rick moved, opened the driver door of the police car and stood in the space. She recognized this as a way to mask the state of his clothes, keeping the distorting glass of the front windshield or side window between him and whoever was making an approach. That told her he didn't recognize the vehicle, or maybe he did. *Which actually doesn't tell me anything*. She grimaced, flexing her knees as best she could in her crouched position.

A swirl of dust washed out in front of the SUV when it parked about forty feet away. Too far for easy conversation, close enough to see details without getting out of the car. Seemed the SUV's driver had his own countermeasures he was putting into place.

The driver's head twisted back and forth as he looked around the clearing, and the spit in Alace's mouth dried, leaving her tongue a foreign-feeling wasteland. That profile looked familiar, a terror-inducing familiarity that fixed her in place. She watched as Eric—*fucking, fucking Eric*—opened the driver door and stood, placing one hand on the roof of his SUV. Less than six hours to Denver from here, she'd mapped that months ago. She must have given away more clues to her location than she remembered of their call if he'd not only found the national forest but this individual cabin on the reservation, following a trail of breadcrumbs she couldn't recall laying out. She was frozen, staring at him, the well-known lines of his clean-shaven jaw making her fingers tingle, longing to touch him again.

Rick called a gruff greeting, his voice harsh with anger, a sound that would surely discourage Eric from doing anything stupid. "Can I help you? This is private land." A park ranger standing next to a reservation cop car might ping strange to someone like Eric, and she knew she was right when he didn't move from his position. With the waders and jacket, maybe Rick's profession wasn't recognizable.

Alace shook her head, racking her brain to remember if Waterdrum had left any weapons in the car. Of course, Rick could have taken any multitude of things out and placed them inside, and if he intended to use the vehicle to leave, he probably had. *Think, Alace.* There'd been nothing in the front seat as she'd driven out here, and she'd stripped Waterdrum of any dangerous items before bringing him inside, storing everything in the back of the car, where Rick had been stacking boxes. He'd probably either moved or shoved them to the side. Rick had left his knives inside the cabin. His Taser was likely in the park service SUV in the creek. All of this meant he was likely unarmed. *This might not be as big a cluster as it could be.*

Reluctantly approaching the carcass hanging from the ceiling, she soundlessly lifted the knife from where it lay across the edges of a container, shifting it in her hand until she found a balanced grip.

Voice now holding an edge of anger, Rick asked, "What do you want?"

Her lids slipped closed for an instant when Eric answered, his voice rough and hoarse from disuse on his solo trip. "I think I'm lost. Can you help me?" It was a good ploy, people did that kind of shit all the time. Get on a road and just drive, thinking whatever they were looking for would be around the next corner, waiting to reward their persistence. "I was looking for Cuba and think I got turned around." Back at the window, she watched as Rick's shoulders lost their stiffness. Cuba wasn't far from here, and if Eric had been a tourist who was seeking out the far backroads, it was easy to get off track as roads wound around mountain peaks. In some cases, you had to go east to go north, or vice versa. "Can you help me out?" He hadn't moved from his position, tucked behind his opened door, keeping a layer of protection between him and the unknown man.

"Easy enough." The comfortable jocularity had slipped back into Rick's voice; this was his helpful ranger mode, and Alace's lip curled at the lie. "Head back down the track to the second road, turn left and follow that down to 550. You'll take another left there, and be in Cuba in a half an hour or so."

"Oh." Eric looked around, making no effort to hide his curiosity. Also a good ploy, since a real tourist wouldn't care if they seemed rude, most of them falling into the "these people will never see me again so I can act an ass" train of thought. "Nice place. Is this yours?" He stared at a peak in the distance. "Gotta say, I love the view. You ever rent it out?"

"No." All friendliness had left Rick's tone, leaving it harsh and flat. "Safe travels." With that blunt dismissal, Rick turned with a jerk and took a step towards the cabin, slamming the vehicle door behind him with an angry swing of his arm. A look of shock hit his face when he saw her in the window, his movements too abrupt for her to take action to hide.

Thinking quickly, she dropped the knife to grab the strap on her backpack, placed conveniently near the door and walked out onto the porch, glad Rick's back was towards Eric. That meant he didn't get to see Eric's reaction to seeing her, their positions hiding the jolt his body gave that shouted recognition. She hefted the bag, slinging one strap over a shoulder, feeling the weight bearing down.

"Hey, did you say you're headed to Cuba? Can I get a ride?" If Rick thought him a tourist, he might not be willing to involve him in what was going on here. When his partner was unknown, she'd been convinced Waterdrum had to be the hunter of the two, but now she remembered how Rick had continually surprised her today. First by linking her together with Waterdrum's death, and then by Rick's efficient abduction of her, a person trained in the kind of countermeasures that should have kept her safe. She stepped to the end of the porch and off, dropping the three feet to the ground, landing balanced, with soft knees that still complained about the impact. "I was going to hitch with Rick, but he's tied up with something for a while. I need to get to Cuba. Any chance of you helping me out?"

"Sure." Eric's calm voice didn't match his expression, which bordered on freaked out. "Climb on in."

"Thanks, Rick." She called over her shoulder, twisting to see the ranger had swung to watch her walk away. "Love what you've done to the place." A reminder that his interior decorations held secrets he would probably prefer to keep hidden. "See you around." *You won't see me coming*. She held her breath as she dropped into the seat, hearing Eric's door slam shut, closing them inside the vehicle. Shifting the bag to her lap, she wrapped her arms around it. *Will he really let me drive away, knowing what I know?*

From his position on the steps, Rick watched, unmoving. Alace locked gazes with him and he didn't blink, didn't flinch. He was letting her go. *Time to get the fuck out of Dodge.*

Alace turned her head towards Eric who was staring at her, equal parts terror and exhilaration in his expression. "Drive. Turn around and drive." Surprised out of his shock, he reached and started the car then reversed into the field next to the cabin, pulling out onto the rocky track. "Not too fast, you'll tear up the car." Tearing her gaze from Eric's face, still not believing it was real, Alace angled her eyes to the mirror, seeing Rick growing smaller with every second. "How'd you find the place? How did you find *me*?"

Eric didn't respond, and she glanced at him. Fingers tight around the wheel, his knuckles were stark white from the force of his grip. He was alternating looking at the road and flicking his eyes towards her. Back and forth, as if he were afraid she would disappear in an instant. The vehicle was rapidly picking up speed, and he looked about half a second away from that promised freak-out she'd seen on his face earlier. Keeping her voice 'soft, she repeated the question, "Eric, how did you find me?"

Motion in the mirror pulled her attention, and she saw the cop car slowly pulling away from the cabin. It turned the other direction, towards the loop that ran through the back of the property, and Alace wondered if she'd missed something up that way. "Slow down. You can slow down, he's leaving. We're good." The SUV immediately decelerated to a crawl, the punishing bounces from the rocks in the road lessening.

Alace was pulled, finding herself unaccustomedly uncertain what to do. Should she bail out and head back to follow Rick or stay with Eric and make sure he got out of harm's way? *Shit*. Her inclination was to keep Eric safe, no question. *I can always come back and track Rick. I'll need to gather the kids' IDs anyway.* She would send those to someone Regg kept on retainer to report things like this, since attempting to give every family closure was part of her standard gig.

With Rick headed away from them, it felt safe to turn her full attention to Eric, so she twisted to see he was no longer pretending to watch the road, staring across the car to where she sat. "Hey." His eyes widened at the greeting she'd worked to keep casual. "You saved me."

"You're really here?" Eric's hands slipped and tightened on the wheel as a pothole threatened to rip it from his grip. Then he gifted her with something she longed for every day, playing each utterance of her name in his voice in her dreams. "Alace, baby. You're here?"

"I am." One side of his mouth pulled down, and he quickly turned to look out the windshield. She drank in the sight of him. Hair slightly longer than before, curling softly at the nape of his neck. He bore lines of tension she suspected would smooth out once things had calmed down, but they didn't look bad on him at all, giving him a veneer of even more rugged handsomeness.

She studied him, impressing every detail on her brain, storing up the tiniest of things for later. The way the muscles in his forearms shifted as he wrestled the SUV down through the creek and up the other side.

The DNR vehicle downstream fifty yards or more, wedged against the bank in a crush of tree branches and logs. Alace shivered, remembering the chill of the water as it seeped into the vehicle. She dragged her gaze away and stared at Eric again. *He's really here.*

"Eric, you saved me." Not that she'd needed saving, really. When he drove up, she'd been two seconds from exiting out the back door and into the woods, where Rick would have been hard-pressed to find her. Eric pulling up when he did certainly made her escaping easier.

"This was the place? Where you called from last night?" His voice dipped a register, adopting a husky drawl that teased along her spine.

How odd that it was just last night. A handful of hours ago, she'd been drunk off her ass and crying on the phone with a man. *This man.* Someone who had made it a mission to hunt her down, but not for reasons most men searched for a person like her. Not to take her to the nearest authorities and turn her over for a reward. Fear drilled into her head, stiffening her spine. *What if he is?* It had been more than two years since their short-lived romance. People changed all the time. *Hell, I've changed.* She thought of the small cache of mementos she carried with her now. On the phone, he'd told her he knew people, folks who could make things go away. That implied confronting her actions, something she wasn't willing to do anywhere near anyone who wore handcuffs as a uniform accessory. "Where are we going?"

"What?"

"Where are we going? Where are you taking us?" If she couched it like that, he might be less inclined to immediately hit up the nearest authorities. "Yes, that's the cabin I was at."

"How...why would you come back? Did you ever leave?"

"Yeah." She shrugged off the backpack and settled it on the floor between her boots. "Rick found me and brought me back." She plucked at her shirt, pulling it away from her body, wincing as the material stuck to the oozing burn on her chest.

"He brought you back? Why?" She ignored his questions for a moment and hooked a finger in the neck, dragging the fabric out to expose the spot and angling her chin down to look at where the Taser barb had impacted. There was a quarter-inch hole with red, raised edges flaring from the site. "What is that? Did he hurt you?" The vehicle slowed. Glancing up, she saw his eyes fixed on the burn, then flicked to her wrists, raw and torn from the repeated sessions with zip ties. He scowled, expression hardening, and Alace realized Eric was about a half a second from deciding to go back and do something stupid.

"He used a Taser. Got the drop on me because he didn't ping like he was dangerous. The man—" She hesitated a moment, then continued. "—I told you about the man last night." Eric nodded. The SUV had drifted to a complete stop, the quiet engine leaving the silence of the wilderness nearly unbroken. "Rick, Ranger Rick...I don't know his name because he didn't fucking factor." She let go of her collar and slammed a fist against her thigh. "He didn't fucking factor, but he was the partner. The one I couldn't figure out, and I'd talked to him nearly every day for weeks."

"Baby, I don't understand." A sweet pain swept over her with his use of the word, and Alace let her eyes close for a moment. Sound in the distance alerted her, and she looked in the mirror, staring at Waterdrum's car as it returned to the front of the cabin. *We gotta go.*

"Drive, Eric. Get us out of here. I'll explain everything, just..." She couldn't wait any longer, needed to reassure herself that this was real, not a drug-induced hallucination. Alace reached out and covered his hand with hers, flesh and bone fingers spreading to let hers fall through, tightening around and trapping her as their fingers threaded together. "Get us safe first."

He released a deep breath, heat gusting over her hand where it was joined with his, and he brought their clasped hands to his thigh, adjusting his other hand on the wheel as he started the SUV rolling again. "Okay. I can do that."

By the time they'd reached the highway, she'd thrown caution to the winds, no longer caring if he might have a recording device in the vehicle. She had explained what brought her to the location, a scattering of reports on the darknet about how kids who hit the local state cops radar fell off when they headed west through the reservation. Those disappearances had eventually led her to Waterdrum. He'd been the last contact for many of the cops dropping the runaways at the edge of the reservation, as far as the treaties would allow them to go without a clear invitation. She talked through her process, and how she'd been hiking and camping for months, working a grid pattern to try and find his base of location. The process of identifying which of the many remote cabins held not only the tools, but as of last night, graphic evidence of his murder and mutilation of so many kids. She'd skimmed over her involvement in his death, not certain what pitfalls her failed memories held for things she must have told Eric last night.

Through it all, he'd listened quietly, not asking questions, just taking in the story. His fingers had tightened on hers at places when she'd gotten too detailed, those reactions letting her map out when to back off. When she got to today and her disgust at not picking up anything from Rick, irritation at herself for allowing him the opening to scoop her up, Eric made a tortured sound, and she looked at his face, seeing lines of pain drawing his mouth down and to the side. *Too much.* Skipping to waking up at the cabin and what Rick had been doing hadn't alleviated Eric's distress, so she quickly drew her narrative to a close, ending with her relief at seeing Eric in the vehicle.

When he turned towards town on the highway, they were only minutes away from whatever came next, and she pulled in a hard breath. *Reality time.* "What are you going to do? Where are you taking me?" His fingers clutched hers, knuckles grinding painfully against her bones. "Eric, what—?"

"I'd checked into a motel room, but he knows I was coming back to Cuba. That was it." He gestured over his shoulder at the brown building they'd just passed. "I'd rather…" Trailing off, he loosened his grip slightly, adjusting to pin her hand between his palm and thigh. "Come home with me, Alace." She opened her mouth, but he cut her off. "You're injured, exhausted, and you have everything you need from here to sort out what's next. You have everything you need, baby. What's a day or two? Hmmm? Come home."

Not a mention of cops or his friends who could magically fix everything. Eric didn't give any reaction to the things she'd said, any guilt she'd claimed. *Come home.* Like anything could be that easy. "Your home?" Five and a half hours away waited the place that still was a balm to her soul. "Just leave this unfinished?" That went against the grain, and she knew he heard it when he pressed her hand farther into the giving flesh of his leg.

"Just for a couple of days. We'll come back and sort it out."

Her head was shaking back and forth before he'd even finished spitting out the lie. "No. That's not what you mean. Not at all." The tone of his voice had given it away. Up to that point she'd believed, but not now. He would take her home, right. "You'll pick up the phone first chance you get. First time I doze off, you'll be up and making a call."

He shook his head, the quick motion exposing his fear. *Fear of what?* "No, Alace—"

They'd pulled up behind a car turning left, stopped in the middle of town in light traffic. She evaluated her options, reaching down to grab the strap of her bag as she tried to yank her hand out of his grip. Tried and failed, and they were moving again, faster, turning a corner with the vehicle's frame rocking violently before he screeched to a stop, tires barking as they slid on the pavement. "Alace, don't." He slammed the gearshift with his hand, reaching over to grip her arm.

She twisted in his grip, willing to leave skin behind if that was what it took. He was ripping apart every dream she'd had about him. His words down in Alabama making her believe he could look past what she'd turned herself into and see the person she wanted to be. "Alace." He sounded frustrated as she opened her door, sliding half out of the seat, one foot and one hand still inside the SUV. Yanking hard, she nearly broke free. Then he stripped her of movement with a word.

"Baby." *Fucking, fucking Eric.* He pulled, and she slipped halfway across the seat towards him, foot leaving the ground to dangle uselessly in the air. "Don't. I'm not going to do that. Not a chance, baby. I get it. I do." *Fucking liar.* No one could get it, especially not someone like him who had lived such a good life. Her words to Regg echoed through her head. *He's a good man.* "Baby, I get what you do. I want to help." That stiffened every muscle as if she'd been Tasered again, and she stared up into his eyes. Honesty and something else shone out at her, the something else undefinable, outside her wealth of experience. Honesty she could deal with, and she stopped struggling, choosing to believe him. "Baby, I want to help. Get back in and let me bring you home. We'll sleep and eat and plan. I'm good at planning. I can do that with you."

"Help me?" He nodded, pulling her closer, her head nearly in his lap, neck craned so she could look up at him. "Not turn me in?" She needed the reassurance. In her experience, people could say things on their own, volunteer lies through smiling lips, but if asked a direct question they didn't like, you could see it on their face as they answered.

"*Help you*, baby. I want to help. I get it." He'd said that several times now, over more than one conversation, but it still confused her. *How much has he looked into me?* He'd had two years and then some to put everything together and come to peace with how her chosen life's direction went. He was staring straight at her, gaze locked on her face, and nothing in his expression told her he was lying. He meant every word and was so willing to back it up he'd driven down to what she'd described as a slaughterhouse to find her. On the strength of her words, he'd dropped everything to come to her. She hadn't allowed herself to do more than cursory searches on him since she'd left his bed in the middle of the night. Her searches had dug a little deeper after Alabama, just enough to find out he'd taken paid vacation time to drive down. She didn't know what methods he'd used, what markers he'd called in, but she did know that nothing he'd done to find her had raised an alarm with any of the countermeasures she had in place against that kind of thing.

You'd think I'd have worried more after Alabama. She hadn't, though. Getting away and sorting out her next plan of action, she'd laid aside any misgiving about his actions. *It's like I've known all along I could trust him.* She stared at him. *Can I trust him?* Multiple adrenaline crashes were clouding her brain, making every thought more difficult than it had to be. She might have slept until nearly midday, but that didn't count for much when she'd been up more than twenty-four hours previously, and only laid down her head after six o'clock. Add in all that had happened today: Tasered, drugged, hit with bear spray, choked out, then rescuing herself again—exhaustion made her muscles weak, biceps and quads quivering from the strain of holding her position.

He stayed still, not shifting his grip on her arm and hand, not moving. Eric watched her, his gaze seeming to drink her in, eyes flicking side to side as he tracked down her features. No doubt she was a sight. Face covered in dirt and blood, flushed red with fear and anger, probably paling now as she came to a decision. *Am I deciding right now?* Once again, their penchant for having single words alter their trajectory together came into play, and she gave him what he wanted.

Gave herself what she wanted, too. More than anything. *My dream.* "Okay."

Without another word, he tugged, and she slid all the way into the seat, swung her legs around and dropped her bag as she reached out to close the door. Only once it was shut did he release her arm. Eric glanced down and his eyes closed, an anguished expression on his face as he turned away. She looked at her arm and saw the white imprint of his fingers there. *That's gonna bruise.* Snorting, she regained his attention. His eyes flew open and he stared at her. "Smallest of prices." She was already leaning his direction when he hooked a hand around the back of her neck, abandoning her hand for a more secure grip.

For the first time in more than two years, she kissed a man. Not any man, but Eric—*fucking, fucking Eric*— and just like that, she was gone for him again.

His lips softly questing across hers led to a firmer pressure as their mouths worked together. Her palm hit his chest, fingers twisting into his shirt to pull him near, pull herself closer, anything she could do to reduce the gulf of distance between them. The tip of his tongue slipped between her lips and tenderly touched hers, sliding and withdrawing, testing the waters. A breath later, she knew he found the waters to his liking as the kiss did what every one of their caresses had done and exploded into a corona of heat.

He made love to her mouth, breaths mingling as they separated to draw in air, panting and groaning. "Beloved." His murmur covered her like a blanket, separating her from the knowledge of what he was, letting her fall farther under his spell, no longer caring if she ever crawled out. She shifted, angling her body towards his, slipping between the wheel and his chest, and he adjusted on the fly, lifting and supporting her. Cradled in his arms, she explored as much as she could reach. Nips and licks drew more groans from him, making her smile when he arched his neck, giving her access to the sensitive underside of his jaw. She worked along the edges of muscles and bone, mapping his skin and charting every inch with her touch.

The whoop of a siren yanked her back into her head, heart pounding as she looked through the SUV and out the back window, seeing a cop car parked behind them. Eric had done a half-assed job of pulling over to the curb when he stopped, leaving them blocking part of the lane. *God. Sloppy and stupid.* She eased back across the seat to her side as Eric recaptured her hand, rolled down the window and propped his arm on the wheel. When he squeezed her fingers, she realized this was intentional, a way to partially block the cop's view of her.

"Officer."

"License, please." The nameplate on the cop's breast said Smith. An innocuous name, and Alace decided to tell Regg to use it as her last name when it was time to pull that letter out of the hat. "You're not quite parked, partner." The spring of tension in her breast eased slightly as a narrow band of teasing looped through Officer Smith's tone. "Got a good reason?"

Eric laughed, sounding so natural and easy she wondered at his acting abilities. With a father like his, and knowing the many decades of intimate involvement in so many political campaigns the man had demanded from Eric, it shouldn't be a shock he was quick on his feet when confronted by fast-changing events. "My girlfriend just hiked out of Mesa. I haven't seen her in a few days. Sorry for the bother." Eric shifted in the seat, pulled his wallet free and plucked out his license to hand to the officer. Smith gave it a cursory glance before handing it back.

"Figured as much." Smith tipped his hat to her. "Ma'am. Good hiking?"

Alace nodded, slipping a tiny smile into place on her face. "Not easy, but good." It was, too. She'd hiked all over the Mesa de Cuba area. "The erosion gives it a surreal feel. It's awfully pretty." The entire area was peppered with channels from flash floods over decades, troughs scratched into the dirt and rock by the force of rushing water.

"Beautiful in the right light." Smith agreed with her then tapped the window frame. "Be more careful where you stop to reconnect next time, Mr. Ward." Teasing and playful, his tone gave no sense of danger. "Travel safely."

"We will, Officer. Sorry again." Eric dropped his wallet into a cubby in the dash instead of replacing it in his back pocket. Turning away from the cop still standing there, he asked her, "Hungry, honey?"

She smiled shyly, letting what she hoped was a little sexy curve lift one corner of her mouth. Knowing full well the cop was still looking and listening, she tapped the frustration left in the wake of the kiss they'd just shared, infusing the single word response with everything dirty she wanted to do to Eric. "Starved."

Smith laughed, the sound light and airy, his saunter knowing as he moved away.

Still staring at her, Eric fumbled the vehicle into gear and with a shaky voice that belied the entirety of his cool performance, told her, "He's watching. Buckle up."

She leaned over and brushed the corner of his mouth with her lips. "Okay." The click of her buckle slipping into place was loud in the quiet car. "You okay?"

"Scared the fuck out of me." He waited for a break in traffic, then signaled, pulling out and making a U-turn, blowing out a hard breath as he paused at the stop sign. "What do we do now?" Alace waited a beat, verifying her feeling that this was what safety felt like, that Eric would no more hurt her than he'd hurt himself. That he wouldn't betray her, and his action that long-ago night had been misguided, but done with the best of intentions. *Didn't help Pandora when she opened the box.* Still, her gut was seldom wrong.

"There was a gas station just back over there. We'll need to go north through some remote areas to get to Colorado the fastest way. So I vote that right now, we drive back the way we came. We stop at the gas station, and then we hit a drive-through because I really am hungry." His neck twisted, and he looked at her. "I *am*." She nodded. "And you probably are, too. Unless you ate just before driving into the wilderness to rescue me?" She tried for Smith's tone, but it fell flat in the face of Eric's somber expression. He shook his head, a muscle in his jaw pulsing just under the skin. *Okay, he doesn't like me making light of what just happened.* "We get gas first. Then food. And then..." She paused and studied him closely. Time to take a leap, trusting in her gut. *God, catch me. Please.* "And then, we talk while you drive us home."

CHAPTER NINE

Eric

Holding the wheel steady as he steered across lanes to pass a semi, Eric glanced to his right, devoting a moment to study the face of the sleeping woman leaning against the door. From the moment she'd stepped from the shadows of the cabin in the woods, he'd been running on fear and panic. Even when she convinced him to eat, he couldn't choke down much, focused on getting them up the road and towards home while studying traffic behind him, looking for any vehicle that seemed to stick around for too long.

Alace Sweets.

She hadn't asked about what he'd found out in her background. Not yet. She would, though. Someone who lived on the verges of society as she did wouldn't pass up a chance to know where the holes in their walls waited. There hadn't been any real holes in her story, though. Not that he could ever find. Querida Pansy O'Dell had a life story, one that was well-crafted and believable.

If he hadn't been in bed with her when she had that damned panic attack, he would have never known Querida wasn't real. Everything pointed to the thick paper trail painted over her past being exactly what she'd portrayed on the surface. Sweet-natured, middle-income child of boomers who hadn't wanted to rack up education loans so bypassed college and had been working her way through various cities along the front range of the Rockies. A good waitress was in high demand during tourist season, and she'd been good.

That flashback had been his only crack in her story, but damn, it had been a big one. With a name to anchor it, he'd set about tracing every fact he could pay for. Using investigators recommended by a friend of a friend, Eric had kept everything at arm's length, not associating his name with any of the inquiries. It had been nearly six months in when he had the first real break. Alice Swete was considered a person of interest in the death of a man acquitted for charges of molesting and killing a nine-month-old baby. The man had been murdered about a month after a six-man grand jury refused to issue a warrant. Information found with his body identified four of the six men who had accepted payoffs to juggle their vote. The other two finally broke their silence, reporting they'd had family members threatened. It seemed the pedophile had been thorough in his efforts to remain free.

The killing was inventive, showcasing a raw anger the authorities felt would be the killer's quick downfall. The lead investigator on that case said in a press conference that rage made slipups inevitable. Unorganized killers were opportunistic. The investigator had refused to speak regarding how he felt about the molester's death, but his face said a thousand words. As part of his studies back in law school, Eric had voluntarily enrolled in several micro-expression training sessions with a renowned researcher. Learning to see emotions people weren't even aware they were communicating had given him a major advantage in a number of high-profile cases. It had also allowed him to see the investigator's glee that the man had been killed by impalement, just like the infant.

Eric twisted his neck and studied Alace for a moment, seeing her toned muscles stretching atop a wiry frame. Much of the cushioning she'd carried previously had been worn away in the months since he'd last seen her. Alabama Alace had looked much like Denver Alace. Cuba Alace, on the other hand, looked like someone who had spent the past nine months hiking in rough conditions, never eating enough, and sleeping in only limited quantities.

She'd been on the hunt at least that long, he knew, based on her recitation of what she'd been doing.

After they gassed up and grabbed a bag of burgers, he had driven east to swing through the campground so she could collect her things. Parking two curves away from the site, he had waited outside the vehicle, heart in his throat as he watched her fade into the scrub and trees. Fifteen minutes later she had reappeared, sleeping bag and some other bags dangling from her fingers as she moved through the undergrowth. One instant she hadn't been there, the next she was, and he'd let out the breath he'd been consciously holding.

Once on the road, she'd shown a voracious appetite in spite of everything, spending the time eating and talking. So much to say, there were so many things she seemed to want to explain. She'd talked herself hoarse, head weaving on her neck from exhaustion until he put a stop to it, lifting her hand to his lips to kiss the backs of her knuckles. "Sleep, beloved." How fitting that word. Not only had she been Querida when he met her, but her real last name, Sweets, also held the same meaning. She'd done as he asked, and the trust shown him made his throat tight. So much time had passed, but when caught up in an urgent need, she still hadn't doubted he would drive away from that cabin with her.

When she'd called last night—he shook his head at the thought, *only last night*—he'd known immediately that whatever...case—in his head he didn't know what to call them, but knew she spent significant time investigating, so case seemed most likely—she'd been working had gone horribly wrong. The tidbits he'd pulled from her over the hour they'd spoken, tiny hints carried through the call in slow, single words at a time, had taken him nearly too long to thread together. *Thank God for tech*, he thought, knowing he'd have to eventually explain to her the trace he'd worked on her phone. Having the location gave him a direction, one he'd embarked on almost before she'd hung up on their call.

Since his lucky break to locate her down in Alabama, Eric kept what his friends laughingly referred to as his bugout bag packed and ready to go. A lightweight, biometric-locking folder held copies of everything he'd learned about Alace, along with pictures of her taken the night of his stepmother's party. He'd been surprised at how those, paired with images of a much younger Alace, traced the line between her truncated childhood and the adult woman he'd met. So little to go on, it had been a wonder he'd found even a trace of her. Her small-town high school yearbooks granted access to a single image per year. Shy, or self-isolating, Alace didn't do band or choir. She wasn't in drama club, and didn't play sports. Her test scores and eleventh-grade GPA told him she was far more intelligent than he'd believed. The notes her grade school teachers had written about her shone a spotlight on the losses a bad environment could wring from a person.

Her brutal rape had taken so much more from her, nearly ending her life in an alley. *I think in some ways it did end life as she knew it.*

He tipped his head to the side and watched her for a moment, trying to reconcile the worn beauty seated next to him with the wretched child on the video. The men and boys had targeted her, that much was clear from the get-go. With the money and determination to dig deep, Eric had located more footage than the single file those local cops had found. Dozens of minutes captured on devices. The entire event had taken a long time, and to watch the pack as they spread out around her, shoving her back and forth with brutal strength, Alace's expression frozen into a terrified mask, suffering with clear disorientation from repeated blows to the head and face—it had been all Eric could do to hold on and watch.

But he had.

From that point, he had studied her case. Spent untold hours with his head bowed over his desk as he pored through trial notes and documents, had forced himself to watch the videos a dozen times, trying to isolate and identify her assailants. Strangely, most were still alive. The ringleader had died of disease, and his inner circle through a series of weirdly tidy accidents that when you were looking at them in a group were clearly not as advertised, but they'd been spread out enough and were different from each other so law enforcement never twigged to the ties. A small group of the men lived untouched by tragedy, and it didn't take a rocket scientist to see the similarities there—family men, every one. He had no doubt she'd verified they were good to their families, because just having children wasn't enough to save them. Many of the dead men had children. It hadn't taken his PI long to sort through information on those men, and as their private lives were uncovered, Eric had no illusions about the countless children saved from ruin by Alace's actions.

That had given him the first inkling she *was* what she seemed, a good woman and not a straight-up psycho. In each case—*I'm sticking with that until I have a better word*—the death fit the crime. Or crimes, in so many of the cases.

Alace moved, just a tiny motion, but it caught his attention, and he turned to see her looking at him. She'd gone from asleep to alert within a breath, and her gaze was locked on his face, studying something she'd seen there.

"Hey, did you sleep okay?" She didn't respond, and he couldn't keep his mouth still. "Not that I think sleeping propped into the corner of my truck is going to be comfortable, but at least you got a little shut-eye, yeah?"

He let the silence lay between them for a time, fixing his attention back on the road. False dawn lightening the eastern horizon made the shadows stretch in odd ways. Movement announced by a soft brushing of fabric against the seat preceded heat from her hand on his arm, fingers curling around the bend of his elbow as she braced herself against the vehicle's movement to lean in and brush her mouth across the corner of his jaw. Pausing near his ear, she whispered, her response scarcely loud enough to make out the words over the rush and rumble of tires against the pavement. "I slept very well, thank you."

Eric pulled in a breath, trying and failing to keep it steady, the heated rush of her breath against his skin an unexpected aphrodisiac. Her head settled against his shoulder for a moment, fingertips digging into his skin as she held on, and he wanted to shift, get his arm around her, pull her close—but with a woman like Alace, trying to hold on would get you empty hands. He already knew that from experience, so he relished the fact she'd initiated this contact, giving himself over to having her lean on him even this much. "I'm glad, baby." Her seat belt clicked, and her ass slid across to the inside edge of her seat, so her body was folded tight against his arm. "You hungry or need a bathroom break?" With his other hand, he gestured ahead, knowing she'd see the motion by the dashboard lights. "There's an exit in another five miles with a truck stop."

She was quiet for so long, he wondered if she'd slipped back into a doze. Then her head rolled to press her cheek against the curve of his chest. He rested his chin on top of her head, holding her in place for a moment before she sighed and shifted away, stretching up to drop another tiny kiss along his jaw. "I could use a stop." Back to her seat, she secured her belt again. "You're taking this all very well, Eric."

He parried with a quick, "You studied me, right?" She would have had to, and it wasn't like he was ignorant of why she might have shown up in his hometown. Not once he knew what she did for a—*Is it a living? Does she make money from her cases?* He shivered. *Father.* No, he'd considered her motives for going after the esteemed Amos Ward and none of them had to do with money. Every allegation through the years shone a spotlight on his father Eric would much rather have never seen.

Ignorance is bliss. Knowledge is power. Eric shook his brain free from the trite sayings his father was so good at.

A pattern had emerged, and it was clear to Eric there had to be something behind all the accusations. Smart, or lucky, his father had been careful to only target interns and staffers with little influence, and in those circles, having little influence meant even less money.

Alace hadn't responded, so Eric forged forwards into the silence. "So, you have to know I'm not stupid, Alace." He marked how she first jolted at his use of her name, then slowly eased back into the seat, affecting a relaxation he was confident she didn't feel. "While we've been driving, you talked about New Mexico, and told me a lot of what you uncovered there. You need to know I've a good understanding of the man in Alabama, too. I kept watching, hoping you'd resurface. Instead of you, though, your evidence hit the news centers a month after I made you run out of town. I know it was you, because until it was brought forwards, everyone else in that town believed the lie that man shoved in their faces."

"Eric—"

He didn't let her interrupt, talking over whatever argument she felt compelled to provide. It was still dark enough to feel intimate in the truck's cab, and he didn't want to lose that feeling, wanted to keep her comfortable, safe, even while he laid out a few things for her. "But what I'm getting at is, you know I'm not stupid. I didn't come find you without knowing what you do. I'm sure I will never know everything, and God...I'm also sure I'm okay with that, because what I do know is—" He cast around for a word, finally settling on how he'd felt when it all came together in his head. "—unsettling. Stunning. But, I think I've come to know you, and I believe in the woman you've shown yourself to be. It doesn't matter what name you wear, you're always still Alace Sweets underneath. I've had the past few hours to think on your words, on the story you told, and, baby, I gotta say, I'm not disregarding the differences in our positions, but that man, Waterdrum...he was a monster."

"You're romanticizing this, Eric. I'm not a monster slayer." She paused, and he heard her quavering inhale before she said, "I'm not a nice person. Don't make this...me something I'm not."

Straight to the heart of everything, even afraid of rejection, his Alace didn't shy from head-on confrontation. Wasn't a surprise, not really. "Yes, you are. And no, I'm not. You took a man's life. He'd killed countless kids. It's not a tit-for-tat thing. I'd venture to say you don't do anything on a whim."

"No, I'm not the impulsive type."

"Except with me." He didn't turn, didn't look at her, just tamed what wanted to be a broad grin down into a smug smirk. They'd be home in thirty minutes, and then he could take his time convincing her of how he felt.

"What?"

"I seem to remember one night you did something entirely unexpected." He reached out, latching onto her hand again, pulling it over to rest against his thigh. Her fingers tensed in his, holding tightly. "You told me to stay, against everything we both knew were the right things to do." He gave her a squeeze, holding until she returned the pressure. "That's kinda impulsive, baby."

CHAPTER TEN

Alace

Exhausted as she was, Alace still took a few seconds to orient herself inside Eric's home.

She'd been here less than a handful of times when she lived in town before. Two times, if she were being precise. Once the night of the party, that fucking, fucking night when she let her weakness tear down every wall between her and the outside world.

The other time had been about a week before the official meeting at the diner, when she'd dropped by while Eric was out, just to scope the lay of the land. *And duplicate data on his encrypted external hard drive, access his password key chain on his computer, and sort through his not-extensive collection of porn, looking for anything that might indicate he was more like his father than any of the reports had shown.* She stuffed her internal wince down hard, shoving it to the side. *It was my job, then.* He'd said in the truck he knew she had dug into his past, stated it without any kind of bitterness, and she believed him. Eric was a straight shooter, always. One of the things she'd admired about him, even as she'd played him.

A lifetime of studying people and their things gave her the advantage in so many situations. This was another one of those.

"Why did you stop going to visit your mother?" Framed collections of images hung on the walls of his living room. There'd been artwork in other areas of his house, at least when she was here before, but in his living space, he kept reminders of people and places that meant something to him. His bedroom décor had been neutral, lending weight to a gut feeling that the framed pictures of his many vacations to Malibu had been provided by his mother. Hung by Eric on the wall in a growing, concentric circle where the oldest images were in the center and newer ones spiraled around the outside, likely sent to him as reminders when the next visit came due. From what she could see, there had been only a single new image added to the arrangement, and it was from the trip he'd taken just before she'd "met" him.

Shuffling footsteps approached behind her as she scanned the pictures, the images of Eric captured in each marking again just how handsome this man was. Strong arms circled her body, bands around her chest and belly tightening to pull her back against his frame.

The rustle and scrape of his whiskers through her hair preceded words whispered in her ear by only a breath. "I spent every moment I could looking for you."

She stood still, letting the weight of that settle into her gut. There was a building pressure to acknowledge how she felt, how she'd felt since the first moment they'd locked gazes. Alace swallowed hard, and he gave her a squeeze that told her the internal struggle wasn't so internal. *In for a penny*. "I have a kind of partner." The soft, reassuring sounds of his breathing stopped, things held in stasis for a moment before she realized what he must be thinking. Giving her head a shake, she said, "Not like that. I've never met him. But I talk to him a lot."

"Okay." Quiet encouragement with a thread of interest. Not curious, but ready to listen, and it seemed he valued what she had to say. Alace closed her eyes, the wonder of that sweeping over her for a moment.

"When I left—"

He interrupted, voice firm, "We don't have to talk about that night."

They hadn't yet, true. But it needed to be explained. "This isn't about that"—*not yet, at least*—"it's about after."

A squeeze that pulled her shoulders in, holding her firmly, a silent confirmation that no matter what she said, he promised to catch her. *Answer to prayers I didn't know I was praying.*

"Okay."

"He's been my associate for a long time." Understatement of the truth, but still a fact. "About twelve years ago—" She knew she was pulling the curtains back on secrets by even revealing that kind of timeline, but this was Eric. Fucking, fucking Eric, who hadn't stopped looking for her. Who had found her, twice, when law enforcement agencies had expended thousands upon thousands of man-hours trying to do the same thing and failing. Fucking, fucking Eric who for months had ignored family and friends to track her down. Anything she gave him, he'd earned a hundred times over. "—he met a woman. He called me that same night. Not to brag like he sometimes did. He sounded different, talking about all these nuances of emotions she'd shown him, how he'd responded, how it felt being away from her after only a single encounter." She shrugged, feeling Eric's arms shift with her movement. "She was his 'one.' That's what we decided. She was the one person he was made to be with. Not in a romantic sense. He didn't sweep her off her feet, and she was understandably wary. He met her in line in a coffee shop, bought her drink and muffin, talked her into sitting down with him when she'd intended to take it back to work. After a five-minute conversation, he knew. She was his one."

"His one." Certainty infused his voice, already following where she was leading them.

"I left here and bugged out." Her hair shifted with his nod, bristles of his beard tugging gently at the snarled strands. "When I called him to explain..." She trailed off, then whispered softly, "I told him I'd met mine, too."

Groaning, Eric moved, whirling her around, wrapping one arm low at her back, the other thrusting up her spine to tangle in her hair. He fisted at the back of her skull, fingers gripped tight to angle her head as he leaned down. Their mouths met in a crash of hot breath and gliding tongues, and Alace could have wept at the beauty of being possessed by him like this. His demanding kiss forced her lips apart, and she opened without thought, needing to be as close to him as possible, take him into her however he'd give himself. Eric's hand shifted from her hip, heat from his palm sliding across her low back and around the front, fingers pulling impatiently at the fastening of her jeans.

She had wound her fingers in his hair at some point, hands clutching on either side of his head, holding on. Shoving one hand between them, she managed the work the tang of his belt, attacking the button and zipper next, abandoning her efforts once she had enough room to shove her hand down and in. He gasped when her fingers encountered the molten heat of his erection. The perfection of soft skin slid across the hardness as she wrapped her palm around and stroked, slick liquid easing the way and taking her breath.

Then Eric's hand flattened against her belly, pushing down and in, one finger gliding through her wetness and deep inside as he ground the heel of his hand against her clit. He captured her sobbing moan in his mouth, breaths mingling as he worked her hard and fast, her strokes of his cock trying to match the ferocity of each movement.

She released her remaining grip on his hair, pushing frantically at the waistband of his jeans, shoving them to his thighs. Ripping her mouth from his, she bit the side of his neck hard, then lost his finger as she turned in his arms and placed her cheek on the wall, working at shoving her own pants down. His hands wrapped around her hips, hot as sin in contrast to the cool air of his house, and he yanked hard, angling her ass up. Alace held her breath as the tip of his cock nudged and prodded at her folds. She bent at the waist and pushed back as he shoved forwards, and Alace felt the rumble of his groan when he slipped inside, the exact amount of pull and drag needed to light every nerve in her body aflame.

"Jesus, baby." Every movement caused a ripple through her. Out and in, hard and fast, he pulled her back and forth, and she went willingly, giving him everything. Legs as wide as she could manage with the fabric of her jeans bunched at her knees, she twisted her neck, seeking. From this position, he had to hunt for her mouth, but with an elbow to the wall to brace himself, he gave her what she needed, mouth meeting hers in a wanting gasp before he kissed her hard, lips working across hers with bruising pressure.

Lifting to her toes, she clawed at the thread of pleasure rising inside her, chasing it as she brought her body down against his with a smack of flesh on flesh that sent a pulse through her clit. "Faster." Again and again, each thrust of his cock tearing her control to shreds. The demanding stance pulled bright aching from her muscles and that paired with the burn of stretching inside felt so good. Sweat stung her eyes, and she tasted salt on his tongue when it next plunged into her mouth. She opened her eyes to find him staring at her, dark pupils blown wide in pleasure and the look was so erotic she cried out, distorting his name as she came. "Eric."

"God, Alace." He bit her lips, sucking her tongue before chasing it back into her mouth with his own. "Baby."

His hips moved faster, so fast it seemed impossible, but it was like he needed to drive as far into her as he could, looking for his own release. Still coming, gut tight as a drum, her muscles pulsing around him, she watched his head go back, lifting from hers with eyes closed. Mouth pulled open in a silent cry, he stiffened as he thrust without rhythm now, bucking against her as he came hard. Settling deep, he sheathed himself far inside and bent forwards to bury his face against the side of her head. Breaths still coming hard and fast, she felt his heart pounding through her back.

Languid now, lips to her neck, he kissed and caressed with his mouth. His hand against the wall slipped down to settle on top of her head, fingers stroking slowly through her hair. His other hand shifted from her hip to her waist, then down her thigh and back up as he pumped, gliding out and in. Soft and slow, he moved inside her again and again until he stilled, finally letting his weight rest against her back.

Alace lifted a hand, giving herself permission to play with that intriguing hair long enough to curl at the nape of his neck, fingertips drifting along the shell of his ear with a gentle touch. He moved slightly and opened his eyes, staring at her. Staring into her. He pierced and plundered her with his gaze. That look told her what they had shared against the wall of his living room had been just as earth-shattering for him. They remained like that for long minutes, close enough to share breath as he softened and she lost him.

She shifted, pushing against the wall with little conviction. It was a fruitless move, and she hummed a soft laugh, admitting a truth, "I can't walk yet." Eric's chuckle lifted the corners of his mouth, curving his lips in an inviting way, and Alace sealed her mouth to his for a moment.

"That's flattery." His palm stroked down her leg and back up, coming to rest on her hip for a squeeze. Then she lost that welcome pressure as he rested it against the wall, pressing to lever himself off her back. "It'll get you a lot." He moved, standing as he adjusted his pants around his hips. Arm around her belly, he steadied her as she regained her balance.

"Will it get me a shower?" It took both hands to yank her jeans up—they'd been twisted by their movements.

"Anything you want, baby." The earnest promise rang through the quiet room, and Alace froze for a moment.

"Let's start with a shower."

***

Eric

It still seemed surreal.

Head propped in his hand, Eric leaned back slightly to better look along the entirety of the form lying in bed beside him. Alace slept quietly, her face turned away so he could see the curve of her cheek and the jut of her determined chin. The fluttering of her eyelids told him she was dreaming, and he wondered if he dared hope her dreams held him.

He had led Alice up the stairs after taking her against the wall like he had, unable to stop himself from burying himself inside her. The kiss had inflamed them both, and he'd had a moment of fear that had him looking back every other stair tread and checking, verifying she was still with him.

She's my dream, he thought.

In the bathroom, he had taken his time undressing her. Moving slowly to take the tie from her hair, he'd slipped her shirt over her head. Fingers stroking the hot flesh in the middle of her back to release her bra, he'd kept his eyes on her face as she'd let it slide down her arms. Kneeling at her feet, he'd held her gaze while he fumbled with the laces of her boots. She'd laughed softly, bent close to graze across his lips in a kiss that left them on fire and told him, "They're double knotted, honey."

His boots and jeans had joined hers on the floor. Then he'd reached beyond her and turned on the water, adjusting it with a few deft flicks of his wrist. As he'd stepped into the shower enclosure, he had twined his fingers with hers and tugged, pulling her towards him, letting the door swing shut behind them. Her time on the trail had been written clearly on her skin. Dust and sun had marred skin long exposed to the elements and the events of Waterdrum's cabin.

Working the soap to a lather, he'd begun to wash her, long luxurious swipes of his hand along her skin where every touch felt like a reward. He had turned them, moving her under the spray as she tipped her chin up, letting the water run through her hair and down her back. Fingers tracing tan lines and scars, he had worked his way down her body to between her legs, freezing for a moment when the evidence of their haste met his touch. "Alace," he'd begun, but she'd silenced him with a finger to his lips.

"I'm covered." Her thumb had brushed across his chin and up along his jaw until his cheek rested in the palm of her hand. "No worries."

Eric had taken his time bathing her, reacquainting himself with her body. Fingers in her hair, he had worked lather through her locks, laughing as she quietly grumbled about the masculine scent. He sucked in a breath now as he remembered the feel of her fingers touching his reawakened cock, slippery with a handful of suds.

He felt his dick stirring, filling with blood at the memories, aching to be inside her again.

It hadn't gone any slower the second time. He'd lifted her against the hot tile wall and slid her down his cock until he was buried balls-deep inside her. Mouth locked to hers, he'd kissed her until they were both starved for breath. Hard and fast, not that he could've slowed down, not with her hands on him pulling him eagerly. She'd tipped her hips, moving with him, his name on her lips a reward of a different kind.

Afterward, he'd wrapped her in a soft towel and lifted her in his arms. Carrying her to his bed, he'd placed her in the center before he followed her down and arranged the covers around them.

Eric glanced over her shoulder at the clock. It was past 3:00 a.m., and he found himself wide-awake, curled closely around the woman he'd been searching for over the past two and a half years. Her hair was shorter than he remembered it. Shorter even than when he'd seen her in Alabama. Her time in the national forest had leaned her body as it strengthened her muscles, and he traced down one taut bicep with a fingertip.

There were no maps where they were right now. Eric and Alace were as off the grid in terms of relationship as she had been while on the hunt. Just the fact she was in his bed seemed a miracle. *A gift.* Something he hoped to God she never took back. *Can I do this? Can I really be the man she needs?* He smiled and tipped his head to trace his nose along the apple of her cheek. With her acknowledgment that she'd felt the same instant attraction between them, it felt like the narrow precipice upon which he'd stood for so long had suddenly grown in size, able to support the weight of his desires.

There'd been lots of talking in the truck, and little to none after they got to the house. But with just a few words, she had proven to understand exactly where he was. "Beloved," he muttered, bending to press his mouth to the column of her throat.

She murmured something unintelligible, arched her neck, then murmured again, this time uttering a very clear, "Eric."

He slid down the mattress, pressing closer. She moved, rolling her hips slightly, meeting him halfway as her eyes opened a slit. Eric took her mouth, kissing her softly, slowly, questing and caressing with his lips. Scarcely awake, no pretense as she gave up all control to him, and Eric pressed his advantage. Locking an arm around her back, he lifted and arched her into him, hitching one knee high across her thighs. She squirmed, fingers threading through the hair at the back of his neck. Her hold tightened with a quick sting

MariaLisa deMora

then backed off to grip firmly. He kept the pace of their kiss slow, deliberate, raising the heat by measured increments, stretching out these moments as if they would be the last he could spend with her.

"Baby." He dragged his teeth along the top of her shoulder, then angled his head to take a breast in his mouth. Sliding a hand down the sleek skin of her belly as he sucked, he slipped his fingers between her legs. "Jesus, you're wet." The needy sound she made as he touched her fed the hunger he'd been banking for so long. *Fuck*, he thought, *I've never stopped wanting her*. From the moment she had sat in the seat across from him at the diner, she was everything he ever wanted.

"Alace." He moved, shifting over her, and she adjusted, thighs spreading, knees rising to cradle his hips. Elbows to the pillow beside her head, he lifted, releasing her breast with a pop. "Wanna make love to you." She was breathing shallowly, her nails scraping along the muscles of his back. "Fucking gorgeous. You feel so good, beloved." He moved his hips, angling and thrusting, and watched as her mouth dropped open when the head of his cock slipped between her lips. "Gonna make you love me." Wet heat engulfed him as he pushed deep. *So fucking tight*.

Alace turned her face to the side, eyes closing, an expression that looked like pain crossing her features. Eric stopped in place, and ignoring the insistent demand of her hands moving on him, asked, "Baby, what's wrong?"

"Eric." Her hips pumped up, taking more of him inside.

So fucking good. Sleek and hot, her muscles gripped him with a promise of exquisite pleasure. Needing to understand what that look had meant, he held to his fraying control and pulled back, slid out so he was poised at the edge of her entrance, and held there. "What's wrong?"

Her neck moved, head rolling back to center, only then did her gorgeous deep green eyes open, staring up at him. "I already do."

She loves me.

The profound meaning of her three words struck him, and groaning, Eric crashed his mouth against hers and pushed hard, hips rocking against her. Shouting when she met him stroke for stroke, his hips moving, pistoning now, each thrust burying his cock, each response an instinctive and animalistic need to mark her as his. "I love you, too." He forced the words out between grunts, all thoughts of going slow this time lost, and he abandoned control to her demands.

Soft whimpers combined with his name stroked the air, much as her hands caressed his skin, competing with the slapping of their bellies. He moved, shoving a hand underneath her, curled his fingers around her ass and pulled her up, holding her in place. Swiping a fingertip through the wet evidence of their mutual arousal, he traced the puckered ring of her asshole, the tight grip of her pussy around his cock a clear invitation. Thrusting gently, he slipped one finger inside to the second knuckle, holding there.

"Yes," she hissed, nails scraping along his spine, the sharp points of pain giving him permission to move faster, deeper.

He found a rhythm, sliding his finger in at the same time his cock pierced her. She whined, head tossing to the side as her arousal peaked and held there, trembling on the edge. Eric laid a series of hard, sucking kisses along her throat, then, mouth to her ear, gave her everything. "Jesus, baby. Come for me. Please, God, *come*. Wanna feel you around me, wanna know you're coming with me. You're so fucking hot, beloved." She gasped, and the muscles in her arms and legs tensed, locking around him. Her pussy was a vice, sucking him in, threatening to never let him go. "So fucking hot like this, under me. With me, right where you belong, baby. You're mine, you know that."

His name was a rising wail in the room, a signal flag that the finish line was in sight. Alace seemed beyond words now, guttural sounds drawn from far inside her.

"Everything for you. Jesus, Alace. Anything for you." Her head turned on the pillow, and he met her lips. Between kisses, he told her, "I love you. I love you. *God*."

When he came, hips bucking as heat surrounded the head of his cock, she groaned along with him. It seemed to pull another wave of climax through her, and he rode it for a long minute like a high. Exhausted, muscles relaxing, he settled against her and held tight, loving how everything about this felt. Her limbs wrapped around him, not letting go either.

This is my dream.

Alace proved she was right alongside him, once again, when she whispered, "If this is a dream, Eric, I never wanna wake up."

CHAPTER ELEVEN

Alace

Fingertips lightly resting on the sides of the mug of coffee placed on the counter in front of her, Alace kept her eyes on Eric as he moved around the kitchen. Heat soaked through the heavy ceramic to her skin, and the scent of a full-bodied dose of caffeine wafted to her nostrils, but she chose to ignore those sensory inputs, focusing instead on the way his ass was displayed to perfection in his jeans. "We had a sex-a-thon." Her blurted statement earned her a glance of his whiskey-dark eyes from over his shoulder, an amused smile crinkling the corners. "What?" She made the mock exclamation with a grin of her own. "We did!"

Spatula in hand, Eric reached out to stir the in-progress scrambled eggs, and Alace was treated to a play of muscles all across his bare back. The time between had changed him in subtle ways. While he hadn't been soft before, he'd definitely lost a couple of inches around his waist, going from firm to definition, the difference highlighting his physique in an extremely attractive way. Her smile faded as she wondered how she appeared to have changed to him. *Better or worse?* Ducking her head, she lifted the mug and sipped the hot liquid, grateful to have something to keep her hands busy.

Eric transferred the fluffy, yellow mass from skillet to platter. Bacon was already on the counter in front of her, English muffins toasted and wrapped in a basket at her elbow, and an assortment of jams and jellies set out nearby. *Very domestic.*

When they'd come downstairs looking for food, Eric had surprised her by offering to cook. One detriment to her decades-long transient lifestyle was a serious lack of skills in the kitchen. She'd never really had a chance to learn, and no overwhelming desire to create an opportunity. Sure, she could do small meals, more than suitable for a single diner, but nothing complicated. *Not that eggs and bacon are a complicated dish, but he makes it look so easy.*

"We did," he agreed, placing the eggs on the counter as he moved around to where she sat. "And I—" He cupped her chin in his hand, fingers steadying her face as he swooped in for a kiss. "—loved every minute of it."

If it seems too good to be true...

For an instant, she was transported back to the SUV on the side of the road, cop in the window and Eric—*fucking, fucking Eric*—showing he had serious acting chops. She swallowed and tilted her face for another kiss, forcing down the idea before it had a chance to take root. "Me—" She kissed him a third time, settling back to her stool as he lifted, putting slight distance between them. "—too." This was an unfamiliar mindset and one that didn't yet sit comfortably on her skin. He knew her name and what she was, and she was sitting in his kitchen as if this were normal when it had jumped the crevasse between ordinary and bizarre the moment he'd shown in that New Mexico forest. *It'll take work*, she reminded herself of what she'd told him last night. Change always does.

He perched on an adjacent stool and waited for Alace to serve herself before spooning food onto his plate. To Alace, the silence wrapping around them felt confining, as if it were a constrictor, slowly tightening to starve them of the air needed to keep living. Every movement felt awkward, forced, as if she were following unfamiliar stage direction from an untrusted source. She opened her mouth twice, discarding the conversation starter that had popped into her head each time, which meant the silence stretched on. Eric clearly did not feel the same, and she understood why when he began talking.

"You can't leave that man out there." Fork frozen in midair, slowly Alace twisted to stare at him. Eric wasn't even looking at her, eyes focused on his plate, mouth pulled to one side with a look of distaste. *For me, or for what he's saying?* "He'll just find another partner, and then it will all begin again." He glanced up and his lips bowed down as he shook his head, looking pained. "How do you do it?"

Spine straight, Alace rested the tines of her fork against the edge of her plate. "Do *it*?" *Is he asking how I killed Waterdrum? Coach? Does he know about any others, really, or is he fishing?* Alace ran every word spoken inside this house back through her head and drew a shaky breath. *Nothing damaging said here, but in his SUV?* Nerves thrumming under her too-tight skin, she unhooked her ankles from around the legs of her stool, a scarce breath away from fleeing. "How do I *do* it?"

"Yeah." He gestured with his fork, drawing aimless circles in the air above his plate. "Deal with knowing people like that exist. That they are able to just go on about their business every day? No one does anything. Fuck,"—he shook his head—"most people wouldn't believe the things you've had to witness could even happen.

"I remember there was an in-service for volunteers in the school district last year about human trafficking and two of the female teachers stood around afterwards complaining about the time spent talking about something that was never going to happen here." His voice rose in register, mocking his coworkers, "Not in our neighborhood. We're good people." He scooped up more eggs and then stabbed a piece of bacon. Pausing a moment before shoving it into his mouth, he said, "So blind to the criminal things in the world they couldn't even spend a half an hour making the world safer for the kids they teach without bitching about it, and you have to be immersed inside it every day. How do you do it?"

That was so different from what she'd expected, it took her breath away. A kind of boon, really, his ability to put himself in her shoes even if he'd never taken a step down this path with her. "I just...it's my life, Eric. I've put myself in the position of being exposed to evil." Fingers trembling, she managed to lift the fork without clinking against the plate. "Since forever, it's how I see the world. I have to. Even good guys get painted with the same brush until I really get to know them." A reminder to herself to trust her gut where Eric was concerned. *He's not one of the bad guys.*

"I can see that." He spoke slowly, his tone musing as he smeared purple jam on a muffin. "Like in court, my go-to is innocence, and I hold tight to that until I've been given overwhelming evidence to the contrary. It has to be proven in my head—no doubts—before I can walk up to that table with a clear conscience, ready to do what I need to in order to take the bastards down." He nodded, getting onboard with the idea. "With your experiences, it would be natural to swing far on the other side of the spectrum. Everyone would be guilty by default and have to earn a place on the good-guy scale." Teeth flashing white, he shone a smile her direction. "Even me."

"Even you," she admitted softly, letting her toes curl around the rungs of the stool again.

"I can work to get there, baby." He accepted her statement at face value, and Alace was stunned with the sense of ease creeping back in the room where a few moments ago she had nearly convinced herself to run. "I'll work to stay there, too." He leaned sideways in invitation, and she met him halfway, lips brushing lightly against his. "You're entirely worth it."

"If we're...are we going to try and make something work here?" Alace winced, but didn't know how to finesse the question, glad she'd finally decided to just lay it out there and see where his head was. She just didn't have the patience for any kind of a mating dance to see if he felt the same. The fact she was in his house and had been in his bed gave her some confidence, but her radar was all off where Eric was concerned. After Ranger Rick, every instinct was in question. Everything inside her was screaming to move forwards at warp speed with Eric, but what if she was wrong?

"Yes." His response had a firmness her question had lacked, and left no room for doubt. "You and me, baby." He grinned and bit the muffin, leaving a smear of purple in the corner of his mouth. *Great, now I want to lick him.* A heavy tingling hit between her legs, and she shifted on the stool.

Focus. He needed to understand how it would be with her. Not that she'd ever had anything that could remotely be called a relationship, but she knew it all had to start with having both parties on the same page. "I can't talk about what I do." He stopped moving, his expression attentively focused on her. "I can't tell you...anything. You're going to hate it."

As she watched, his face softened, a gentle look coming over his features. "Alace, I can't talk to you about my job, either."

Her head shook, the motion sharp and quick, hair falling across her forehead. "It's not the same, Eric. You know it's not the same."

"What are you afraid of?" Head tipped to one side, he offered her a crooked smile. "Is it of this—" His brows drew together, and he motioned to the space between them. "—working out? Do you want it to work out?"

Alace sat and looked at him. The expression on Eric's face didn't change, patient affection was blended with the tiniest bit of amusement, all of that holding strong. He didn't get impatient, just gave her time and let her work through what he'd asked. *What if it does work out, for a while? What if in four weeks when I have to go and do a gig, he gets tired of the secrets? What if he won't let me go for a long job?* With a start, she realized she didn't want to go. For the first time in her memory, she wasn't looking forwards to the next mark. Hadn't even logged into the servers to see what might be next. *I still have to deal with Ranger Rick. That's all. It's not done, yet.* She knew the thought was a rationalization. Dealing with the ranger wouldn't take long, not knowing what she did now. If she worked it right, there might be a single overnight away from Eric, maximum. *I want this.* Heart in her throat, she opened and closed her mouth, constructing and rejecting a dozen statements she knew would reveal her desire. *"Stay safe," Regg always tells me. He'd never steer me wrong.* "Maybe." She offered the uncertain word like a compromise, relieved when Eric accepted it with grace.

"Maybe," he repeated with a half smile. "I'll admit, it's not the answer I'd hoped for, but I'll take it with the caveat it's only until you can say yes."

"I have to go back to New Mexico. But," —she shook her head—"that's all I can say. I have to go back, and then if you want, I'll come here again."

"Always, always come home."

***

Curled into the cushions of a broad bench, Alace watched the flickering flames of a fire Eric had built for her in his patio firepit. She had been out here for some time alone, explaining that she needed to place some business calls—at the time she wondered to herself, *That's what I'm calling it now?*—and Eric hadn't argued, simply making certain she'd be comfortable as she worked. *I don't know if I've ever met someone who could just...roll with it like he does.* Even Regg would have had questions.

And that was the core of why she was still out here, phone in hand, eyes on the fire. Regg needed to know what had gone down, and she couldn't delay having him monitor any and all news, both public and darkside, looking for whispers of what Ranger Rick might have thrown into the mix. She also needed to check the servers for what came next. Regg needed to know, but he would want to understand what the fuck she was doing up *here*. Here being Denver. She knew he would not be pleased when she told him the conversations she'd had with Eric. Forget the fact she'd returned to a site without any kind of cover, just as herself. Once Regg knew everything, he would then rightly expect a certain amount of situation management that she was unwilling to undertake.

So, I don't tell him.

She shut down the idea hard, shoving it back into a corner room in her mind and blocked it in place by setting a thousand reasons why she had to tell Regg in front of it. They were all valid, every one of them. Honor among thieves meant, in order to trust Regg not to screw her over if a bigger price tag came calling, she had to be trustworthy. Keeping him up to date on every aspect of a gig allowed her to stay in front of the leading edge of any repercussions for her actions. Regg was her out, every time, and had never failed her. But he could only do his job if she gave him the right tools.

Don't tell him. It's not part of the gig.

It was. Eric had tracked her down to a cabin that her marks had used to slaughter untold kids, and God knew what else might have gone on in that small building. He'd tracked her down, and she'd used him for egress, to escape. *He saved me.* She rolled her eyes. *Okay, maybe I'd already saved myself, but he made walking out of there tons easier.* Regg wouldn't take to that news. Eric tracking her down not once, but twice. *I never told him about Alabama, either.* What she'd said was she got a feeling, and Regg knew enough to understand she followed her gut.

So, why am I so resistant to the idea of following my intuition now?

Through the years, Regg was the only one who'd had her back. The only one she'd let close enough to have information that could save or bury her, and she trusted him to keep her above ground. He had *never* failed her. Always on the other end of the phone, and more than once his willingness to go to extremes on her behalf had kept her breathing. Not telling him felt uncomfortable, like a woolen sweater worn over naked, sweaty skin. A body could do it, but it wouldn't be an enjoyable sensation.

She sighed and shifted, lifting her feet to the cushion. Wrapping her arms around her bent knees, she dangled her phone in one hand as she looked towards Eric's house. Flickering lights in the living room told her he was still watching TV. No shadows near windows or doors, he wasn't lurking and keeping an eye on her. She could see wine glasses from dinner sitting on the counter near the sink. Eric was trusting her and giving the space she'd requested.

He's no threat to Regg.

The same could not be said in reverse.

If Regg knew Eric had knowledge about what Alace did, that would be on her to deal with. But Eric knew she had a partner, and given his track record, it wasn't out of bounds to think he could be successful in tracking down Regg, too. If given the right motivation, he would. That meant he was a threat to Regg. At least that's how Regg would see it.

Eric's not a threat, though.

She knew that in her bones. Not a threat to her, and not a threat to Regg.

Eric would probably shake his hand and thank him for watching out for me all this time. She snorted. Not like Regg hadn't profited from the arrangement, but she knew he wasn't in it just for the money. They were friends.

She lifted the phone and woke it, tapping in her password to make her call.

***

Regg

About halfway through their conversation, he allowed himself to lean back in the computer chair and stare blankly at the ceiling as Alace talked him through what had gone sideways in New Mexico. Nearly two days ago.

When he'd seen the call coming in, he'd pointed to it as he stood, getting a tolerant nod from his wife. She knew business came first. Most of the time, anyway. Hell, the hunters he worked with depended on him being available. Sometimes their very lives rested on his ability to work a solution on the fly. *I'm good at my job.* Work often came in waves, so it wasn't as if he were on call all the time, just full-time during the end phases of a hunt.

Alace was a special case. Not only was she his first full-time hunter, but she was also the longest-lived one. He knew her inside and out, upside down and right-side up. He'd known her for half her life, and had enough intel on her to guide his every step. He knew when she was dragging and needed a quick, life-affirming job to motivate her. Could recognize when she needed a more intricate puzzle to solve, a cerebral exercise ending with her exorcising her demons by dealing with a despised monster. He could also identify when she needed him to surprise her with special treatment, and spot those moments that told him she needed some downtime to settle her nerves.

She trusted him. Alace was open to a degree most of his other hunters never reached, because of their own life experiences pre-hunter status. She'd started so young, she didn't have those defenses in place. Not his Alace. His Alace was special in a lot of ways. Until a couple of years ago, he would have thought her incapable of being anything other than his Alace, open and real. Alace trusted him and gave that back in spades, never holding secrets when it came to debriefing during or after a job.

Until about two years ago.

Colorado.

He stumbled at the memory and frowned.

When she'd bugged out of Colorado, she had lied to him for the first time. Ever. Her evasion such a novelty, it had been her own fault he looked closer. If she'd just told him what happened, he'd have understood. Playing at being someone else all the time, it would be more unusual if she didn't occasionally fall into the emotional trap of becoming who she was pretending to be. That one had been different. For one, it had been the wrong job to fuck up on and then her unwillingness to fess up had made him dig until he'd found what he needed. Eric Ward was supposed to be her route to access his father, not her fuckbuddy. There had been nearly three mill hanging on her getting that access and coming out the other end with the older Ward down.

It wasn't the first time a hunt had been interrupted by circumstances beyond her control. But it had been the first time she was unwilling to circle back around and take care of business the way he expected. The failure was a first, and a smear he wasn't happy having on his otherwise spotless record. But it had been her lie that bothered him the most.

Then it happened again. In Alabama, she'd lied a second time. Only after taking care of business, thank God. That meant she hadn't gotten in the way of the deposit into his accounts, and with Lena's lifestyle demands, it was critical to keep that cash flowing in. But she'd lied again, and he'd dug even deeper, finding CCTV footage of a certain vehicle licensed out of— *gasp*—Colorado. Ward the younger. Again.

So tonight, he listened. Eyes closed, he listened and judged.

Alace spun out thousands of details, a wealth of shiny information to distract him, no doubt. She'd been days out of contact, an unexpected absence, and most of her details lined up. The things that didn't, though? They were glaring.

She would be headed back into the job tomorrow, and he had no question she'd deal. The niggly details were different than he'd anticipated, so throughout the first part of the call, he'd made lots of notes on the computer. Just in case he ever saw another situation like this, he could leverage the knowledge differently. Now she was talking about the extraction, and it was just one more thing that wasn't ringing true.

"No, I'm not far. I'll be back midafternoon. I'm beat, planning on sleeping in." Alace's voice was tight, the cadence of her words slightly askew. He lifted his head and looked at the computer screen to see validation in the oscillation lines mapping how stressed her voice was. *Liar.*

"Okay, honey. You need me to order you a pizza delivered or something? Anything you need?"

"No, I'm good. Just going to crash." He studied the screen and shook his head side to side. *Liar.*

Mouse in hand he clicked, and clicked again, green lines filling the screen. He clicked and scrolled, zooming in on the steady red dot, making it large enough to see the town name, then scrolled again, zooming out. With a click and drag, he moved the map to show the outline of the states.

"Okay. Rest well. I'm glad you got out safe. Do me a favor, leave the phone on when you go back in so I can track you?"

Silence, and that itself was telling.

"No, I'll follow normal protocol. Contact you once everything is complete. I'm planning on a few weeks here afterwards." He heard her swallow through the call. "I'm tired, Regg. I was thinking of taking some time off. I haven't done that for a while."

He grimaced, remembering a recent conversation with Lena. Her car was nearly a year old and she wanted to trade up soon. If Alace took time off, that would delay the next payday. Turning the chair, he looked at a computer screen on the desk beside him. Fourteen viable contacts, three of which would tweak her if she saw them. He'd already built info cases, documentation and details filling folders ready to drop out onto the server. Click and drag, and it was work of moments to do exactly that. "Okay, honey. I put some new gigs on the server, but they can wait a few days." Best to set expectations. "Let me know the moment you get out of the woods, okay?"

"Okay." She hesitated, and he waited, rewarded when she told him, "You know how much I appreciate you taking care of me, right?"

"We're a team, Alace. Always will be."

She disconnected, and he watched the map, seeing the red dot disappear, knowing that was her turning off the phone. Less than twenty yards from where that had last been visible was a steady green teardrop. The tracker in her backpack. Hundreds of miles from where she'd claimed to be. Regg slowly shook his head. *Liar.*

CHAPTER TWELVE

Alace

Seated in a booth next to the front window of the diner in Cuba, Alace felt as if a spotlight was being shone on her. Playing up the role of a backpacker fresh from the trail, she'd just ordered her third entrée and was waiting for the tolerantly amused waitress to bring it to her. There were not many customers in the diner right now, which suited her just fine as she watched the brown forestry service vehicle circle the block again.

Ranger Rick.

He'd seen her on the street, his face white and stricken as his SUV rolled past, head on a swivel to keep her in view as long as he could. She hadn't made any bones about seeing him either, locking gazes through the dusty vehicle window before turning to bound up the two steps at the front of the restaurant.

The plate of food clinked against the tabletop, and she turned her head with a smile, thanking the waitress. "This'll probably be it for me. You can go ahead and get the ticket ready if you want. Hey, do you know if there's a motel in town that's not too expensive?" She needed to lay a trail, even if it was a false one. Oh, she might rent a room in the motel she'd already scoped out, but she wouldn't be waiting inside like a scared bunny in its burrow.

"Yeah, sugar. Slumber Inn, just two blocks to the north." She scribbled something on her pad and ripped it off, putting it on the table. "Pay me when you're ready." Alace dug into her pocket and pulled out some bills, turning the ticket face up as she calculated a carefully generous tip. *Memorable, but not too*. Brown moving back into view pulled her attention back to the street, and she watched as the SUV parked against the curb on the other side.

Rick—even knowing his name was Terrence Tresca, he would forever be Rick to her—stared at her through the two panes of glass that separated them. He'd lost the sick expression over the past hour and a half, and the look on his face now resembled wary anger. With effort, she controlled the wry twist her lips wanted to make. Ranger Rick was pissed she'd dare come back to his hunting grounds.

She laid the money on the table next to the ticket, sliding it towards the other side. Without looking back out the window, she picked up the burger and adjusted it in her hands, turning it to get the best bite possible. Once she walked out these doors, she was back on his turf and had no idea what it would take to get another meal like this. *Take advantage of the chance*, she thought, dipping a french fry into a puddle of ketchup and slipping it into her mouth.

Eric had fed her well last night, knowing that she'd be leaving with the sun in an old beater car she'd paid cash for. This one was nearly two decades old, and could be easily abandoned if needed. Right now, it was parked on the outskirts of town behind an abandoned grocery store, keys in a magnetic storage box attached to a rusting garbage bin nearby. Egress if needed, no loss it if were left behind in the hustle and bustle of her gig coming to a close.

The next bite of burger nearly lodged in her throat as she caught sight of Rick stalking across the street towards the diner. She hadn't expected a direct confrontation and, coughing, kept her head bent over her plate as he walked towards her. Every muscle drawn tight, she had palmed the serrated steak knife near her left hand as his measured footfalls approached. Without pausing his advance, his knuckles rapped on the end of her table once. The sound echoed in the bubble of silence collected around her, and then he was past, seating himself in the next booth along the window. The waitress approached and Alace heard, "Terry, we haven't seen you for a while. Where you been keeping yourself?"

Alace's pulse pounded in her ears, maintaining the racing pace it had reached when she'd realized he was coming inside, and she could barely hear him over the rushing sounds. "Busy. Lots of careless hikers these days."

"Oh, no. I hope everyone's okay." The waitress's alarm wasn't fake, a rich concern in her tone loud and clear over the gurgle of pouring coffee.

"Hope so, too. Still to be seen. I'll take the special tonight." More casual words between them and then the sound of the waitress moving behind the long counter.

Alace quickly checked all available reflective surfaces, finally finding an angled window on a car outside that gave her a view of the table behind her. Blurred through the glass, Rick was more nearly a blob than a person, but it at least would give her warning if he moved.

The waitress came into view, moving towards him as she dropped off his salad and cutlery. Then it was just Rick at the table. Over the clinking of forks and knives against plates, the low murmur of conversation all around her, she heard him. "Thistle, did not expect to see you again. I wish you'd stayed away. Now—" A pause as the waitress approached again, leaving behind a steaming plate of pasta and bread slathered with fragrant garlic butter. "Now—" His voice dipped low, becoming inaudible for a moment. "—have to deal with this, too."

Alace wasn't certain if Rick thought she heard him, or if his words were entirely for his own benefit. Either way, they chilled her. Regg had pulled and provided a wealth of information about Terry/Rick. He'd been part of an elite military unit, his element one that had taken out multiple high-profile targets. He was accustomed to being the hunter. Regg had even joked that this was the kind of guy who often wanted to do Alace's job.

"He's got the skills. You're going to want to be wary of him. I'd peg him as a planner and executor, and once he catches sight of you, he's going to be putting all his experience into play." Regg sighed. "Maybe you could talk to him first, see if he'd be willing to partner up? That would make it so you didn't have to do the grunt work on every job."

She mashed the phone tighter to her ear, frowning. "I don't do partnerships. You know that."

"Maybe it's time to reconsider. You're wanting to take time off, but what if what you need is to shake things up a bit? You've done well enough on your own, Alace, but imagine what you could do with someone else who could think on their feet as well as you do."

The sound of flesh being ripped off Waterdrum's body echoed through her head. Never, not with Rick. Not with anyone. "No. Just get me what I need."

Regg knew he'd pushed her too far, and for the first time ever, he'd backpedaled. "No worries. I always get you the info. You should stay holed up at that motel for *a couple of days, make sure there won't be a media splash if Waterdrum is found." As far as Regg knew, she'd never left the area. She felt like shit keeping something as big as Eric from him, but Alace wasn't ready to share yet.* Might never be ready.

"Okay. I'll call you in two days."

She'd done that from a burner in Eric's backyard, telling Regg her phone was damaged. Without the app, she couldn't access his servers, but for finishing this gig the access didn't matter. Regg had fed her the info during their chats, and she had an excellent memory.

Alace set the remainder of her burger aside, wiped her fingers with a wad of napkins, and nodded with a studied casualness at the waitress as she pushed out from the booth. Head down, she reached across to the other side and lifted her backpack, swinging it up and settling it into place on her shoulders. A glance towards the back of the diner showed Rick's face turned towards her, wide eyes glaring, mouth set in a firm line. Once out the door, she used the windows of cars to keep track of what happened behind her. Alace was surprised Rick hadn't come out of the diner by the time she turned towards the motel.

Just a slight change of plans.

No doubt he'd get the info on her from the waitress. All Alace had to do was rent a motel room, lay her traps, and wait.

***

Alace silently shifted with miniscule movements as she carefully stretched one set of muscles at a time. She'd been holding this position for nearly five hours, which was about four hours longer than she'd expected. *Serves me right for thinking there'd be a quick resolution.*

Nothing about Rick had matched expectation. Why someone who had gone through the training he had would settle for a forestry service job was a puzzle. Normally—she liked to think she'd had enough experience with this type of person to be able to draw normative values from interactions—an adrenaline junkie retained at least some aspects of that facet of their personality regardless of how they tamed it back.

She'd missed the fact Waterdrum had a partner until after she'd dealt with him, and after significant review, decided it likely meant Rick had not been an active participant in the abduction, or killing of the victims. *What's his role? Maybe he's the sales guy?* She mentally shook that off, centering her thoughts and pulling stillness and composure over her like a calming blanket. *It doesn't matter.* She could figure it out after, since the truth was he'd been involved in some fashion. He might not have the right pattern of disappearances to be the delivery boy for the parted-out kids, might not have been the abductor, but he was involved. *He's awfully good with a blade.* The memories of his butchery of Waterdrum swam to the surface, and Alace swallowed hard.

Maybe Rick's appearance was a coincidence?
Frustrated with her brain's inability to drop the topic,
she tried to shake that off, too.

He'd come hunting for her after their early morning
encounter where she'd teased him less than previous
days. Even if he hadn't known about Waterdrum until
after entering the cabin, he'd still stalked and Tasered
her, trussed her up with available supplies, persisted
in the face of adversity to get her to the cabin, and
then...what? He'd lost interest in her once he'd found
the cop's body. She'd been discarded while he worked
on the available carcass. *That doesn't make sense.
Nothing about this makes sense.*

At the diner today, he'd surprised her again. *I don't
like surprises.* Instead of fleeing when he saw her,
something she had prepared for, he'd approached,
veering off to sit by himself at the last second. Not the
actions of a man who felt he had anything to hide. His
talking, even if it sounded directed at her, hadn't been
pitched to carry. She believed as he had in the car and
at the cabin, he'd been talking to himself.

Movement across the parking lot had her angling
her eyes and squinting. Instead of what she expected
to see, the broad-shouldered, green-clad body of Rick,
she saw a smaller version. Distorted and distant, the
reflection in the motel windows was off and a breath
later everything registered, and she was up and
running. Shocked that he was on her side of the lot,
creeping up on her position instead of approaching
the empty room, she tapped her inner reserves and

put on a burst of speed. Somehow, he'd known where she'd be, and then scouted without her catching sight or sound of him, and—her brain stuttered with data, so just as she rounded the corner of the building, she swung wide, ducking in response to the sudden conviction that seeing him when she did was deliberate. *He was flushing me out*. The glint of a moonbeam on metal proved her right; there was a passive trap in her previous path. If she hadn't changed trajectory at the last moment, the pitchfork wedged against the wall would have gutted her.

Clever. Head up, actively scanning now, she continued. Arms pumping as she reached for greater speed, the heels of her sneakers never quite touched the ground as she lengthened her stride. Her approach to the edge of the forest managed without an outcry, she plunged into the darkness for a handful of yards before reaching out to grip the rough bark of a tree. Using it as a pivot, she swung around and allowed her momentum to bleed off abruptly, coming to a stop facing the field separating the motel parking lot and the woods.

Not running, not even looking as if he were in any particular hurry, Rick followed the path of her retreat, his feet falling within the swath of long grass dark and devoid of dew, brushed free by her passage. The rest of the field was silvered in the moonlight, tiny reflections of the sun's balance dancing on the tip of each blade, shivering as a breeze stirred the tall stalks.

He walked within ten feet of the trees and paused, head cocked to one side. "I hear you, Thistle."

He can't, no way. She was holding her breath and hadn't moved, no snap of a dead branch to betray her position.

"I don't know why you came back." Three strides and it took her a moment to discern why he suddenly seemed so much closer than he should be. The damp grass gave him away, showing where he'd diverged from her path to angle across the triangle of space between them. Head snapping straight, he twisted his neck to stare where she stood in the silent shadows. "But, we need to talk."

Without waiting, not caring to listen to more, she whirled and ran. Staying parallel to the wood's edge, she dodged branches that came out of the dark like slung baseball bats, and hurtled over deadfalls that reached up to scrabble at the bottoms of her shoes. The loud pounding of Rick's footfalls chased her, echoing off the trees in a way that made it impossible to determine if he were gaining or not, if he'd entered the woods or was pacing her through the simpler-to-navigate field, or if he were perhaps an illusion cast by her mind.

A blueish flicker betrayed his intentions, and she dodged left around the next tree, ducking low to avoid the angled trunk of its fallen neighbor, hearing the thud of the barbs as they bounced off the bark. *Taser.* The information that he was again playing for keeps settled her, and Alace angled left, breaking through the edge of the woods and across the field to where she'd laid her best trap. A metallic snap told her he'd rearmed his gun. The trap was one she'd fully expected to never activate, intending to come back and correct things after all was said and done, not wanting someone to fall afoul of her skills if there were no need.

At the last moment, she leapt, arching her back to gain another inch of distance without exposing how far she'd jumped. She continued to run hard, not faltering until she heard a thud of impact and Rick's low cry of pain. Stumbling a bit, blowing hard, she swung in a tight circle and trotted back, Rick no longer in view. She slowed, still breathing fast as she came to the edge of the pit. Toes dangling over into the empty space of the old well, she stared into the depths, not seeing any movement. No sounds emitted from the hole in the ground, and as she watched the water standing at the bottom settled, all ripples stopping after a couple of minutes. Palm pressed against her ribs, she stood and watched until her breathing was easy, still without spotting any movement. *It's done.* The breeze danced through the dew-laden grass, drying the sweat on her skin, bringing a rush of gooseflesh in its wake.

Alace retreated to the woods and came back with her supplies, including a telescoping metal bar and rappelling rope. She extended the bar, locked it in place across the opening and anchored the rope to support her climb down. Five minutes later, she was on her way back up, his few personal effects stowed in a sling bag over one shoulder.

Naked but for his briefs, she'd left him for the scavengers who made their home in the dark. Still, even with that act, this was one of the least intimate culminations to a gig that she'd ever experienced. As always, her planning was what kept things from driving sideways.

Dew lubricated the maneuvering of the heavy cover back into place, locking Rick's body underground. He would undoubtedly be found someday, but she would spend the next hours ensuring that when he was reported missing, any search for him would be conducted far from here.

Back at the motel, she changed and spent a few minutes arranging the room to look as if a tired hiker spent all night in the comfortable bed. She left the TV on to show the weather, and dampened towels scattered on the floor of the bathroom. Sling bag carried in one hand, backpack over her other shoulder, she located and retrieved the forestry service vehicle, aiming the headlights of the SUV up the highway and into the wilderness.

***

Alace stood in the front room of Waterdrum's cabin and turned a small semicircle as she stared, eyes darting from surface to surface. The survey left her surprised and yet not at the pristine state of the building. Clearly Rick had cleaned up after butchering

Waterdrum. Very well. Obsessively well. *It doesn't line up*.

The last time she'd stood here, the floor had been tacky with drying blood and gore, the ceiling splattered with arterial spray, stacks of victims' belongings crowded along the walls. She angled her neck and looked up. Even the holes for the suspension rig had been filled in and painted over, erasing every iota of evidence available to the naked eye. *If I didn't know, I wouldn't know.*

Once out the door, she turned and jumped off the end of the porch, softened her landing with bent knees and angled into the trees where she'd found several of Waterdrum's burial places. Those were still in place. Undisturbed. She shook her head, wisps of her hair catching in the sweat along the nape of her neck and pulling with a sting, leaving her uncomfortable in more than one way. Given the state of the cabin, leaving the bodies behind wasn't what she would have envisioned from what she knew about him. Now, she'd never know if it was because Rick hadn't found them or hadn't cared. *Out of sight, out of mind.*

Nothing here fit any profile she could identify. Rick had proved more of a ghost than anyone she'd experienced, and she didn't like when things weren't as expected. He'd been military, was stringently controlled on multiple assignments, then back home and retired—literally blending into the woodwork—as a forestry service employee. She could take some of that and twist it to make sense. But, when she added in his apparent partnership with the body-part-trafficking Waterdrum, an efficiently executed kidnapping of her, his callous butchery of a human carcass...well, none of that went together with a man she'd seen earlier tonight who'd seemed slightly frightened of her. "Dammit," she muttered, the sound of her voice startling in the quiet of the woods. *He can't be both sides of the coin. It just doesn't make sense.*

Back at the cabin, she inserted the battery into her phone and turned it on, walking from the front room through the back. She turned left and entered the bathroom. Just as clean as the rest of the building. Finally, the device buzzed in her hand, letting her know she had a message waiting. She looked back through the doorway. Clean. Obsessively so. This was the work of a highly organized person. Given his background, Rick could be that person. *It had to be him, there wasn't anyone else.* She shook her head and looked down, angling the phone to see the screen.

Check the server now.

The text was timestamped ten hours ago. She'd been stashing the forestry service vehicle at that point, at a national park nearly 200 miles away from her current location. Alace's eyes narrowed as she read what had to be a message from Regg a second, then a third time. This was a burner phone, and Regg should know that meant she didn't have the secure app. On a burner, all communication was necessarily cryptic. Regg had taught her that.

She unlocked the phone and her thumb moved over the screen.

I'm sorry. Who is this?

The phone buzzed in her hand, letting her know the text had been sent.

Not even a breath later, the response was immediate and scarcely cryptic. Startlingly so, as she had found several things with Regg recently.

If you've finished the job, check in.

Then came a final text, one that drove her to rip the battery from her phone without even turning it off. She twisted on her heel and ran out of the cabin, leaping off the porch and angling directly towards the cover of the forest. A short time later, she arrived at her car and, in a movement which probably looked practiced but wasn't, simply the result of her rabid desire to vacate the premises, without opening the car door, she swung on the frame and angled her body feet-first through the open window, landing on her bottom in front of the steering wheel and brought her legs down even as she viciously twisted the keys left in the ignition. A roar and jerk of the shifter had the car in motion, and she drove out of the forest with much less care than she'd used entering, not even wincing when the undercarriage repeatedly scraped on rocks heaved from the earth through the efforts of frost and rain.

The phone was shoved into her pocket, but she didn't need to have it in her hand to see the device in her mind. Logically, she knew the letters hadn't been writ in red, hadn't been pulsing malevolently, and surely hadn't grown in size as she looked at the screen. Logically, she also knew that it was highly unlikely anyone had noted the brief text exchange.

Still the two words stayed with her as she drove out of the woods where she'd ended more than a decade of terror for unsuspecting young kids. A place so steeped with blood she wouldn't have been surprised if her steps had forced thick, red fluid from the ground, could nearly imagine the look and smell of it oozing around the soles of her boots. There was no planning in this retreat, no lists to process for her drive back to Eric's—she wouldn't let herself think of it as home, might never be able to—and afterwards she would likely try to downplay the fact she'd felt such an overwhelming urge to flee.

She reached the end of the dirt track, and Alace ruthlessly controlled the vehicle's trajectory, wrestling the wheel as the rear axle attempted to skid sideways across the highway. Well and truly away, she took in a shaking breath, then another, waiting for her heart to stop racing. She reached with one hand to secure the seat belt across her body, and forced her foot to cease mashing quite so desperately on the gas pedal.

Through the hours of driving in the dark, she kept her mind carefully blank, refusing to focus on what had frightened her beyond measure. Still, she knew as soon as she reassembled the phone and battery, she'd see it again. Regg's text to her on an unsecured phone, when he'd never done anything close to that even when they'd spent thousands of dollars on devices and systems to guarantee no hitchhikers and no eavesdroppers.

Her name.

Not Sutton, the name picked for the gig.

No, this was *her* name.

Alace Sweets.

* * *

Eric

He paced.

For the past three hours, after Alace called to say she was on her way back, Eric had paced through his house. Kitchen to den, back to the empty kitchen to stare unseeing out the window. He knew exactly where she'd been, calling from one of the only places where you could still reliably find a payphone—a dump of a truck stop a couple of hundred miles down the interstate. He retraced the path through his house again, trying to shake off the fear that had held him in its grip since he'd stood and watched her drive away. Alone.

Before she'd left, he'd pushed her to talk and kept doing that. Even as she tried to gracefully avoid the topic, he kept bringing it back to the forefront. Attacking it from all angles, he'd pushed her until she gently but directly refused.

"Eric, please. Don't do this to yourself. I will not put you at risk. That subject is off-limits."

That had stung. Wasn't he the one supposed to be protecting her? If she couldn't invite him along—and he understood that, at least—she might at least allow him to help her plan. He was good at strategizing, putting together a plan and laying track for a secondary path just in case the first went awry. He'd told her as much, hoping to sway her. Unsuccessfully in the end.

"I've got my assets in place, and Eric—" She paused, laying her hand flat against his chest, the fine tremor in her fingers stilled by the contact. "—this is what I do. I'm not going to ever let it touch you." Turning her head, the brush of her hair against his bare skin sent a thrill through him as she pressed her lips to his chest. "Above reproach. It won't touch you."

"Have you forgotten that I've already covered any trails leading from me to you?" The only thing he couldn't change was the memory of his friend Todd, from the call Eric had made in alarm over the state of the woman left sleeping in his bed. Every other avenue of investigation that had led him to her had been erased as thoroughly as money and skittish effort could manage. "We're in our bed." He knew she liked

hearing that, couldn't have missed the way she leaned into him when he said the word "our" as if it melted her somehow. "And nothing can touch us here."

That argument won him a kiss that blazed out of control, a consuming combustion that led to another bone-melting orgasm for both of them. A battle, but not the war.

So in the end, he'd promised to respect her mastery of her job, and she'd called her handler, or whatever the fuck the man was. That had set in play a variety of plans Eric was not privy to. Then Alace drove off into the sunset to battle her own demons. Now he knew she at least was on the other side of things, but from the brief conversation, he had no idea how it had shaken out, if she were injured—the Taser barb burns on her chest, ragged abrasions on her wrists, every mark on her skin burned brightly in his memories—or anything. Just that whatever had happened was in her rearview and she was on her way home. Not that she'd called it that, but he wasn't surprised. She'd only been here a handful of hours total; they had a tenuous connection still, no matter how solid it felt to him, how involved his heart already was.

I should be thankful she called at all, and grateful she's on her way back to me. He was. Still, the knowledge she didn't trust him to assist with anything was eating at him. If something bad happened, he might never know. Eric turned on his heel, stiff strides taking him across the room, angry at the idea of anything happening to her.

Can this work?

His stomach rolled as the traitorous idea slipped through his thoughts. It was an entirely different role than he had ever been cast in, and the only time he could remember feeling this helpless was the call to tell him Ariana had died. He'd taken his grief—and a tiny bit of perverse relief, which made him feel incredibly guilty. While they'd been good together, he had already decided they were better friends than lovers, and had planned on having a conversation with her—and turned it into good, building the foundation for a funding effort to make outdoor activities safer for everyone involved.

How can I do the same here?

She wasn't doing these things for glory. Alace had made that clear, and if the haunted look in her eyes as she talked about the things she'd done was any measure, they did nothing to bring her satisfaction. There was no gratification in what she did. It also wasn't about trapping the evildoers in their acts to bring them to the notice of the authorities. It wasn't even about punishing them. In no instance did it sound like she had made it an act of redemption or absolution. For Alace, it seemed to be a drive to even the scales. They were atrocious crimes, and after the legal system failed, she took them out of the equation.

If she wouldn't trust him to help her, then how could he be supportive of her mission? A dozen different situations ran through his head of terrible crimes where the guilty had walked free. He winced.

Some because I was good at my job. Those were the days that had nearly broken him, before he swapped sides and moved to prosecution after learning how to better judge the people who walked through his door. *Could I really give her a list of names, knowing that I would be sentencing someone to death? What about innocent until proven guilty? Jesus. Could I?*

He whirled, stalking back the other direction. He couldn't do that. Couldn't set himself as the judge and jury, aiming his pet executioner at a target and effectively pulling the trigger. The longer he worked through this in his head, the more frustrating it became. His memories called up an image of a victim's mother, body shuddering with sobs as he delivered the news her son's killers would walk free due to of a laboratory glitch, her wounded eyes brimming and spilling over with tears when Eric gently explained that double jeopardy prohibited him from bringing them to justice, ever. Her son, beaten to death with an iron pipe because he was gay, one of a connected string of deaths and his had been the best chance of justice. Denied when one tech failed to fill out a log entry, the killers hooting and joking as they strolled down the courthouse steps. Their arrogance deserved. He couldn't touch them. *Can't I?*

Lights swept through the windows and across the back wall. He watched for a moment as rectangles of illumination moved across the surface, bringing things momentarily into focus. Hands shaking, he strode to the door and ripped it open.

Alace was just climbing out of the car, and every line of her body told the story of a bone-deep exhaustion. Even though it had only been two days, just looking at her would convince anyone she'd been gone far longer. The tiredness suffusing her face was a kind that wouldn't be shaken off by a single night of good sleep. She lifted her head and looked at him, anguish and fear on her features. At her side in moments, he took the keys from her, closed and locked the door, then swept her into his arms. Legs around his waist, she propped her elbows on his shoulders, leaning in to place her forehead against his. Any thoughts of conversation fled his mind, and Eric focused on getting her what she so clearly needed.

"Hey." The single word gave voice to her fatigue, and he threaded a hand up her neck, cupping the back of her head and urging her closer. Brushing his lips across hers, he carried her to the house, pausing only long enough to close and secure the door.

"Hey," he finally returned, as he carried her to the bedroom. "You hungry?" She shook her head, her temple bumping against his jaw as she sagged against his shoulder. "Want a shower?" She shook her head again.

Voice faint, she whispered, "Tomorrow."

Alace burrowed against him after he set her on her feet, and her arms moved to wrap around his waist. He made quick work of stripping her to her panties, retrieving one of his shirts from the dresser and tugging it over her head, smiling at how the hem swirled just above her knees, the fabric swallowing her small frame.

He pushed the covers back, urged her to bed, and crowded in behind her. Eric fit his front against Alace's back, one arm shoved under her head and the other locked around her waist. This was what she needed. He knew instinctively, just from the expression she'd worn. Recognized how terrifying it had to be to come back to him. And even without her saying anything, he knew she'd expected him to turn her away after knowing what she'd come from doing.

This, he thought. *This is what I can do.*

Her body shook and a sound escaped, a broken gasp that told him tears were threatening. He bent his neck, nuzzling into her hair to place kisses on the soft skin behind her ear. Alace needed a rock. Without someone to hold her together, she handled everything as best she could, but she needed more.

She needed *more*.

She needs me.

He tightened his arm around her, angling a leg up and pushing close, tangling his calf between hers. Fingers twined with his and she tugged, bringing his hand up to rest between her breasts so their clasped hands rested over her heart. He traced the hinge of her jaw with the tip of his nose, going back over the same surface with his mouth, laying a line of kisses there, too.

Alace drew in a hard breath and then blew it back out, her body relaxing underneath the weight of his.

Yes, this he could do.

CHAPTER THIRTEEN

Alace

She'd woken in his arms yesterday.

Alace twisted to look out the back windows of Eric's home and into the silent darkness from where she sat in the safety of his house. She smiled at memories of their activities immediately following that awakening, not knowing her face had turned soft.

Eric wasn't here at the moment, and wouldn't be for hours. Since there was no real way of knowing how long she'd have before she had to go out again, his absence cut deeply. She understood, and yet wished he could have begged off this fundraiser. If it had been for his stepmother, she knew he would have. But this was for a good cause. It would benefit the basketball teams at the high school where he volunteered, and he was one of the coordinators of the event. With her back in his house, he hadn't wanted to go, and she'd laughed at his attempts to talk himself into ditching it and staying home. When he failed at that, he tried hard to convince Alace she should accompany him, something she'd turned over in her mind for seconds longer than she should have before shaking her head no. The resigned look on his face told her he hadn't been surprised at her refusal. *It'll get old for him*, a voice that sounded like Regg muttered in her head.

But she couldn't bear to go, not once she learned his father would be presenting a cardboard check representing a sizable donation from local businesses.

He has to know. She'd thought this a number of times. Eric was far from stupid, and while she might never have come out and detailed why she'd been in town when they'd met, he had to know it was because there was a gig in the area. Maybe he didn't realize the depths of his father's depravity and sense of entitlement, or maybe he was just blind to the faults of family. Lots of folks were. Throughout the years, she'd learned that blood was thicker than nearly anything, and sometimes the most resolute denial could be rooted in an effort to reject a relative's betrayal.

Not with Eric, though. First his behavior at that long-ago party, and then the involuntary expression of disgust that crossed his features every time he spoke of his father—all of those underlined a strong desire to avoid the man at all costs.

Movement at the far edge of the yard caught her eye, and she stared hard into the darkness, trying to force vague lines and shadows into something recognizable, and Alace watched with awe as a deer materialized out of the shadows. Walking carefully, cautiously, delicate legs took tentative steps towards the house. Alace was spellbound as the doe came closer, head lowering to sniff at the grass, every movement guarded. *I feel ya, honey.* Alace pulled her mouth to one side. *I've lived my whole life like you.*

Lights swung across the trees and the deer's head jerked up, freezing in place, every muscle taut with the need to be gone, to flee. Ears flicking back and forth, the doe quickly assessed the danger and, at the slam of a car door, gave up whatever edible delicacy it had been stalking. With wide leaps, her tail flagged high, the flashing white signaling danger, it took only moments and she was gone. The yard as empty as if it had never held a living, breathing being.

With the deer's disappearance, Alace rose and shifted over to a wall, placing her shoulders against the surface, palms braced to push off. Poised thus she waited, unsettled, knowing it was too early for Eric to be back. He'd kissed her goodbye with a reminder that she was to sleep in his bed, telegraphing his need for her with hot hands and hotter mouth, cementing on her skin the desire running through him and she'd soaked it in, appreciating how he mastered himself while managing to stoke her fire ever higher.

A key clattered against the lock, finally seated and turned, and the door opened boldly as a body stepped through. Briefly silhouetted against the ambient streetlights, the man's frame looked like Eric, but Alace knew better than to believe what she wanted to see, and stayed where she'd be partially hidden. Ready to bolt, her own version of wide leaps would come with pumping arms and racing legs. The door latch slipped into place, and the man shrugged off a jacket, the work of a moment to fling it over the back of a chair as he took long strides towards the stairs.

Alace didn't speak, still not certain of the visitor's identity. She hoped, but couldn't force herself to make a sound. She didn't have to. Eric seemed to have an innate sense of her location. He paused in his advance, head swinging so he could look into the shadows by the back wall, calling softly, "Alace?" Changing course, he approached her fast, barreling towards her on an inescapable arc until his arms swept around her, pulling her to him. "God, I couldn't..." His voice trailed off when his mouth became busy, working along her neck to her jaw, and she turned her head. She wrapped her arms around him, one low around his hips and one higher, fingertips in that damned hair curling at his nape. Then his mouth was on hers, possessing her with a kiss that started heated and flared to molten as he quested inside, and she tasted him. Whiskey and good cigars, a light fruity sweetness mixed with the heady woodsy flavor of Eric. He groaned in her mouth, and she captured the sound, working to pull a second one from him. A third and he pulled back, harsh breaths gusting across the sensitive skin of her neck. "Jesus, baby."

He lifted her and pitched, tossing her slightly into the air to settle her in his arms, laughing when she squeaked in surprise at the motion. "Eric." Voiceless no longer, she leaned into him, arms twined around his neck, feeling the heat from him baking through the fabric of his shirt.

"I couldn't stay away." His words were murmured against her mouth, and she stared into his beautiful eyes as he confessed, "I didn't even tell them I was leaving. I just...wanted to be here more than I needed to be there." He jostled her as he climbed the stairs, cool air wafting over her bare toes. "Baby." She smiled at him, and he stole it by dropping another kiss to her mouth, leaving her gasping open-mouthed.

"I'm glad." A vision of the startled doe slashed through her, and Alace forced it down, reminding herself that this wasn't frightening. Eric held no danger for her. "I've been waiting for you."

He stopped in place and angled his head down towards her. Meeting his motion, she folded her elbows between their bodies and lifted her hands, reverently cupping each side of his jaw with a palm as she tilted her face up to his. Crushed to his chest in a fierce hold while he kissed her, it was a wild crash of lips and teeth, contrasting with the gliding satin touch of his tongue against hers. The joining of their mouths taking full attention as she tried desperately to convey to him how much it meant that he had come back to her. That he would come for her. That he'd exhausted precious time and energy to find her and bring her here for this.

She was the one to break the kiss, twisting to bury her face against his neck, blood drumming in her ears. She drew a ragged breath, feeling an echoing pounding of his heart under her hands. Then he proved once again that single words were what signaled important things for them both by telling her how he felt.

His lips touched the top of her head, then her temple, gliding down to nuzzle softly just in front of her ear, and Alace shivered with need as he said, "Blessed."

***

"No." Frustrated, Alace clipped the word out as if it were offensive to her. Tipping her chin up, she looked at the angle where the wall met the ceiling. She was seated in a chair by the window in Eric's study. They'd finished breakfast half an hour ago, and when she told him she needed to make a private phone call, intending to do so outside as she'd done over the past few days, he had turned to glare at the dusting of snow in the backyard and then escorted her in here, pointedly closing the door as he exited.

Now Regg was on the phone, and he not only wasn't supportive of her newest idea for Ward, he was actively resisting it. His last suggestions were so absurd she didn't want to itemize the reasons why they were bad ideas, simply dismissing them out of hand.

"Jesus, Alace—"

She cut him off, deciding in an instant to finally get into what had sent her running from the woods. "Why did you use my name?" There was a hush on the other end of the line. Weighty silence, a quiet that felt like the instant between the detonator being triggered and the heavy whump of the resulting explosion. "You knew it wasn't a secure phone. Why would you do that, Regg?"

"You'd gone dark for too long, I worried."

This pronouncement, made in a dull, bored tone caused Alace's back to straighten, her shoulders moving back as she heard not only what he said, but what he meant.

"I go off the grid all the time. It's what I do." Normally she wouldn't consider reminding Regg of this. It was how he'd taught her to work the gigs, and she shouldn't have to remind him, given it was his wisdom in the first place. "It's part of the gig."

"Let's get back to Ward." Regg sighed, and that heavy exhalation held a note of disappointment. Alace's neck angled, her head dipping so she could stare at her feet.

For the first time in their long partnership, she wondered if that sigh had been carefully calculated to be audible without being condescending, because usually when he sighed like that, she capitulated, not wanting to upset him. Regg mattered to her. He was her friend.

My only friend.

She glanced at the door, carefully closed by the first person in her life other than Regg who knew what she did. True, Eric was more than an associate, he was a close confidant, a lover. But he also was a good friend—a person with influence and leverage. Was that why she was suddenly so much more critical of Regg than she'd ever been? Before Eric, would she have taken Regg's recommendations more to heart? She shook her head, knowing before Eric they wouldn't even be having this conversation. Leaving a mark alive wasn't how she worked. But because of Eric, they were. The idea of removing Ward another way had become so attractive, she hadn't even tried to talk herself back into the original plan. A relief, and not just because he was Eric's father.

Alace set that feeling aside, knowing she'd have to circle back around to it, but time for consideration was not now.

"Yes, lets." Alace pushed for brusque, knowing it wasn't something Regg heard from her often and she wanted to make a statement. If they were blazing new paths in their relationship, then let them not be tentatively crafted. "We're doing this one my way, Regg." She paused, hoping for a word, a breath, anything that would tell her he would be all-in on this. Regg gave her nothing, and she hesitated for only a breath before forging ahead. "Here's what I want from you."

For the next twenty minutes, she laid out her carefully crafted strategy, and at the end, even Regg grudgingly admitted it not only would work but might have the side benefit of flushing additional marks from cover. "Damn, girl. Might be less brutal to just kill him."

Alace lifted her gaze from the toes of her shoes where it had been directed and glanced towards the door again. Eric might not appreciate her methods, but in her gut, she knew it was the right thing to do. "Sometimes having to live with it is harder. For the rest of his life, he'll regret what he's done." *I could be the poster child for regrets.* At the thought, her brain tried to drift down the path of memories, wanting to catalog the people fallen in her wake. With effort, she pulled away and twisted, putting her back to the door, facing the windows instead. The glory of the Colorado Rockies filled her view, beauty that resisted every effort of nature and man to change them. "I'll call you in three days."

She disconnected without saying goodbye, still annoyed with Regg over their near argument at the beginning of the call. She pulled in breath after breath, shoving down the feelings of fear and regret, refusing to rethink the decisions she'd made in the past.

Gotta go with my gut on this one, too.

***

Regg

Scowling, he laid the phone on the desk in front of him, staring at the computer screen without really seeing the things displayed there. It wouldn't have mattered. There wasn't anything new to be seen, and he'd long since memorized the contents.

Images of Alace, laid in a collage, taking her progressively through life. He'd uncovered photos of her in grade school through the unsuccessful trial, had those pictures arranged in chronological order, youngest to oldest. Following those were additional images of her pulled from a multitude of sources. Tourist photos where she'd appeared in the background, security cameras from banks and grocery stores, employee ID photos that were nearly as unflattering as any state licensing branch pictures he'd ever seen. This cache was where he pulled his pictures from to create her new identities.

He'd taken the call today expecting them to have that conversation. What was next, where would she go, which gig would she pick. He snorted. *Picked with my guidance, of course.*

Regg reached out and clicked the mouse, minimizing the images, clicked again and then again, bringing up a folder on the server. Machine named, the string of characters and numbers held nothing to indicate the importance of what was inside. The contents of the folder held a man's life in the balance, and Regg studied his documentation again, opening files and adjusting terminology slightly here, redacting a detail there. Nothing huge, he'd spent countless hours on this file already, making it into a story that Alace would find compelling. Irresistible.

It needed to be.

Regg clicked again and the screen filled with security camera footage. Angles showing the inside and outside of his home with Lena, the rooms filled with expensive and attractive furniture, the backyard landscaped to showcase the in-ground pool. His children were grouped in the media room, draped across couch and chairs, his youngest stretched out on a rug he knew was plush and should have been, given it cost nearly eight grand. Another image showed the garage, and he watched as the outside door slid up, Lena pulling her new luxury sedan inside, the door silently lowering behind her.

I like my life as it is.

He hid the camera views, bringing up the case folder again. He reviewed a few final details and then closed everything. He logged into the server via a different path and typed in a series of commands, entering the directory location of the folder before triggering a script that would change the metadata on all the files, adjusting all dates to indicate they hadn't been opened or changed in months.

Alace would read it and want updated information. Information Regg already had, but needed her to be invested before he gave anything else to her. It was how she worked. The longer a case sat idle, the more driven she was to solve everything. She was a sucker for the cold case, the idea that justice had been waylaid for too long. She also needed to be the one in charge, so if he had already investigated on his own, she'd discount the case. He'd learned that a long time ago.

"Alace, baby, you're too easy."

The script finished running, and he reviewed the contents of the server in general. There were three other cases she'd expressed interest in before New Mexico, but they didn't have the same potential for a payday. The one he wanted her to accept would reap nearly two million. Not that Alace would ever know.

"After this little display, I'm thinking you need to be brought to heel, Alace dear."

Regg clicked over and brought up the collage of images again. His eyes flicked from picture to picture, cataloging the differences he'd noted in her after each of the jobs. Once she had enough money in the bank so she didn't have to worry constantly about how to afford the work she did, she'd stopped being interested in payoffs at all. *Not me.*

"Okay, Alace. We'll do Ward your way. But then we get back to normal."

He fired off a dozen e-mails and messages, priming his resources for the push that would come in a week, a date that lined up conveniently with the kickoff of Ward's latest campaign. Every two years like clockwork, the man refused to give up his stranglehold on his state and ran for reelection.

Regg grinned, getting into the groove of things now, relishing the idea of his work bringing down a man of Ward's power. Normally he was the man behind the curtain, pulling Alace and other hunters' strings to achieve the final goal. This time he'd be more hands-on than usual, and he liked the idea.

After Ward—who didn't have a payday if done this way, the idea causing Regg to roll his eyes even as he pulled another chess piece into place—he'd force Alace to pick the job he wanted.

CHAPTER FOURTEEN

Alace

Eric stirred behind her, stretching as he reached across her body towards where the remote sat on the coffee table. "What's next in the queue, baby?"

Alace smiled, turning her face into the pillow bunched underneath her head. She'd never done this before, a lazy day spent watching movies with someone. When Eric found out, he'd loudly declared it was a criminal oversight that needed to be rectified immediately, and proceeded to arrange his day so he could stay home with her. So many firsts with him. She felt languid, relaxed to a level that was unique in her experience.

They'd begun the day with soft, slow lovemaking followed by whispered conversation while he held her against his body. Every movement, every touch had been tender, just the memory making her throat tight with emotion. Then had come the closeness on the couch. No urgency, no agenda—nothing but Eric and her and a day full of comfortable exploration taking the form of shared observations about movies and shows, how the world had changed since the days of Clark Gable, and what it meant when reality shows held people's attention as if they really were reality.

She rolled against his chest and looked up into his face, memorizing the gentle smile he was directing her way. *I love him.*

That thought ripped through her like lightning, setting every alarm blaring as her heart clenched in her chest, stomach twisting painfully. His brows angled together slightly as he asked, "What?"

Alace held the mouthful of bitter saliva and forced her lips into the curve of a small smile. Only when he was again focused on the TV as his thumb worked the buttons on the remote did she allow herself the reactive swallow. "Probably should eat something."

His hand dropped to her belly, fingertips tracing a circle just above her panties. "My baby need me to feed her?"

"You're too sweet," she teased him, seeing one corner of his mouth pull sideways as he tried to hide a smile. "Put the weather on or something. Let's go see what we can throw on a tray and bring back." She shifted, preparing to slide off the couch and to her feet, barely getting a leg off the furniture before his hand at her belly turned into an arm at her waist, yanking her back against his chest.

"Gimme a kiss first." His demand was a mutter, mouth muffled against the skin of her neck as he worked his slow way up and across her jaw. She opened under the demands of his lips, meeting every thrust and glide of his tongue, swallowing down his groan when his arms tightened around her. Wiggling her hips backwards, she felt the hot hardness of his arousal against her ass as he crowded forwards, molding himself to her.

His arm loosened, hand sliding under her shirt to find and cup her breast, flicking her hardening nipple with the edge of his thumb. She found herself gripping his wrist tightly in both hands, holding on as she arched against his touch. Flick and a glide across her nipple, then his fingers were grasping hard as his teeth grazed her bottom lip.

Every inch of her lips burned fiercely, his stubble rasping them until they were swollen and sensitive. "Eric." Nothing else, just his name, her voice breaking on a gasp when the kiss turned slow and lazy, his mouth traveling leisurely from one side to the other. Tracing along the side of her nose with his, he pressed their foreheads together tight, breaking the caress.

A final brush of his lips against hers, then a whispered, "Food." She nodded, not moving, eyes fluttering open to find his gaze fixed on hers. "Alace, you gotta get up, honey." She nodded again, and he grinned, the predatory curve of his lips telegraphing a masculine satisfaction that made her toes curl, knowing she gave that to him. "Come on." He lifted, hovering over her for a moment as he found his footing. Arm locked around her waist, he raised her off the couch and set her on her feet, bending to press a final, final kiss on her mouth. "Lemme feed my woman."

***

Two weeks later, she was again seated with Eric on a couch, this time in Malibu, California. They shared the piece of furniture with a distinguished-looking older woman and an equally distinguished-looking man, Eric's mother and her husband, all four of them staring at the TV as Eric's father gave his resignation speech.

On Alace's part, she watched with a great deal of satisfaction, seeing the plans laid with Regg come to fruition so quickly and thoroughly. Every step of the way had been orchestrated by her, revelation after revelation delivered to the media so they couldn't mistake a single clue, and they had leapt on it all, creating their brand of circus out of a mix of facts and conjecture—facts from her, conjecture from the networks' talking heads—until Ward had no choice but to leave public office.

Eric was tense, every muscle primed for action, impotent as he watched this final appearance. When the writing was on the wall, his mother had called and demanded he come away from Colorado, bringing him to her in a move that left no question where he, or she, stood on the things his father had been accused of doing. With the media already knowing she'd abandoned Ward years before when the first allegations had aired, by placing himself at her side, Eric's innocence of everything was assured.

At their first meeting, Phoebe Mayer, Ward's ex-wife and Eric's mother, had shocked Alace by greeting her with both open affection and excitement. Proclaiming her to be "exactly like Eric described," a statement which had Alace whipping her head sideways to see Eric's grin grow impossibly wide. In the days following their arrival, Bebe, as she preferred to be called, had effortlessly won Alace's heart.

Even so—seated on a plush, leather couch in a sprawling multi-million-dollar home overlooking a beach near Malibu, nestled close to a man who continually introduced himself as her "boyfriend" and whose mother had given her tacit approval of their fledgling relationship in the form of a shared bedroom with a California king bed, and having gone for more days in a row as herself than she'd done in years—Alace still felt separated from everything. Only slightly at times, and then in some moments, it was as if she were watching a colorized newsreel from decades past, any resemblance to reality only passing. Surreal didn't come close to covering it.

On the TV screen, Ward stepped back from the microphones and lifted both hands to shoulder height, palms facing the camera signaling an end to not only the interview and press conference but also an era of terror for young, naïve interns and assistants. *Never again*. He turned and walked through the open door behind him, alone, as he had been since the second day of the barrage of accusations. Various gossip rags had published pictures of Ward's young wife abandoning him as she boarded a private plane and departed, her destination no doubt a sunny beach somewhere where she wouldn't have to watch her life implode. That meant Ward was alone, something that had fleetingly led Alace to consider making his retirement permanent.

But then her words to Regg had come back to her, dousing those thoughts with the realization Ward would pay far more this way. Even if no criminal charges were ever brought against him, it was very likely there would be multiple civil cases. Either way, he was done. *Toast*.

Alace leaned against Eric's shoulder, reached for his hand and threaded her fingers between his. They hadn't talked about it, but he had to know she was behind his father's humiliation. Had to know, but clearly didn't care. He held on tightly, and she turned her head, pressing against his chest, lifting her other hand to his cheek and angling his mouth down to hers. Softly, she kissed him, keeping the closed-mouth caress tender. "Let's turn this off, go for a walk." He nodded, pushed to his feet and pulled her up behind him.

Bebe smiled up at her, the expression on her face so clearly approving, Alace felt a sense of wonder sweep over her again at how her life had changed.

Surreal.

***

Regg sighed, the sound loud through the phone. "Look, Alace, I get that you're enjoying playing house with Ward." Alace flinched, glad he couldn't see how he'd scored. It had been just that morning she'd thought nearly the same, wondering for a moment what it would be like if she could just settle down with Eric. They were still in California, planning on staying for another couple of days before heading home. She let her lids drift closed. *Home.* Eric probably didn't realize it, but every time he said the word and she was near, his hands went to her, palms gliding up her arms, or he'd give her a quick nuzzle against her cheek. Without words, he communicated she was his home, and even just thinking about it now Alace's belly dipped. "You should have told me sooner, in case I had to run interference for you while we took his old man down. But you need to know about Charlotte."

Alace lifted her head and stared out at the ocean. Charlotte meant Regg was talking about a mark on the east coast they'd been hunting for years.

Following a cycle it had taken far too long to become clear, a killer stalked the streets of Charlotte, North Carolina. With rigid precision, she—Alace believed the killer was female, unlike the police who were clearly unwilling to look at the fucking evidence—mechanically strangled her victims at intervals that halved the previous break in activity. At the end, as her kills became much more closely staggered, she would enter a frenzied period of activity. When this window closed, it would be another four years before she surfaced again.

"Cadence? Where are we in the cycle?" Alace tried to remember the last time she'd reviewed the case notes for Charlotte. It had to be at least a couple of years ago, when the gap was enough to make it impossible to do much more than she already had with digging through the pilfered police information and documentation, scant as it was.

"Two months. He's beginning to devolve." Alace winced again, this for a very different reason. That would mean there was less than a month to unravel a puzzle that had remained unsolved for two decades. Two months meant the next kill would be in a month, then two weeks, then a week, and so on.

She focused on her reflection, familiar lines falling into place on her face as she realized that this time with Eric was coming to an end. *Doesn't have to be forever.*

"You want me to send the files? Let's tackle this guy, together. Me and you, just like always." Alace realized she hadn't responded, and Regg was trying to sell her on the mark. Not their style, and his pushy tactics felt strange. She held her tongue, letting him continue. "I've already been digging. Got things laid out. You didn't tell me everything that went down last time, but I guessed using your little trail name wasn't a real request, so I put together Tonia Sage. Figured if you couldn't be a Thistle, you wouldn't mind being a Sage." His tone was cajoling, and that also was new, so she focused on it. Cajoling, and threaded with false humor. "I've got everything ready to go, just say the word."

Regg had never pushed her towards a gig before. Not once. He facilitated her choices, didn't direct them.

"Let me think about it."

Regg huffed, the sound loud in her ear. "He's going to hit again soon." Alace's neck twisted and her eyes closed as Regg's aim struck true. "I remember last time, you were a mess when you missed the chance to catch him."

Eyes flying open, Alace looked at her reflection again, seeing a clear look of puzzlement on her face. "No, I wasn't." She'd been absorbed by a gig in Texas, working a human trafficker who preyed on the kids who flocked to the Gulf beaches every summer. It was never a choice once she was on track. Too much went into the process for her to consider pulling just in case a different gig heated up.

"You were upset." Regg asserted, and she watched her reflection squint. *Why is he pushing so dang hard?*

"Upload what you've got. That way if I decide to look at the gig, I can." He made a sound of agreement, and Alace cut him off. "I'll call you." Clear lines, known expectations—that made a good partnership.

She disconnected the call, disassembling the phone by rote, shoving the battery into one pocket, the reassembled phone into another.

I need to look at Regg and this gig. Alace made a face. *Something's off.* Off didn't work for her. Off meant mistakes, or bad decisions, either of which would put everything in jeopardy. She heard Eric's voice calling her name and felt her expression grow soft. She couldn't afford to make mistakes, not now.

Twisting on her heel, she strode from the room to find him.

Far too much to lose.

***

Alace stared at the screen of her battered laptop. Purchased used at a local pawn shop, the device didn't look like much, but it had all the processor speed she needed. The laptop sent by Regg to the drop box established for the New Mexico gig sat inside an RFID blocking bag tucked into the trunk of her junker, and that was parked in a long-term lot far from Eric's house.

Alace had found a tiny bug in her backpack.

She hadn't been looking for it. Hadn't expected to find anything like that on or in any of her garments or possessions. The strap on the bag had come loose, and she'd been threading it back through the clasp when she felt it. Tiny and so ultra-thin she didn't credit it at first, but after poking and prodding for fifteen minutes, defining the boundaries of the oddity, tracing the outline through the padding and fabric, she'd taken the tip of her knife to the strap and within a few seconds had extracted it.

A high-quality bug in a nondescript bag meant to be discarded after a gig? That didn't compute. She'd sat and stared at it for a long time, lying innocently on the edge of a table in case it had a temperature sensor. Then, gut twisting and heart sinking, she'd methodically detected and removed another half a dozen tracers from articles of clothing and shoes. Affixed into seams, hidden underneath liners, each of them would be worth hundreds of dollars on the black market, and they'd been placed in items she normally would pitch when she started a new gig.

So engrossed was she in her discoveries, she hadn't heard Eric come home and he had surprised her. One look at her face and he'd come to her, arms tight around her shoulders as he'd asked, "Can I do anything?"

She'd shaken her head, which was the truth, and then gave him something that was also the truth. "You already are. Just hold me for a minute."

"I can do that." He'd twisted and sat on the edge of the couch, stretching out, folding Alace into the space between his body and the back of the couch. "That I can do."

That night, she'd put the trackers into a bag, tossing it and every stitch of clothing she had with her into a big box, wedging that box into the back of the closet in Eric's guest bedroom. She'd already been working off a locally purchased burner phone, so she put her other phone into the same box. It had taken a few days, but when she talked to Regg next, he'd asked how things were, asked if she were ill, asked enough questions that she understood he'd noted they hadn't moved. That had solidified her fears.

Regg was tracking her without her knowledge.

Before New Mexico, she would have given her permission without pause, trusting Regg would have her best interests at heart, that he would use the info to help extricate her from a tough spot if needed. But she'd been in a tough spot in New Mexico, and he hadn't put anything into play. If he were tracking her then, it was clear he would have hung her out to dry.

Since New Mexico, she had a different set of rules. With Eric, things were different.

If Regg is keeping tabs on me without a word, what other secrets is he holding?

After a few moments spent cataloging Regg's behavior, she dialed in on the serial killer he had pushed hard to get her to consider taking as a gig.

Alace went to work. She'd been doing this long enough, had enough connections independent of Regg, she'd been able to cast a series of queries into the darknet, and wait. Through the years, she'd cultivated personas online, creating pockets of influence that she didn't often leverage, given Regg had been doing the same thing for far longer. That meant his ability to gain whatever intel they needed far outstripped her own. Still, she'd found it advantageous enough to warrant maintenance of these identities. Now, they were paying off, and in a big way.

Alace worked quickly, saving a report she'd been given to a folder on a secure server hidden as a virtual machine on another very secure VM. The one linked from a message had a timer on it, and in about fifteen minutes, it would be as if it never existed. Except for the single copy she had in her possession now.

Hunched in front of the computer, she read enough of the report to know what additional tags to look for and then patched several queries together. She paired what she knew with what she expected to find, hoping it wouldn't be a self-fulfilling prophesy. Even as she cast the final query wide, more fruits of the first were looping back around to her. Virtual money exchanged hands—she'd kept pods of reserves for this purpose—and once payment hit accounts, the flow of data became a flood. Four more reports were saved to similar servers, and so certain was she of what they contained, she didn't even review them first.

She stayed online long enough to see the ripples from her activity die down, nothing bouncing against them to agitate the online community with counter-queries, waiting around to verify everything in her little node became calm and quiet. Then she logged off the darknet and crafted a connection to her secure virtual server, slamming her way through the security questions and passphrases until she had downloaded all five reports to her old, used, but very un-bugged computer.

On her feet, she stalked away from the computer, leaving it sitting open on the coffee table as she made her way to the kitchen. Downing one tall glass of cold water, she refilled the glass and drank this one slower, trying to control her racing heart.

If I delete the reports now, nothing has to change.

But she knew the fabric of what she had with Regg was altered the moment she found the trackers in items provided by a source assumed dependable. She could never go back to the same level of trust, never believe without questioning, never feel safe. *Regg did that.* Alace shook her head, drained the glass and tipped it upside down in the dish strainer sitting alongside the sink. A single drop of water trailed along the inside surface of the glass, making its slow way to the rim where it trembled on the edge, all animation suspended. If she'd asked Regg about the devices, he may have come clean, or he could have lied. Either way, the trust was lost, and she didn't really want to know if he'd lie. *That would take things to a whole new level.* The droplet lost its grip and gravity took over, it fell, vanishing into the shadows.

Seated in front of the computer again, she clicked, and clicked again, opening the first report, using the password she'd assigned the file when she stored it. It would be saved with a different password when she closed it, the progression sequence known only to her. Two failed attempts to open the file would delete it.

Staring at the wall for a moment, she thought again, *Regg did this to us*. Glancing at the clock, she saw she had at least two hours before Eric came home. With an intent breath, she enlarged the report on the screen and began reading.

An hour and forty-five minutes later, she closed the laptop with a slap that echoed around the room, flinching as the latch slammed into place. Her stomach had started out rolling with nervousness, but had settled during the time spent reading the reports she'd purchased. Now instead of feeling shaky and afraid, she had only one emotion. *Rage*.

The killer in the Carolinas would have been one she would do because it needed to be done. Too many people had already lost their lives when law enforcement couldn't put the clues together. She would do it for no reward, but there would have been one. A huge one. The payoff on that one gig was enough to keep her living comfortably for probably a decade or more. *Not that I need much*. She shook her head, folding her arms across her chest.

Regg apparently did. The other marks she'd examined, retroactive though her investigation was, and cold though the trails had become, all told the same tale. The higher risk the marks, the higher the payoff. Payoffs in some cases, plural. None of which she'd seen. He had never alluded to them, not even mentioned in passing. Not that she'd have wanted the money. Often she took the payment only when the retaliation client felt the desperate need to feel they had contributed to the retribution in some fashion. Even that was typically split not just with Regg, but with a charity that matched the victim's personality.

Over the past four years alone, from only the handful of marks she'd looked at, Regg had cleared more than fifteen million dollars. Add what the Carolinas' killer would bring in, and he'd be sitting at twenty.

Twenty million dollars.

She snarled silently. *Hell, I paid for the destruction of Ward out of my own account.* She hadn't wanted to make Regg suffer for her change of direction on the gig.

Alace felt the rage burn cold through her veins as her brain worked at lightning speed.

By the time Eric walked through the door, she had the beginnings of a plan. She just had to make it work.

***

Eric

Alace sat beside him on the couch, cuddled warm against his side, but Eric knew she was miles away in her head.

The past several days Alace had seemed distant. Not cruelly so, just a casual preoccupation that he found could be interrupted, so he did, as often as he could. It wasn't as if she were angry or upset with him, more that her mind was entirely taken up by something...not him.

He knew this was a change for her. They'd talked about how she'd never had a set base. Normally if taking time off between gigs—as she called them— she'd insert herself into a medium-sized resort somewhere. Not to rest and recover, just to blend. Staying somewhere with hundreds of other people meant she wasn't an anomaly, and a rent-by-the-week place lacked the inconveniences of an actual lease where you'd have deposits, and neighbors. Eric figured it was easier mentally, too. Since she spent her life fitting into places where people were already established, all while pretending to be someone she wasn't, it was probably a relief to be herself around people who were out of their element and somewhat pretending, too.

She hadn't done that this time. Instead, she'd gotten involved with him, which meant she was in his house. Unless he organized something specific, she seemed content to stay home most of the time. Their time in Malibu with his mother was a different thing, and he'd spent hours going over those days in his head. From the time they got into the car to drive out, she had subtly changed, becoming a more public version of herself. Behind closed doors, she'd been just the same as always, but it made him wonder which was her playing a part.

He suppressed a grin. She'd actually taken the announcement that they were going to visit his mother in stride. Only after they were back here did she admit to the normal nerves a woman might have when meeting her future mother-in-law for the first time. Not that Alace knew those were his intentions. Not yet. He'd decided to keep that question—and the ring—under wraps until she was more comfortable with him.

More comfortable. He stared at the TV. Instead, she seemed less.

He needed to at least address the possibility that she was getting bored with this. His life, his home...him. She was here on her terms, not his. That had been clear from the beginning, but she'd exposed so much of her life to him it had felt like she was making room for them.

If she leaves, what then? He'd gone from having no one, to this. Eric tightened his arm around her shoulders, and she leaned more heavily, giving him her weight as she rested a hand on his chest, fingertips drawing tiny circles on the fabric of his shirt. He liked the way she snuggled into him, fitting herself there like she'd been made for him. *If she has to leave, she'll come back.*

When they'd started things, he'd wondered if he could handle that kind relationship with her. One where she might be here for a few days or a week or two, then gone, and then eventually return after who knew how long. At the time, he'd been convinced part of her was better than nothing. Then she'd gone back to New Mexico, leaving Eric afraid things could go wrong and he might never know. As if she were going off to war, leaving him behind to tend the home front.

He bent his neck and touched his lips to the crown of her head, breathing in her scent. *Can I do that again? And again?*

She tipped her head back, offering her mouth, and he took it in a gentle kiss.

When he next looked at the TV, it was without a clear answer.

CHAPTER FIFTEEN

Alace

Slipping her knife free from the back pocket of her jeans, Alace sliced through the thin piece of plastic affixing a price tag to the duffle bag resting on the foot of Eric's bed. She methodically did the same for the clothing piled around the bag, empty store sacks lying on the floor near her feet. She glanced down and curled her toes inside her new shoes.

Nothing to chance. Over the past two days, she'd laid her plans, borrowing Eric's car one day to make a day trip to a small town near the New Mexico border. Her first stop was the extended PO box rental place there where she'd stashed the money from Waterdrum's cabin. In the flurry of activity that went on after Eric had shown and she'd escaped, she'd never gotten around to mailing the cash to Regg.

Never mentioned it to him, either, so it was a clean stash of money he had no knowledge about. She'd also reactivated an old identity, one she'd intended to use last year between gigs, instructing the ID associated with it be mailed to the same PO. That was another thing Regg didn't know. It had been her first foray into using another paper guy. Since it was already created, it had been no problem for the guy to send it along.

Three stops on the way home had garnered her a new burner phone and the clothing, a new(er) junker, and carryout from the local restaurant Eric liked. Since she didn't cook, it was her way of making dinner.

Finished with the packing, she tucked the bag inside the closet and disposed of the detritus, gathering all the tags and plastic pieces and carrying them to the garbage can inside the garage. Then she sat in one corner of the couch to wait.

Eric woke her, one hand at her waist while he traced her features with the fingers of his other hand. "Wake up, sleepyhead." He murmured this while smiling, and she knew that because she felt his lips curving against her mouth. "Beloved." Alace melted inside like she always did when he gifted her with that endearment. He followed it with the second punch of his one-two combination by dragging his lips along the sensitive skin behind her ear, whispering, "Baby."

"Hey" was her unimaginative greeting, but his eyes lit with warmth anyway. "You're home." He bent closer, pushing his face into her neck as he nodded, arms shoving behind her to lift her, holding her close.

She wrapped her arms around his neck, twisting her head to drop a series of soft kisses along the edge of his jaw. "I didn't mean to doze off."

"I like coming home and finding you like this. You're all warm," he squeezed her, arms tightening deliciously around her, "and snuggly." Alace fell backwards and tugged, pulling at him, silently urging him to lie with her, and he accepted her invitation, stretching out beside her, thigh across her hips holding her in place.

"I need to tell you something," she whispered against his throat, face held there by his palm at the back of her head. "Listen all the way through, okay?" He nodded. But the way he'd gone tight told her he didn't expect this to be a good talk. "It's not bad. Nothing's changed between us. But I have to do something. Will you listen?" Eric pulled in a hard breath before releasing it slowly, the outrush of air stirring the hair on top of her head. He nodded again on a second sigh.

"I told you about my handler." That's the term she'd used for Regg, while careful not to divulge his actual name. She didn't wait for Eric's response, needing to get past the background and into the information that was most critical. "He's done some things that I find concerning. I need to see what's up with that. I've taken measures to hide my tracks from him, which might still have the effect of him noticing something's not right. I'll be gone just a couple of days, and then back here. It's not..." She trailed off for a moment, trying to find words that didn't sound pretentious to her own ears. Leaving off anything about it being dangerous, or not, she decided to focus on what it definitely wasn't. Regg wasn't a mark. Couldn't be. "It's not a gig. Just something I have to look into."

"You're leaving?" Every muscle under her hands was taut, tight with anger or fear, she wasn't sure which. "When?"

"Tomorrow."

He didn't respond, didn't move, just lay on the couch with her, and she wrapped her arms tighter, wanting to give him whatever assurances he needed. "Couple of days, Eric. I'll be back here."

"You'll come home." Alace's breath caught in her throat, because while his words were certain, his tone was anything but.

She nodded and kissed his neck, giving him what he needed. "I'll come home."

***

Driving cross-country was a great way to prepare. And, all reassurances to Eric aside, this was as much a gig as anything else she'd ever done.

She was headed to do an initial reconnaissance against Regg. Tongue tracing the edges of her teeth, she snorted. Laying it out like that in her head felt weird, wrong. Regg was meant to be her partner, not someone she used her skills against.

Still, she had a fistful of trackers that said things weren't what she'd thought they were.

If she were wrong, it would mean someone else planted the trackers, and that was a different concern. She had to make sure first.

So Alace did what she was good at, putting together the information she knew and outlining the places where it didn't fit well, or where there were holes.

She had found more holes than info. Having never met Regg, never seen him, she had no idea what he looked like. She'd talked to him more times than she could count, knew every intonation of his voice over the phone and felt she could read him there, as well his attitude via electronic communication. He probably never thought she'd know where he lived, but she did. Tidbits dropped one at a time over the years had built a map in her head. Community information, the schools his child attended, the coffeehouse where he'd met Lena, a neighbor's name—all hints laid down by mistake, things he wouldn't credit could be built to a location profile, but she had.

Alace didn't realize until she began cataloging the small bits of information that she'd made a lifelong study of Regg.

From their conversations alone, she'd had a sense of the size of his house and how many bedrooms, understood the scope of the landscaping well enough to peg the size of the backyard pool, measured the distance between the house and garage, and knew while his office was underneath the garage, he had a window to bring in natural light. He'd had dogs in the past, but his daughter was allergic, so they'd put off replacing the last one when it had died of old age. From conversations in his car, the manufacturer's satnav voice had been distinctive enough to identify. Now, with her electronic surveillance, she knew so much more, and found a few of her assumptions from his innocent clues were wrong. *Satellite imagery doesn't lie, not like Regg.*

Still, there were a lot of holes.

Steering the car off the highway and down into a residential neighborhood, she made her way towards a copse of woods that stood nearby. At nearly 4:00 a.m., the houses themselves were dark, windows lit from inside only infrequently by dim nightlights, the outsides awash in attractively placed spotlights, setting off the charms of the enormous homes while providing the illusion of safety. She parked and turned off the engine, sitting for a moment with her hands resting on the wheel.

Flashlight in her pocket, Alace climbed out of the car and reached her arms up to stretch. Working out the kinks from a long drive, she bent side to side, pushing her muscles until the strain built to a pleasant burn. Locking the car, she wove her way through the chill underneath the trees, keeping to the edges of the woods until she was directly behind the house she believed belonged to Regg. Cautious, she knew he had a residential alarm and might have environmental ones, too, so she made her way to his neighbor's property, keeping close to the fence line that separated the homes.

About halfway along the fence, she found the tree she'd marked from the satellite maps and braced her back against the trunk, using her feet against the fencepost to work her way several feet up off the ground, putting her at an advantageous angle to look over and into Regg's yard. She adjusted slightly, making herself comfortable for what could be an extended vigil, and then, wedged securely in place, able to maintain her position with little effort, Alace surveyed Regg's home for the first time in person.

Large, opulent, meant to house a big family, what looked like a lavish home stood three-stories high. The back of the house was awash in windows overlooking a yard which housed a pool sized for a community, not a single family with one child. There were toys floating on the surface of the water, bikes piled alongside the back of the garage, a grill that even from this distance gave off the odor of cooked meat, and enough furniture arranged to entertain to testify about the frequency with which this backyard oasis was used.

She remembered him telling her, "Oh, big enough for her to paddle around in." That had been in answer to a casual question about the pool he and Lena just installed, spoken as he found a quiet corner so they could chat about the next gig she would take. Big pool to go with a big house. Big house to go with a big family. But, as far as Alace knew, Regg had one child. That was one of the things he'd commiserated with her about during their long, intimate talks that tracked the path of the moon through the sky, when she had admitted wanting kids in a someday kind of way, and he claimed to have wanted a big family, sadly truncated at one.

Before leaving the car, she'd slung a small bag over her shoulder. Tugging it in front of her now, she unzipped the top and dug around inside, withdrawing a device about the size of a pack of playing cards. Pushing at the hidden latches, she flipped open the vanes and rotary wings. The controller was larger than the drone and offered her a small screen that displayed the camera's view. She balanced the tiny device on her knees and pressed a button. It whirred to life, and she let it hover for a moment before sending it higher. Even if Regg had pressure-sensitive environmental, it was doubtful he would have defended himself from the air, and if he did, then her drone was so small it would likely slip through undetected.

She focused on the screen, approaching the house at an angle, edging the drone into the shadows along the wall to reduce the chances it would reflect light in a way to draw attention. Along the bottom level, she let it hover for a moment while she scanned what she could see on the screen. Rotating it slightly, she zoomed the camera view in on a picture mounted on the wall to the side of a fireplace. An attractive man sat next to a gorgeous woman, a child on each of their laps, two standing behind what had to be their parents, and one seated on a tiny stool in front. Four of the children shared the man's distinctive hair, bright red. Curly on the little girl, of which there were two total, and springing wildly from the little boys' heads, of which there were three. His wife had contributed her chin to the girls, and a mix of nose and eyes to the boys. Clearly these adored children were the product of the two loving adults, sharing enough mixed characteristics that parentage was undeniable.

Liar, party of one, your table is ready.

She piloted the drone across the width of the bottom floor windows, mapping the house's layout, looking at the parts of his life Regg surrounded himself with. Refrigerator cluttered with magnet-fastened photos, drawings, party invitations, and lists. School backpacks lined up under hooks holding five jackets, the children's name labels unreadable from this distance, but it looked as if all but one began with the same letter, a shared initial with their father.

She zipped the drone to the second floor, looking in windows on children sleeping, one to a bed, one bed to a room, furniture high quality as were the toys littering their spaces. Computers, TVs, gaming consoles, snow skis standing in a corner in one room were balanced by a snowboard in another. Five bedrooms occupied, and two left vacant for guests. Plenty of room at the inn, but no invitation for someone he'd known for years.

Third floor now, and she kept the drone along the edges of the opened curtains, peering around the fabric to see an enormous bed with a single occupant. The beautiful Lena lay on her side facing away from the windows, and Alace found herself glad. She didn't want to see what the love of Regg's life looked like in the flesh. *Wonder if anything he told me about her, about how he met her was true?*

The next window was a sitting room, furnished with a mix of leather and fabric. Undoubtedly it was stylish and classic, but all Alace could do was apply imagined price tags to each piece. Then she started thinking of the people, the ones who haunted her dreams, their faces superimposed on things throughout the house, drawing correlations between the terrible things she'd done, and what Regg had at his fingertips.

Everything I ever wanted, right here. A home. A real home, a place to return to where there were people who loved her. A family ready to sweep her into their arms. Children, even just one, a baby to cradle and sing to, to raise in the way children should be raised, a chance to prove her mother wrong, prove everyone wrong. A being in the world who would always love her, never leave her, and believe in her.

Everything.

Alace's mind flitted back over the past handful of years, through the flophouses and cheap apartments, her transient existence that wasn't living. The constant reinvention of herself, clawing her way into someone's life only to end it. Regg urging her to take another gig, and another, everything leaving her as dead inside as she'd been while laying in that alley. *Two minutes and forty-seven seconds.* All while he had this.

Even now, if he could manage it, Regg would rip her away from Eric, she knew. Pull her away and insert her into the gig they'd discussed. Well, he'd discussed at length, she'd sat silently through most of it. He would have her leave Eric behind and focus on their version of vigilante justice. While he had everything she'd ever wanted.

Rotating the remote control with her fingers, she eased the drone back from the window, going the other direction across the back of the house, passing the bedroom again and looking into the attached bathroom. No Regg.

She glanced at the garage, following the drone with her eyes before concentrating her gaze on the screen again. She flew the device around the corner and out of sight, focused instead on the small window set just below ground level, light streaming from it. Easing the drone in closer she saw a man with bright red hair, slightly thinning on the crown, head angled over a tablet he had balanced on one knee.

Regg.

***

Regg

He drummed his fingers against the desk in front of him, flipping over another page on the electronic report currently on the tablet's screen. He quickly highlighted and copied a section of text, shifted to a second document and pasted the snippet, adjusting a few phrases and deleting a sentence or two. Once he had it crafted as he wanted, he went back to the report and continued reading, stopping in a moment to repeat the process.

On the computer monitor, he had the evaluation open that pertained to the hunter he was going to promote this job to. He found it helped keep him focused on what motivated each of his operatives.

Pausing to drink from a bottle of water he had on the desk, he glanced at the phone again. Alace should have called in by now. Leaning towards the computer, he minimized the open document and navigated to her folder. Double-clicking the shortcut to her tracking profile, he looked at the markers on the map. Markers that hadn't moved for days. A few of his tags had gone offline, something he chalked up to defective equipment. His supplier swore by the units, but was still sending replacements. Not that it helped him right now. They weren't sophisticated enough to indicate which article the tag belonged to, so replacing them would be problematic. *Until she heads to the east coast, at least.* He could strongly suggest an entire reset on clothing and accessories, which would get new tags into her hands just in time to deal with one of the largest potential payoffs he'd ever worked on.

Glancing at the phone again, he startled when it rang. It was like he'd called it to life through sheer willpower. The burner number Alace was using lit up the screen, and he quickly opened the eval on Alace while he set the tablet aside.

She always required his full attention.

***

Alace

Through the screen on the remote, she watched as Regg reached out for the phone. He didn't answer immediately as she expected, but allowed it to ring another two times before he lifted the device towards his ear, his rough, just-woken-from-sleep voice managing to sound both pleased she called and exhausted.

"Hey, honey. I'd given up on you calling tonight."

For all his voice was languorous, he was in motion, fingers flying across the keyboard, and she watched as a half a dozen documents opened on the computer screen. He rapidly sorted them, adjusting so they took up precise sections of the monitor.

She hit the zoom on the camera as she responded. "Sorry, got caught up in something. How you doin'?" They always did chitchat if she wasn't in the middle of a gig. Quiet catching up, mostly her sharing what she'd been doing, but he would often tell her something that seemed personal. "How's Lena?"

He made a small sound she would have assumed accompanied a stretch, but as she could see, he was seated firmly in a comfortable office chair. "Gimme a minute." She watched as he held the phone to his chest, leaning back in the chair and staring overhead. A couple of times he moved the device, and she heard scuffling in the background, sounding like he was walking through a quiet house. "Yeah, she's good. Tired. Work's been a bear."

Lena had supposedly changed jobs not long ago and was now working her way up the ladder in a retail chain. *Probably bullshit.* "That sucks. Does she still think the change is going to be worth it?"

"Oh, sure. She just has to settle in."

More cautious back-and-forth followed, things of no consequence. They could have been any pair of friends catching up after any length of absence. While Regg sounded relaxed—and if things were normal, she would have thought he was lounging in an armchair, collapsed back with his feet up—his posture was anything but. He sat stiffly, back ramrod straight, leaning forwards occasionally to select sections of a document. She eased the drone into a different position, angling to see that window on his screen.

There were segments highlighted in red, and some in yellow, and only one with green. Her eyes flew across the tiny screen as she zoomed and adjusted, trying to read them all. Her name, her real name, was at the top edge of the document.

He was looking at a report on her.

She read what she could, each sentence hitting her like a punch to the gut, stealing her breath.

"anxiety and depression complicate and obscure easy manifestation of trust"

"is currently fragile and emotionally immature"

"doesn't respond well to threats or intimidation"

"better results with a pseudo close relationship or collaboration"

"many symptoms of anxiety, tension, worries and sleep difficulties were observed"

"highly motivated when perceived injustices are offset by internalized responsibility"

She watched as he used the cursor to select one of the sections and heard him ask, "Have you thought more about Charlotte?" One of his hands came to rest on the desk, and she watched as he unconsciously rubbed his thumb and fingers together in the age-old gesture of money. "I don't want to push you if you're still playing house with Ward, but if we don't stop this monster, more people are going to die."

Alace ground her teeth, then panned the camera out, angling so she could see his face as she asked, "What were the financials on this one again?"

Regg froze, then leaned forwards to the computer screen, and she zoomed in on that window, seeing a paragraph of notes from their last conversation. He used the cursor to select two words, then underlined them. "No money. This one is because it's the right thing to do." He toggled to the report and increased magnification so she could see the phrase about "perceived injustices," and said, "So many people are already dead. The cops don't care. They've packed away their reports and given up. Every time it happens again, they deny there's any connection back to the killer's previous victims. These families deserve more. We can give them more."

She forced a sigh, knowing that was what she would normally give him when she didn't want to do a gig, but he was adamant. "I'll think about it."

"Well, think fast, Alace. You've had a good, long break this time, but we're past due to get back to work." Hand on his thigh, he was tapping rapidly with one finger, his words matching the tempo and cadence. No nonsense, all business. "I've got everything ready to go, and have the drop boxes all set up and ready. I think we'll do a full reset of all your gear, so there's no possible cross contamination between the gigs."

And there was his acknowledgment he had noticed the trackers were no longer moving around as they should be. She shook her head. "I'll think about it, give you a call soon. Three days, our normal schedule."

He backed off, probably thinking she had already agreed, but just wanted more time with Eric. *Bastard thinks he can be magnanimous in his victory.* "Sounds good. Be safe out there."

"You too. Give Lena my love."

On the screen, she watched as he rolled his eyes, head shaking back and forth as he promised, voice warm and affectionate, "Will do."

She spent the next few minutes continuing to observe, watching as he shut his office down for the night. Her call had been all that held him here. He set the alarm, and she memorized the sequence, not certain if she would ever need it, but information was information and good to have. Alace lost him for a few minutes as he moved through the garage, then picked him up on the ground floor, padding barefoot through the living area, deftly avoiding furniture and piles of the kids' toys and such.

She expected him to check the kids, but he bypassed their rooms and went straight to the third floor, discarding his clothing in a pile at the foot of the bed. He slipped between the sheets and Lena rolled away from him, further towards the door. Alace noted with some surprise that his side was nearer the windows, which as they were three stories from the ground, wouldn't be the first route of entry for thieves. That meant he put his wife between him and danger. *Just like he places me in that position, every time I head out on a gig.*

Having seen enough, Alace brought the drone back to her, landing it lightly on her knees, feeling the heat radiating from the tiny motors inside the casing. *Best hundred bucks I've spent in a long time.* She packed it away and dismounted the tree, making her way back to the car and climbing inside. Sitting for a moment and thinking, she brought the drone back out and plugged it into a tiny device she'd left in the car, watching as the lights cycled through red to yellow, and then to green, telling her the video was being uploaded.

The entire drive home, made with only minimal stops for gas and necessities, Alace ran what she knew or suspected through her head. Repeating the sequence again and again, she picked apart the inconsistencies and pulled together a picture that made sense, in the end.

Regg had been lying to her for years about what they were doing. Alace swallowed hard, forcing the choking knot in her throat back down. *Lied. To me.* Every conversation became suspicious in her mind. Each interaction through their association suspect when viewed through the lenses of what she now knew to be true. He had deftly maneuvered her to achieve ends known only to him. Wary even of the histories he'd fed to her, Alace shivered to consider what that could mean.

What if he did more than lie to me about his motives?

Ruthlessly curtailing her brain's pursuit of that thought, she tried instead to focus on what she knew about the killer he'd been pushing. The cyclic murders were part of public record, and she had engaged her own investigative elements through the years, so she had connections. *I'll do that, get the guy started on this gig, see if it's got legs or not.*

Alongside the chill of doubt flickered a tiny flame of anger. Alace fed her rage, fanning it higher and higher until it drowned out the terrifying ideas crowding her brain. Regg had done this, climbing the ladder to wealth on her back. Visions of his house swarmed her thoughts. She remembered how big it was, so much larger than it had to be. Lavish and proud. Stolen time—and if she were right—and pieces of her soul to buy the very beds his children laid their heads on. He had everything, and she—

Did it to me. Did it to himself. He's going to have to pay.

She considered and discarded a dozen ideas as too narrow. Regg's betrayal feeling so huge, the retribution would need to be to scale. Steering the car into Eric's neighborhood, she saw a tinge of dawn creeping across the horizon in her mirrors. *If Regg handed me a portfolio this thin, I'd laugh at him.* She had more than one source of information in her pocket, and as she parked the car, she resolved to activate any resources needed to build the folder she'd need to have in order to talk herself into what she felt would probably need to be done.

Her door opened before she could land a hand on it, and she jerked back, seeing Eric framed in the space. His jaw was set, muscles rigid, and the expression on his face startled her. He looked a careless mixture of anger and fear, and she watched as it settled slowly into fury. *He's mad at me.*

This was surprising. When she'd left, he'd been reluctant to let her go alone, but respected her enough to believe in her abilities. She would have expected a warm welcome, not this hot rage.

Alace opened her mouth, but Eric beat her to the punch, his question clipped and terse, radiating his displeasure. "What the fuck did you think you were doing?"

***

Eric

He knew it was the wrong tactic, but over the past three days, he'd gone from cautious anxiety to terror. Ten minutes into her trip, he'd texted her and received no response. The same the next morning, and her campaign of silence continued through the second night. It wasn't until this morning that he'd realized her disassembled phone was in the box shoved into a corner of the guest room closet. By then Eric was so frantic for anything that could tell him where she'd gone, when he stumbled on her cache of things he'd thrown the box across the room, the short-lived flight leaving articles of clothing and her bag littering the floor.

It felt like his greatest fear come to life, that she could walk out of his life as easily as she'd walked in.

Her phone wasn't a tool he could have used to find her, he knew from experience that when he failed accessing it, the damn thing would wipe itself. Alace was good at covering her tracks. He'd spent hours wrestling with the idea of calling his connections, trying to track her, trying to find her any way he could. He'd considered and rejected a hundred plans while he paced through the house, stewing in his frustration. On the one hand, he needed her more than breath, but on the other, he feared bringing attention to her in ways she couldn't escape.

So when the security camera alerted him to activity in the front of the house, he hadn't wasted time looking at the footage, just gone to the door and thrown it open, seeing Alace sitting there. His action and question had startled her, and Eric watched as she brought a mask into place on her features, changing before his eyes from the woman he'd had in his life for weeks and back into a detached observer. *Fuck that.*

"Dammit, Alace." He bent double, wrapping his hand around her arm and urged her firmly to exit the car. "Come inside." It wouldn't do for them to draw attention to her more than they had. One of his father's lessons learned, all disagreements happen outside of the public eye. She came out of the car and then stiffened, moving her body in a way that let him know she didn't want his hand on her like this. *What am I doing? Why am I so angry?*

Closing his eyes, he stepped closer and slipped his arms around her, pulling her unyielding body tight against his front. "Been scared out of my mind, baby." Eric whispered his confession against the side of her head, her response immediate as she became more pliant in his arms. "Couldn't talk to you, and all I wanted to do was hear your voice. I needed to know you were okay."

Her hands sought the hem of his shirt, finding and diving under so they lay flat against the skin of his back, her touch electrifying. "Eric." Her voice shook, and he pulled her closer, needing to impress the feel of her in his mind.

"Come inside." Her hair rasped against the fabric of his shirt when she nodded, and he shifted his hold, moved them away from the car and slammed the door. She squeezed tight against him, keeping her hand on his waist as they walked through the door left standing open behind his panicked exit from the house. "I'm glad you're here safe and sound. *God*, Alace."

Her next words pulled a blanket of calmness over him, the strength of her words more staggering than she could ever know.

"It's good to be home."

CHAPTER SIXTEEN

Alace

"I get it." She wanted to put this behind them, wanted to let Eric know she wasn't upset over his display outside. She also wanted to do this without him mentioning where she'd been. After seeing Regg's house, and knowing the resources upon which he could draw, she wouldn't put it past him to have had Eric's house bugged. Her whole array of countermeasures up to this point required the only devices be in her things. Now? All bets were off. If Regg were listening, he would know she'd been gone, but not where.

The door closed behind them, shutting out the world, and she was surrounded in Eric. His scent in her nose, his body under her hands, his home protecting them both. Lifting to her toes, she placed her mouth to his ear and breathed, "Not safe," hoping he would understand.

Proving once again that he was brilliant and in tune with her, Eric nodded, turning his neck to place his mouth to the side of her head. His response was a simple "Okay." Then he lifted her, hands under her ass, one palm tracing the back of her leg as he wrapped it around his waist. "Fuck, I missed you, baby." He didn't have to say it, but his actions showed her the trust she'd worked so hard to gain remained, even after her absence, even after everything.

Palm threading up the back of his neck, she used her fingertips to bring his head down, meeting his mouth in a blistering kiss. He deepened it, and then deepened it again, thrusting in her mouth, toying and playing with her tongue as he kissed her. He broke away with a groan and pressed his forehead to hers. "Wanna go upstairs?" Evidence of his desire wedged hot and rigid against her, and she arched her back, rubbing up and down slowly, smiling as his pupils dilated, lids dropping to half-mast. "That a yes?" He snaked a hand down her back, flattening his palm at the small of her back and holding her in place as he ground against her. "God, I hope it's a yes."

"Yes." She ran her fingers through his hair and then gripped, holding tight as her head dropped back. He took the movement as the invitation it was intended to be, and she felt his mouth hit her neck, hot and soft as his lips worked along her skin, then a flash of hard as he teased with the edges of teeth, threatening a bite she'd welcome.

"Are you attached to these jeans?" His hand settled on her ass again, and she felt his fingertips tracing along the seam, pushing and pulling at the fabric. "Are they your lucky pants?"

She grinned. "Yes." Bringing her head upright, she gave him a mock glare. "Don't even think about it." One night in Malibu he'd ruined her favorite pair of leggings, ripping the seam between her legs so he could fuck her hard and fast, bent over the edge of a park table, uncaring who might see. He'd laughed when she complained while tying the sleeves of his shirt around her waist, letting the fabric drape over her ass, hiding the telltale damage, telling her that he liked them, too, since he'd gotten lucky while she wore them.

That was one of the things she loved about Eric. As staid as one might think his profession might make him, he had a definite wild side that backed up the man he'd appeared to be from the first night they'd met.

"Damn." He jostled her as he cleared the first three stairs in a jump, then carried her to his bedroom where he proceeded to take her jeans off without ripping them.

But only barely.

It was the next morning before she broached the topic of Regg, and even then, she only did so from an oblique angle, giving her words extra consideration. They were in the kitchen standing side by side near the coffee maker, lifting cups in companionable silence. "Can you arrange to be just mine for a couple of days?"

He bumped her shoulder with a chuckle. "I'm yours, baby. Anytime, anywhere. You want me, you got me."

Alace grinned, flicking him a glance under her lashes. She shook her head at his easy teasing, liking how it made her feel even while she refused to consider the heat building in her chest at his words. "Like, can you take off work and just be with me?"

"I can do that." His easy agreement had her leaning close, chin lifted. He didn't make her wait, pressing a soft kiss to her lips. "My pleasure, baby." His murmured words vibrated against her lips, and she kissed him this time, softly.

"Text me and let me know when?" She knew he'd have to shuffle things to open time in his schedule. Eric was good at his job, and busy. She recognized the heavy load he carried from the amount of work brought home to tackle as they lounged on the couch. It would probably take him at least a couple of days to arrange something, move things around. "I'm going to run downtown today. You need me to pick you up anything?" Downtown Denver was a smorgasbord of shops and stores, several of which sold exactly the kind of bug sweepers she needed to get her hands on.

She would also make some personal purchases in preparation for the trip she'd planned.

They couldn't talk about Regg here. Even sweeping the house wouldn't give her the kind of confidence she'd need to tackle the topics beating at the back of her throat, begging her to confide their secrets. *Hell, most of the things I've already talked about in this house would earn me life and put Eric on the fast track to disbarment.* She wouldn't do that, couldn't put him at risk. *He needs to be above reproach.*

"When I come home tonight, I'll be all yours until Monday." Alace's neck twisted, and she stared at him in surprise. The corner of his mouth quirked up and he smirked, the look sinfully attractive on him. "What?"

"Just like that?"

As with everything Eric had done, he made it just that easy. "Yes."

One word, she thought, leaning over to kiss him.

***

Alace beat Eric home by less than an hour, still enough time to put everything into place. She'd purchased three days' worth of clothing for them both, and used an app on a café kiosk computer to rent a mountain cabin under an alias purchased from who she was now thinking of as her new paper guy. She also paid cash for another junker, trading in the one she'd been driving since it had been out of her sight while she was at Regg's house. That acquisition was probably overkill, but then again, the four bugs sitting wrapped in foil on Eric's kitchen table might tell a different tale. Bugs this time, listening devices, not trackers. The foil wasn't the sexiest solution, but it was a quick and reliable one.

The technology purchased today had worked well, providing silent indicators as she tracked down the devices. Alace frowned, then let the expression smooth from her face. *Nothing to worry about. I have everything covered.* Given the location of the bugs, Regg had likely brokered a deal with a local guy who must have felt Eric was the real target, regardless his instructions. Eric's study, the handset for the phone also in that room, the kitchen, and living room were the locations for the bugs. She'd spent a lot of time in two rooms in this house, as well as the outside patio. Those being the bedroom and living room. Only one of her favorite places had been targeted. She scoffed softly. *Amateurs.* A pro would always cover the bedroom. More secrets exchanged lips there than any other room.

She heard Eric's car pull into the drive and reached out, watching as her fingers curled around the package of bugs, sweeping it from the counter and into the bag with the rest of her things from Regg. They would all be finding a different home in about thirty minutes, and it was likely Regg would be in a frothing rage soon after.

Alace stared at the display on the phone one last time before removing the battery.

No back trail to trace. The only thing she needed to do now was convince Eric to take her newly acquired car. Oh, and strip to his birthday suit in the back seat.

Easy, she thought, then laughed.

***

What will he do? That thought circled through Alace's head, gaining volume with every repetition. *Now that he's learned what I am? What I've been?* She stared at Eric, his expression showing that his lingering frustration with her hadn't left him. She hesitated. If he were already angry or regretting bringing her into his life, the knowledge she'd divulged might be all it took to tip things to the point where he washed his hands of her.

She cleared her throat, wincing as it burned with a dry rasp. She'd been talking for nearly two hours without pause. No letting him get a word in, no stopping for a break—it had been something she needed to purge from her psyche, needed to get it all out, empty herself, and pray there would be enough left of her to go on if Eric stood and walked out the door.

"And that's…that's it." She swallowed, tongue drier than her throat had been, the click of her efforts uselessly loud in the silence. "That's who I am." *I don't know what else to be.*

Alace became hyperaware of her breathing. Tiny sips of air in through her nose, and back out, lips closed tight to hold in everything else she wanted to say. All the feelings that had no place in this discussion, because before they went there, Eric had to understand what she'd learned.

I'm a monster.

She'd killed people. More lives taken than her hands could hold. And for what? *Why?* On the say-so of a man who had played her for a fool. A deadly fool, and a tool he'd wielded with surgical precision, casting her on contracted waters and reeling in blood money.

Eric stared at her from his seat near the cold fireplace. After dropping the bags of contaminated goods at a clothing donation box, she'd driven them high into the mountains, following printed directions to find the remote road that led to the cabin, both their phones left at Eric's home. Their drive had been silent, and she'd been thankful Eric had read her mood so accurately. She'd needed that time to compose both her words and emotions, making it so she could reel off the details of everything learned during her trip out east.

Eric spoke, his expressionless voice huge in the empty space, no wall hangings or decorations to soften the sound. "Are you done?"

She nodded, and he stared, eyes never leaving her face. "Yeah. That's all I had to say." *What more does he want to hear?* A pedigree of the death dealt out at her hand?

"No, Alace." He'd never sounded this cold. Not once. Not since she'd met him. Eric had always held warmth and softness in his voice for her. *This is it.* She angled her chin down, eyes moving, gaze tracing along the edges of a floorboard, tiny cracks in the wood fibers exploding around a nailhead. Damaged by the very thing holding it secure. "I asked you if you're done." She nodded, indicating both acknowledgment of his inquiry and confirmation he'd heard her correctly. "Alace, look at me."

She rolled her lips, then licked them, finding no relief from the terror that bound her throat tightly. Everything felt so fucking precarious, like it could fall apart, the beauty of an autumn leaf crushed under the weight of her life. He moved then, just shifting one foot back as if he were preparing to rise, and she flinched, nearly falling from her perch on the tall stool by the counter. She'd chosen this position because it had no escape routes. There was a single door into the cabin, and Eric was nearest that opening. He could and would stop her from leaving if he wanted to, and she'd needed to know there wasn't an easy out from what she had to do.

"Alace." Pitched an octave lower, he called her name. "Are you done?" The emphasis on the final word finally hit her, and she darted a glance at his face, expecting derision and an ugly hatred, finding instead his expression held caution instead. The question wasn't if she were done speaking, which she was, as her mouth was tied tight, fear of losing everything she'd ever wanted holding her mute. No, Eric was asking if she was *done*.

Locking her gaze to his, she nodded slowly, giving every slight movement the weight of a life-changing decision made wedged in a tree in Regg's neighbor's yard. *I am. I can't go back there, not with this fear lodged in my gut. I'd make a million mistakes, and I'd die. I'd lose you. I am so very done.* She didn't utter a word, didn't say any of what was speeding through her mind, but kept her focus on his face, waiting.

"Alace." He shifted in the chair again, feet angled farther from the seat, knees spreading as the thick muscles of his thighs tightened and bunched. He kept his hands on the arms, and she watched his fingers dig into the leather and wood, the relentless grip leaving his knuckles white, bloodless. "Come here, baby."

She unwound her feet from the legs of the stool and felt for the floor with her toes, her body somehow expecting it to be gone, surprised into a stumble when it remained in the same place she'd left it. One hand on the stool to stop its fall, she let it settle back onto all four legs before she took a step. One step became two, and then she was running across the distance, watching in disbelief as his arms lifted and he leaned forwards to scoop her up. Then she was settled on his lap, burrowing close, taking comfort in his hold. *I never want to leave him again.*

He held her, the sobs ripping through her as the scorching mix of relief and horror flooded her veins. She'd done it, told him the fear that had rooted inside her as she watched a tiny screen. In moments, her belief in Regg and what they'd done together had eroded, gone and falling away like rust as he blatantly tried to manipulate her. Everything she'd thought a firm anchor in her world gone, setting her adrift with a sudden belief she'd done so much wrong. *Evil.*

Fingers twisted in his shirt, she held tight, Eric's arms secure around her. She cried and tried to explain, managing only partial sentences garbled with her pain. "Their families...someone's father...it was me..." She lifted her shoulders, wrenching in a breath that burned the back of her throat, bringing with it the stench of her own fear. "If I was wrong, what does that make me?"

"Are you a sniper? Taking care of things from so far away you can't even make out details?" Her body jolted with his question, and she shook her head, leaning forward to bury her face against his chest, pulling in what might be her final breath filled with the scent of him. "No, you aren't someone who stayed removed and followed orders. No soldier, you've always been an active participant in these 'gigs,' as you call them." She stilled, swallowing past the lump in her throat, not sure where he was going with this. "Did you ever, one single time, ever in your life take out someone without placing yourself in their life in some way?" She shook her head, coming to rest with her cheek to his chest, his heartbeat thudding fast in her ear. "Not one single time? You always got close?"

He paused for a moment, and she assumed he wanted an answer. She gave him the cold truth. *Two minutes and forty-seven seconds.* "I always made it personal."

"And you could make it personal because you found out for yourself what they were. What they did. Who their victims were. It became personal because you lived in some way what they had done. Am I right?" His logic resonated, and a glimmer of hope danced along the edges of his words. "You never took Regg's word for it, did you? You always, always did your own research. Boots on the ground, you dug in until you found something to support what he'd told you." She nodded, eyes flooding with fresh tears. He was right, and she'd somehow lost that perspective, drowning in her fear that she'd become the bogeyman. "Did you ever walk away? Tell him he got it wrong?"

Her head jerked up, and she gasped, hands fisted in his shirt thudding against his chest at the realization. "I did. I *did*. More than once. The first one he argued, *God*, how he argued. But he had the wrong person. I knew it. I *knew* it, Eric. It wasn't the wife who'd killed their foster kids. It was the husband's brother."

She was dizzy, memories slamming into her. "Oh my God. There were more, I remember them. I remember them, now. Thank you." One of his arms loosened and his hand came up, cradling the back of her head and pushing her face into his neck. "I did. I make certain. I never told him, but I always make certain." She shuddered convulsively and sobbed, the release of her fears nearly as painful as their realization.

"Shhhh, baby." Eric's words and hands soothed her, erasing stroke by stroke the tense anxiety that had lived in her bones for days. "I got you." He kissed the side of her face, lips sliding through the sheets of tears flowing from her eyes. "My Alace."

***

Eric

It had taken hours, but Alace had finally calmed enough to tell him about the others, as she called them. The marks she'd turned away from. After her revelation in this Regg's backyard—and Eric wished with everything inside him that she'd trusted him before now so he could have been there for her, but the past was past, and they had to focus on the now— she'd only considered the...successes. *Is success the right word?* He shook his head, not wanting to delve too deeply into the things that covered.

He knew what she did. Wasn't a fool, so he'd realized long ago what she was. An assassin. A vigilante, delivering sentences, punishment dealt out by a tiny damaged woman who somehow had convinced herself to become both judge and jury for people who slipped through the cracks of the judicial system. Executioner, too.

He'd been surprised by her response when he got home from work, anticipating her morning request had covered a need for days where they wouldn't leave the bed for anything other than necessities. Then, she'd been waiting. Met him in the driveway and handed him a note that said she had everything taken care of, they were going away for the weekend, and, oh yeah, by the way, she was afraid they were being watched. He'd changed clothes in the back seat as she drove through the rural outskirts of town, clambering over the seat and into the front when he finished and shoved everything, including skivvies and a favorite pair of shoes, into a bag.

Her discarding their things had hit him with a heavy sense of dread. Somehow the action made everything seem more real, especially since it was only after that she spoke, telling him tersely they had another two hours to get to the cabin. Eric had tried to read her, wanting to be supportive of something that mattered but he couldn't understand. She'd been taut, drawn tight. A thick dread had filled the air until it was suffocating. Since she seemed to need it, he gave her silence for the remainder of their drive, reaching over to rest his hand just above her knee, feeling her relax as the miles rolled past.

At the cabin, he had forced himself to sit and listen to a brutal litany of events so incredible as to be absurd, and yet he believed her. As he had with everything she'd shared with him, he believed her. Somewhere in the middle of her recitation, his head had made the shift from Alace's boyfriend to the lawyer he'd been for so long. Not seeking something prosecutable, but simply seeing the cause and effect in everything she spoke about, drawing different conclusions based on the evidence presented. He could see her points, could empathize with her on many of them, but there were pieces that didn't line up against flaws in her stories.

At some point, he realized this wasn't because she was wrong, just that she was human. This wasn't some fucking movie where everything would be tied up tight and sweet by the end credits. This was a woman who had been handed a shit life and tried to make it different. She'd reached for something that would make her horrifying experience less so, and found in herself the desire—and more, the ability—to create situations where justice could be meted out.

If this were a fairy tale, she'd be the badass hero saving everyone in a life-or-death thriller.

It wasn't fiction, though. Every person's name that fell from her lips represented a life interrupted. Families torn apart, children deprived of a parent, or parents living without children.

Still, the crimes her targets committed—heinous. There was no other word. She'd surely saved more lives than she'd taken. He watched as she deflected any mention of that. She couldn't consider the possibility, and had been so focused on her imagined failing that for her, there was no other outcome. Not until he laid it out for her.

Lying beside her in the bed he'd carried her to after she'd cried herself to sleep in his arms, her body shaking as she was torn asunder by relief that she hadn't turned into the monster in the dark. She'd never killed blindly, hadn't taken anyone's word for the need to erase people from the world. She'd demanded proof, found it herself if it wasn't already available, and—most importantly—she'd walked away when it wasn't forthcoming. He suspected if they looked for those targets now, they'd find them dead and gone anyway, dealt with by a less conscientious agent.

She'd profited from the deaths. It was her livelihood, and she'd made no bones about that. But the payoffs, as she called them, had come from thankful survivors, grateful that she'd ended an unending horror that trailed them through their lives. And based on her scattered recollections, far more money went to charities than she'd banked. She didn't have a home, didn't have anything to pour money into except getting ready for the next target.

So that's what she'd done. That was her life.

Was. He reiterated the claim firmly in his mind. *No more.*

Tracing along her nose with a fingertip, he smiled as she twisted, pressing her face into his palm in her sleep. So much trust. Every word spoken had been a gift of belief that he was the person she thought him to be.

Beautiful and otherworldly, she'd been unflinching in her revelations, vicious in her descriptions of herself, determined to draw the worst out to lay it on the table. He was glad for that. No skeletons waiting to trip them up later, he believed he'd heard the worst of it tonight. She had clearly been bracing for a different outcome, one where he washed his hands of the monster and walked away.

Eric had always prided himself on having a strong moral compass. Exposed to the foulest of humanity by his job and blood, he felt he had developed a good bullshit detector. Alace's determination to only see the worst possible outcome rang true. She wasn't playing some kind of false sympathy card with him. She truly saw herself that way. The damn thing was, she was right. By the laws of man, she had done wrong, taken it upon herself to deliver a self-proclaimed guilty verdict and then deal with the punishment. As the law saw things, there were no differences between her and her targets.

There is, though.

Through the years, there had been many times he'd left a courtroom disgusted with the outcome of the legal system. Watched as murderers and thieves walked free, stepping lithely through a loophole when the ones upholding the system were held to the highest of standards. Innocent until proven guilty was critical to the system, but when you knew in your gut the person was guilty and they walked free anyway—there was a reason for high rates of burnout in his profession. The helplessness of knowing you'd done your best and it wasn't good enough, and there would eventually be innocents who would inevitably pay for your failure.

Alace changed the equation. She balanced the scales blind justice couldn't manage, wedging her thumb against the law until things came back to true. Guilty punished in ways appropriate to the crime, and the victims finally able to move on with their lives.

She'd whispered a question to him just before falling asleep, and he hadn't been able to answer it at the time. He could now, though. After thinking things through, finding his way, he knew.

"Can you love someone like me?" Her words had shaken free from her mouth with a quaver that spoke of fear. Fear he would walk away without looking back.

She told me anyway.

Trust. Something he had craved from her, and she'd given to him by the handfuls today. Baptized him in a rush, plunging into the water beside him, depending on him to not let her drown.

Eric tightened his arms around her, feeling her body curve trustingly into his. Immersed in an exhausted sleep, she shifted, lifted her head and placed her mouth against his throat. Soft as velvet her lips touched him, glided to his chest and her head turned, cheek to his skin.

Alace changed the rules. *Changed me.*

He knew his answer.

CHAPTER SEVENTEEN

Alace

They'd spent most of their two days at the cabin nestled in a cocoon of blankets. Alternately talking or making love, occasionally one of them would brave the chilly air to bring food back to bed. It seemed a sanctuary, Eric's arms her place of safety.

As with everything, it couldn't last.

Alace pushed her hair back from her face with the back of one wrist, scowling at the feel of sweat on her skin. It was hot in the little room off the kitchen where she'd set up her workroom. She huffed a breath, glanced up from the element of the solder gun she was using, and eyed the control board she was attempting to create. The intent was to remotely manage a device she'd use to bypass Regg's physical security as well as other tricks she might need.

They'd been back home for a week. A week in which she'd spoken to Regg for each of their regular scheduled calls. Calls where he became more obvious with his manipulative tactics, pushing her harder each time. Last night Eric said he thought Regg was waiting for her to call him out. She knew he was probably right.

A week of sweeping Eric's house and both their cars daily was thankfully empty of any new bugs. Alace wasn't sure what to make of that. The ones she'd removed could have been an ace-in-the-hole tactic Regg hadn't needed to put into play yet, so he might not know they'd been discovered. Or he might be trying to brazen it out, hoping she would attribute them to Ward's enemies.

Meanwhile, she planned. Beginning at the cabin, she'd bounced ideas off Eric and found to her surprise he had an aptitude for this kind of thing. As did she. Together they were creating an unbeatable strategy, and if the plan hadn't been aimed at going up against Regg, she'd have been damned excited about how well they meshed on the planning side of things.

She'd always considered herself the hammer wielded by Regg and was surprised that not only was the preparation exciting and fun, it also came easily to her. *A hidden talent*. She smirked, huffed again, and bent her head back to her task. With no room for error, she concentrated on what her hands were doing, stopping occasionally to shake the cramps from her muscles. Finally finished, she looked at what she'd made, devices rigged together from Internet purchases and a knowledge of the kind of alarm system she was up against.

A sound from the house penetrated her focus and she turned in time to see the door swing back, Eric appearing in the opening. "Jesus, it stinks in here." He made a face at the smell from the solder, and she grinned. He didn't hesitate, but moved to her and wrapped his arms around her shoulders, leaning over to look down at what lay on the workbench in front of her. "You done, baby?"

"Yeah. Everything's ready."

"Then come eat. Dinner's waiting." His hands slipped down her sides, bracketing her waist as he urged her off the stool and to her feet. "I'm starved, and I'll bet when you stop and breathe for a minute, you're going to realize you are, too."

This was something she'd come to love about Eric. The multitude of ways he took care of her, each showing the trust he had in her. No second guessing, not once their plans were laid, and while he had balked at her role, it wasn't that he didn't believe her capable. His reasons were more personal, whispered across the pillow while still buried inside her, his cock pulsing the final beats of his passion. *"I need you safe."* Nothing about his wants, no posturing about strengths or weaknesses, he just told her what he felt was the most important thing.

She wrapped her arms around his neck and tugged, raising one leg in invitation. Eric wrapped his palms around her ass and lifted, carrying her into the kitchen, using the heel of his bare foot to close the door behind them. She clung to him like a monkey, resting her cheek on his chest, feeling the thud of his heart in her ear as he padded soundlessly to the counter where he placed her, staying close, hips between her knees. Bent knuckles wedged under her chin, lifting and holding her so their gazes locked. "You're ready?" She nodded, his hand moving with her. "You sure, beloved?" Alace gave him a half smile, knowing these questions came from a place of love.

"I'm sure. He's good, but I've known him a very long time. I'm confident I can predict about 90 percent of how he'll respond. That's not great odds, but I've got the best chance out of anyone I know. It's what I do, Eric." She tugged her chin free and dipped her neck, pressing a kiss to the backs of his fingers. "I'm sure."

"And if you get it wrong and he walks in on you?"

Alace's posture straightened, and she pushed her shoulders back, deliberately creating a strong frame with her body. As much as Eric needed her safe, she needed him to believe. "I deal with what I find. If that's a file on me and the gigs over the years, I bring it out with me because he and I are done. If he's there, then his fate is up to him." Eric's eyes widened, and she shook her head. "I mean his reaction will be my cue. He's not been the one out in the field, so to speak. I'm not worried about him hurting me, and I'll be on the watch for any tricks he might pull. Any countermeasures he's prepared, any threats he thinks to make. We both believe he knows something's up, which means he could have put anything into play. But I've trained with the best." She had. Over the years she'd taken every opportunity to seek wisdom from people like her. Setting up meets on the darknet and following the hidden tokens to safe houses scattered throughout metropolitan cities she'd hunted in. It was an elite membership, entry purchased by kill count, permanent enrollment certified by skill and longevity in the trade. Another thing Regg didn't know about her. "I won't let him be a shadow, a stain on our lives." That was as close as she'd come to saying what she really meant. *I'll kill him if he threatens you.*

This was something she'd struggled with, and if it were just her life on the line, the final answer might be different. But Eric didn't deserve to be looking over his shoulder the rest of his life. Regg might be her oldest friend, but Eric was her one.

I'll kill him.

CHAPTER EIGHTEEN

Regg

Fingers tapping in a long-memorized sequence on the keys, Regg pulled up the remote video software he used and navigated through the many location options until he located footage of the not-little, not-large house outside Denver. The listening devices his contact had planted inside had all failed within days, leaving Regg cursing Ward's paranoid father.

The old man had a long reach to be able to deal with things like regular sweeps of his son's house from his exile overseas, and his actions showed he undoubtedly expected his family to be a target. Regg tucked that knowledge in the back of his mind. While Ward might be down, he clearly wasn't out, and someone still in the game might turn into a pawn to be played later.

There wasn't much to see on the footage of the house Alace had made her home base. She and the son had left for several days the previous week, their absence extending over the weekend and coinciding with the mass relocation of every tracker he had in Alace's stuff.

Regg snorted. *Young love.*

The why of Ward needing to shower Alace with a new wardrobe didn't matter, but it made for an inconvenience for Regg because it had triggered a reaction in Alace. One she'd been conditioned to do, so her tossing all her stuff in response wasn't a surprise. Regg had worked hard to train her to not be overly attached to anything. *Except me.*

And now Ward.

He tapped a key, forwarding the video to the first marker indicating activity. On the screen, the front door opened and Ward appeared, briefcase in hand, just as he had each morning. Sometimes Regg caught a flash of Alace in the background, just enough to keep him from believing she might be there against her will. Once the son had paused in the doorway long enough, Alace came into view, approaching and rising on her toes as the man bent his neck. Their goodbye kiss was hidden by the angle, but went on long enough to cause Regg to roll his eyes.

They'd talk tonight. Like clockwork, Alace booted up her phone every three nights and dialed him.

Regg stared at the screen, the footage advanced far past the view of the man driving away, the front of the house now still. No one would ever know one of the most wanted serial killers in modern history waited inside, playing her version of house with a man who walked on the blue side of legal.

He clicked, and clicked again, bringing up multiple views of a sprawling mansion in the hills just north of Charlotte. Picking one, he clicked and waited for the screen to load. Zooming in, he watched as a man lifted a toddler high, cradling the child to his chest.

Raising his hand, Regg cocked two fingers at the screen and expelled a puff of air. "You're my next payday." Leaning back in his chair, Regg folded his arms, staring at the screen.

We definitely need to talk.

CHAPTER NINETEEN

Eric

He drove around the block and parked alongside an empty lot backing up to a house three doors down from his. Within a few seconds of him braking to a stop, the back-passenger door opened and the chassis shifted, then the door closed. He looked in the mirror and out the back window, nothing impeding his view. "Ready?"

"Yeah, I'm good," Alace called from her position behind his seat. He couldn't see her, but knew she'd be burrowed under the lightweight blanket placed there for this purpose. If he couldn't get a look at her, neither could the security cameras dotted around his neighborhood.

He'd never given them any consideration until she began planning this. He'd even scoffed at her dogged insistence in employing what Eric considered extreme avoidance tactics. That was until she pointed out the cameras. ATMs, gas stations, parking lots, fast food drive-throughs, traffic lights—cameras were everywhere. They'd become so much a part of the environmental fabric, they went unnoticed. Except by people paid to monitor them, and people like Alace. He'd stopped arguing entirely when she hacked a dozen cameras and demonstrated how simple it could be to track a single individual through town.

He drove without talking, all their arguing behind them, too nervous now that things were moving to engage in small talk. He would take Alace to a used car lot where she'd pick up a vehicle purchased two weeks ago. She'd paid the lot to store the car until the plates came in, and they'd gotten the call yesterday.

She'd be going from here straight to Regg's, and once she drove off the lot, Eric would only hear from her once everything was done. All the planning and preparation were behind them, and Eric still wasn't on board with some aspects of what was planned, but he'd seen the wisdom behind Alace's position.

It had to be her who went.

It had to be her who dealt with Regg.

So much revolved around what she might find in his office. The outcome wasn't set in stone, not yet, and she was still holding out the tiniest bit of hope she and Regg could end things amicably. Eric had zero expectation this would be the case. Not after listening to Regg's attempts at persuasion. He had dug his heels in, determined to force Alace to do what he wanted, and by now, weeks past when Regg wanted the guy in North Carolina dead, he was still gagging for it.

Alace had wavered once. Regg had sent news article images to her phone, and she'd read them after going back offline. The killings had happened, just like clockwork. Another six people dead by Alace's count and with a sobbing cry she'd claimed responsibility. Eric had stayed up late, holding her, listening and arguing against her beliefs, the gray wash of daybreak sneaking up the walls by the time she let him take her to bed, still unconvinced.

He thought of the fear that crawled into his belly while she was in New Mexico, the hourly litany of terror-filled questions with no answers. *Is she safe? Is she in trouble? Does she need help?*

This would be worse, knowing who she was going up against. Knowing from all her stories and his own experience what Regg was capable of. This time the questions would be harder to keep at bay. He grimaced and told her, "Nearly there, baby."

"I like when you call me baby. Did I tell you that?" Her response was soft, voice ragged in a broken coo, and Eric could imagine her face as she said the words: mouth pulled to one side, eyes squinted to keep pooling tears from falling.

"You didn't tell me, but I knew." Even knowing he couldn't see her, he glanced in the mirror. Turning a corner, he removed a hand from the wheel, draping it over the back of the seat. A moment later, her fingers twined with his. "You get a little funny look on your face when I say it. Not all the time, but sometimes. I like that look, baby."

She snorted, her grip tightening for a moment as she gave him a squeeze. "What do I do that you like?" Eric didn't try to hold back at her question, letting the laugh barrel out of his throat, setting the inside of the car ringing as her hand clenched his convulsively. "Eric, you know what I mean."

"There's that thing you do with your mouth…" He laughed softly. "Honestly, I love everything about you, Alace. Even the parts you think are unlovable." He stretched his fingers, reaching, and she read his need, leaning to press her cheek into his palm. He brushed his thumb across her lips, tracing along the bow of her mouth as it curved into a smile. "You are very loveable, baby." She stilled under his touch and he forged forwards, not wanting her to question anything as she went into this upcoming battle. This one would win the war, and she needed to have all her wits about her. "I just love you, Alace. Take that how you want, but you damn sure can take it for truth, baby. I love you."

She moved, and he felt a rustle of the blanket as she lifted to her knees, arms wrapped around his neck from behind. Eric stared at her shadowed profile, seeing her bowed head in the mirror as she rested her face against his shoulder. "I love you, too."

"I know you do, baby." He turned the car into the lot, steering towards the back of the building. In a matter of moments, she'd be gone. He put as much feeling as he could into his words, wanting to give her something to take with her. "I know you do."

Her arms gave him a squeeze and then chill air crept along the flesh where she'd been pressed. The back door opened and closed, and as agreed before they left home, he drove away without another word.

He stared in the mirror and saw Alace silhouetted against the darkness behind the building for a moment, her pale face turned to follow his car, and then she whirled and jogged towards the junker, keying it open and disappearing as she crawled inside.

Eric watched as long as he could, his heart clenching painfully as he saw the brake lights flash and then the car pulled away from the lot, heading the other direction.

"Be safe, baby." He gave voice to the fears he wouldn't show her, unaware his voice trembled. "Keep yourself safe, Alace. Come back to me."

CHAPTER TWENTY

Alace

She stood on the threshold and stared, eyes slowly sweeping left to right, taking in the entire setup of Regg's office before she stepped inside. She pulled out her phone and took a series of pictures, in case she needed to restore anything as she left. If she found nothing amiss, then Regg would never know she was here, and she'd work to gain back a trust he wouldn't know had been breached.

Propping her phone on his desk, she tapped the display, thin latex gloves no barrier to the pressure-sensitive screen. The six cameras she'd deployed around Regg's property were all connected and showing a whole lot of nothing. A condition she hoped would continue for the next day and a half. Regg and Lena had taken their kids to a family resort in

Tennessee, a trip Alace had learned about through the reminders in Regg's e-mail, and the reservation payment on his credit card.

He'd taught her well, maybe too well, because when she'd turned her talents to investigating Regg, she'd found he might have some of the simplest deterrents in place, but nothing she couldn't best. Alace had learned a whole lot about the man she'd hooked her life to so many years ago. Offshore accounts buried in a trust in his oldest son's name, property in Central America owned by Lena, darknet personas used to bid up auctions for work, others used to contract out to what amounted to the competition. There was so much more she wanted to know about, and Alace expected to find everything she needed here in his office today.

Her looping devices to bypass his video feeds had worked perfectly, even if they'd been fabricated out of parts never intended to work together for that task. Alace allowed herself a small smile. Regg had taught her that, too. Thinking out of bounds, following intuition to a path that granted success, no matter how ugly the tactics looked to the outsider. *It ain't sexy, that's for sure.* She settled into his chair and studied his computer setup closely. *I got this one.* Nothing out of the ordinary, his computer was utilizing a basic connection, nothing that tied to an alarm.

She glanced at the cameras again, then the panel beside the door where the lights all showed a steady green. "Here we go," she murmured, turning the computer around and unplugging the hardwired connection. She followed sensible protocols, ensuring she had control of the computer before reconnecting it to the net. There were few files on the drive, which was not unexpected. It would be too much to think she'd find evidence of his guilt or innocence that easily. She quickly located folder after folder of shortcuts though, all cryptically named, which meant unless she could sort out his naming structure, she'd be shooting in the dark as to where each led.

Nothing for it. She rolled her shoulders and leaned in, fingers flying across the keyboard as she tracked down the electronic ghost trails left behind from Regg's activities online. Three hours later, she had a good sense of what she was looking at, and her blood ran cold. Ten tension-filled hours after that and she knew for certain.

Regg was the monster.

Not me.

She had probably been his first hunter, since she could find no evidence any of this went back farther than her first contact with him. He'd been a good paper man, in high demand, which was why he'd been recommended to her in the first place. Over time, and she remembered each conversation as if they'd happened only yesterday, he'd steered her into dangerous waters. *I went willingly.* That was the argument she made on his behalf. She'd still been a young, heavily traumatized woman, struggling to find a way to survive after a horrific event that had been unsatisfactorily resolved. He'd listened to her and found what would help make her whole, and then guided her towards events that would heal her. *Maybe he really was a guardian angel for a while.*

Any pretense of him having her best interests in mind had stopped about ten years ago, when the first highly lucrative contract crossed his desk. She remembered the gig, remembered the mark, and had slept with the man's death in her head for a long time. Since then, about every ten to fourteen months, Regg had sought out another high-dollar gig. She'd flipped through the pictures Regg had archived, recognizing face after face, shoulders hunching in as she stiffened in response to the overwhelming evidence that he'd played her.

Then she found a picture she didn't know. One image of a dead man she'd never met. No matter how much she questioned herself, sifting through her memories, he didn't exist in her world. That single aberration made her pause and consider, set her to searching around, and eventually she'd found Regg's sideline business.

He'd had other hunters. From what she could tell, there'd only been one in addition to her at any given time. But all told, there were four other people who had traveled the roads Alace knew so well. That being the sole thing they'd had in common, otherwise coming from varied backgrounds, representing different ethnicities and a variety of pre-Regg occupations. It hadn't been until about an hour ago she'd found the last piece of the puzzle, and if she'd thought she'd been on edge before, this put every nerve on screaming red alert.

Five hunters, only one of which was still alive. His first. *Me.*

Her gaze flicked across the hidden cache of images she'd unearthed inside a secured folder. They were all very dead, bodies displayed for the camera, their killers identified only by codename. He'd used Xanadu for her, and she found the rest just as randomly cryptic. The last picture had shaken her, and Alace had fought to control her breathing for long moments. It showed Terrence Tresca, or Ranger Rick, as she'd called him. The wellhead had been removed and someone had gone down to reveal his face. Lips shading to a dark blue, Tresca's jaw was covered with red-stained mud, but his features were unmistakable.

I killed him.

Her ambivalent feelings about what she'd done swelled, bile rolling up the back of her throat as she stared at the picture of the dead man. Then she set it aside, finding Tresca's files and going through them one-by-one. What she learned went a long way towards settling her, because Tresca was no more a forest ranger than she was an elementary school executive assistant.

Regg had pitted him against Alace, and from what she read, Tresca knew what he was up against with her, having been fed a file that painted Alace in the worst possible light. *He probably felt justified*. She was a killer, with a high body count in the dozens. Tresca's specialty was information retrieval, a classy way of saying he tortured information out of his marks before killing them. Military trained, she'd gotten that much right, since the backstory Regg had built for him blended the real and imaginary in creative ways, as he always did with hers. Just enough of the real to make it memorable and believable, but fantasy in the end.

She'd been sent in to kill Waterdrum because he had a business Regg wanted for himself. Tresca had been sent in to kill her so she didn't fuck up that business by doing exactly what she'd done, destroying everything. She remembered Regg joking with her that she should think about partnering with Tresca—it was surprising that she couldn't think of him as Ranger Rick any longer—and how she'd laughed it off. *The whole time he was toying with me*.

Now the chill that had settled into her frame was offset by the building heat of rage. *He's gotta pay*.

She studied the pictures of Regg's hunters again, frozen masks of death staring at her from the digital images. *He did this*. She turned the chair, staring at the images of his children mounted on the wall near the door. The juxtaposition of childhood innocence against what she'd been wading through for hours was surreal.

Regg was responsible for everything, when you boiled it down to the basics. Her first few gigs she'd been well content to expose the marks as liars and thieves, restoring sanity to the world their victims lived within every day. *Would I have evolved to what I am naturally?* Alace shook her head slowly. *I am what he made me.*

Greed.

She might not have caught on ever, if it weren't for Regg's greed.

Alace turned back to the computer and started again. She'd sorted out his naming convention, a mix of date and location, tied together with the code name assigned to his hunters. An hour later, she found it and stared at the screen in disbelief. That kind of payday would have set Regg up for life.

And she'd have still lived gig to gig, no home to call her own, and if Regg had his way, no Eric in her life to anchor her.

Regg would have had everything.

Alace's eyes narrowed, and she began systematically saving documents and files onto the external hard drive she'd plugged into the back of Regg's computer. "You won't have anything when I'm done."

Promise.

***

Alace watched as the family exploded from the SUV that had just parked inside the garage. On her small screen, the individual faces of the children were difficult to tell apart, while Lena and Regg were distinctive. She wondered for a moment at the distance held between the two adults, finally deciding they were in midargument, watching as they trailed the kids into the house. Lena opened the alarm panel and punched in a sequence intended to unarm the system, Alace's override still in place meant it was already disabled, but there was nothing amiss to notice.

She observed via a combination of her screens and Regg's security system, tracking them through the house as they went to their bedroom. Once the door was closed behind them, Regg swung around and asked Lena, "What do you want me to do? I can't make it rain money."

Alace blinked. With what Regg had in domestic and international accounts, he'd amassed more than fifteen million dollars. Why would money be an issue?

Lena threw out a hand to the side, settling her other on a hip as she semishouted, "Just make it happen. Madison deserves to attend that school, Regg. I don't care what it takes, you need to make it happen. That was the deal."

"I know what the deal is, Lena." Regg's tone was scathing even over the speakers. "I've never regretted anything more in my entire life than I do *the deal*." His hands came up and fingers curled as he made air quotes. "I'm not reneging on my side. Maddy will have everything she needs. Attending an exclusive school so you can crow about it to your rival at your next luncheon isn't a need. It's a greed on your part. Give it a rest and go home." *Go home?* Alace angled closer to the screens, trying to see the expression on their faces. *Where does she live if not here?*

He'd turned towards the door, hand outstretched, all Alace had of him was an oblique profile, but she still registered his full body flinch when Lena retorted, "Daddy might have sold me to you for what you knew, but you don't own me." Lena straightened and threw back her shoulders, shouting, "I won't come back this time." *Regg had blackmailed Lena's father into...what? Handing over his daughter because Regg knew something about him?* Alace let her memories trail back over the folders and information she'd studied. Nothing jumped out at her, but she didn't know Lena's maiden name.

"Jesus." The single word was muttered. Then Regg was moving through the door, closing it soundlessly behind him. Regg was in the hallway, walking away when he shouted back at the closed door, "Do whatever the fuck you want." Alace split her attention between screens, seeing Lena cover her face with both hands, an angry wail coming from that feed, while Regg stalked through the house, moving from camera view to camera view.

She knew where he was headed. He was coming to her.

Alace stood, rummaged in her bag a moment before she reclaimed her seat in the chair again. She shoved the gun under her leg and kept the Taser in hand.

Either, or. Doesn't matter to me. On the screen, Lena had pushed past her fit of pique and had left the sanctuary of the bedroom. It looked like she was supervising the repacking of bags for the children, all in the throes of what looked to be an epic case of post-vacation exhaustion. Lena must be cutting her losses, and Alace wondered if Regg knew she was actually going to leave, or if he even cared. *"She's my one."* His voice floated through her memories, having followed her into dreamland more than once as she carved out what she wanted based on what Regg said was important. *One more lie.*

Regg continued on his way towards the garage, and his office.

Bring it.

She was ready when the alarm panel lit up, indicating someone was accessing it from outside. On the screen, Regg's head was tipped far forwards, gaze roaming across the floor as his hand moved by rote, fingers tapping the sequence to disarm the system. As with the one in the house, it gave no indication of tampering. So even if he'd been alert and paying attention, he wouldn't have had a warning. Alace was good at her job.

She heard the click as the mechanism in the wall released, and a sliver of light appeared along the edge of the door. It slid quietly to the side, seating into the wall as, gaze still on the floor, Regg took a step inside. Alace tapped a single key, the smallest twitch of her finger initiating the sound of the door moving back into place. As expected, it surprised Regg and his head jerked up, eyes trained on Alace as she sat with Taser in hand aimed at the center of his chest.

He didn't flinch, didn't utter a sound. Gaze locked with Alace, he stood stock-still as the door locked behind him. The sound of the steel shafts seating in the wall was loud in the silence.

She stayed where she was, waiting. Her position relative to his was intentional, as was the information framed on the monitors. Would he realize all she'd put into building this scene for him? *You made me.* From the corner of her eye, she saw the view on the screens change, motion activated cameras taking over the display as Lena and the kids moved through the house and into the garage above them. Alace noted the silence in the room where she and Regg stood, no hint of his life falling apart could be overheard. Their remote view was blinded by late evening sunshine as the garage door opened, filters flipping into place to accommodate redrawing the vehicle as it moved. The SUV rolled backwards and out of range, the camera display changing to the front of the house as the garage door slid shut. A small white halo of a face was visible in the back window of the vehicle for a moment. Then it was speeding up the street and away from the house.

Regg sighed, and his head slowly tipped to one side before he said, "Hello, Alace." In person, his voice resonated, filled with a rich baritone range. A good voice, a kind one, and the dichotomy made her hair rise on end. Standing thus, he took up more of the room than she'd expected, even having seen images of him in the same chair she currently occupied. When she looked at Regg, it was as if the world was looping back on itself. This man was at once entirely unfamiliar, and at the same time as well known as her own face.

Alace wished for something profound to say, wanted to have it matter that this was the first time in their lives she and Regg were occupying the same space, but after everything that had gone on, and after hours of reading about betrayal after betrayal, she didn't have it in her to care.

"Regg."

Silence folded back in around them, heavy and suffocating with an edge of menace. *Why isn't he doing something?* Alace studied him closely, gazes locked, and she saw his very breath was controlled, muscles held taut, but the giveaway, as always, was in the eyes. Pupils dilated, his eyes jerked back and forth as he tried to get a read on her. Tried, and failed. He didn't know her. Not really. *I know you, though.*

"Madison isn't your child, is she?"

Whatever he'd expected, it wasn't that, and the immediate rage filling his features told her she'd scored with that observation. Alace felt a mirroring pain in her gut, but stifled it with harsh control, governing her reactions. Chin tucked tight to his neck,

Regg looked to be waiting for another hit, so she obliged.

"You've lost, you know that, right?" A fleeting change to his expression exposed fear, muscles in his cheeks pulling the edges of his mouth while his eyes widened the slightest amount, all of this there and gone in a blink. With his family leaving him, this house would be quiet and still and, if she knew Regg—and after all this time, she believed she did—he would want to throw himself into work to disappear. "I control the offshore accounts." His nostrils twitched, but she didn't pause. The money was the least of it, after all. "I have all the information from your servers. I know the names of everyone you've worked with since before me." At that revelation, his eyes narrowed in question, and she didn't leave him wondering long. "I've retired you. No existing contracts will be honored." That was what had taken her the most time today, her reading and investigation worked in between her account and information updates to Regg's various personas. "I might have missed one or two, but I uncovered enough that you're effectively crippled."

"How many?" His first words beyond his greeting showed where his true investment was. Regg wasn't trying to talk his way out of whatever retribution she felt was deserved. He was focused on surviving it, and then would be getting right back to work. He wouldn't stop, she realized now. And he wouldn't leave her alone. Even if she left him like this, crippled without his network, he'd find a way to get back what he'd lost. *Then he'll come hunting*.

She gave him honesty, still uncertain what the final outcome of this showdown would be. "Nine." His lips thinned over clenched teeth, and Alace smiled, tipping her head to one side. "Oh, maybe I did get them all."

"What do you want, Alace?" Syllables forced between tightly clenched teeth, she saw his Adam's apple bob as he swallowed. His carotid pounded, blood rushing through causing the skin above to tremble with every agitated beat. Not as confident as he wanted to project, then. "What the fuck do you want from me?"

"Don't you want to know what I've been doing? What I've done? Who I found?" Alace rose from the chair, leaving the gun on the seat and watched as his eyes flickered down and back up. *Not for you, boyo*. "Who I've talked to? Where I've been?" Tongue tisking in false sympathy, she looked at him and softened her expression with a slow shake of her head back and forth. "No, Alace it's good to see you? No, who's the lucky guy putting that glow on your face?" She shifted, feet braced strongly, leaning forwards at the waist, voice and features hardening. "You aren't going to ask me anything?"

"I did ask you. What do you want? You want something, I know. Everyone always wants something." Before he was even done speaking she was nodding.

"I want the past twelve years of my life back." He froze in place, and Alace shrugged. "Or at least the last five or so." She paused, studying him. "Or, maybe, just since Alabama. That'd be good. Can you give me that back? I'd take even that much."

"What are you talking about?"

"I'm talking about how you had this, all of this—" She pointed to the screens. "—and I've been doing what I've done." He looked genuinely puzzled, and Alace barked out a harsh laugh. "Holy shit. You don't get it. I told you. I'd met my one. Of course"—she affected an eye roll—"at the time I thought I knew what it meant to you. I know what it means to me. When I told you that, it meant I'd met the person who could heal me. Eric's helped me in ways he won't ever know, just by being with me when I needed it."

"Jesus, Alace." Now it was Regg who rolled his eyes, and she suppressed a grin at his attempt to create a posture resonance between them. *Oldest trick to gain confidence in a target, make them believe they're just like me. I'm just like them. Twinsies.* "It's not real. Nothing is real. Just like the little quirky personalities you put together to build a lie, we've been living lies for so long, it's all we've got." He took a step forwards, and Alace went on alert again, waiting. "Your life is a lie. You don't even exist in this world. No birth certificate, no history. I've wiped out what little of you there ever was. It's all a lie."

"Eric's not a lie. The lives I've ended weren't lies."

"Fucking hell, are you really this stupid? How are you this stupid?" It was his turn to shake his head. "I'm assuming you've gone through my things. So, after doing that, how can you not know that—" His torso inclined towards her an inch, increasing the sense of menace. "—the things I told you were lies. I deal in lies, it's what I do. I deal in them, you live them, and together we make things happen."

"No more. I'm done." His eyes widened and stayed fixed, pupils growing to cover nearly edge to edge, opaque white of his sclera and blackness, sucking in her words. Her words had terrified him. *The end of the golden goose?* "I won't be taking any more gigs."

"Is that what you came all the way out here to tell me? You could have said that on the phone." He pulled in a heavy breath, visibly attempting to control his palpable panic. "It's good to finally meet you, though." Regg took another step forwards, and Alace gestured with the Taser still in her hand, watching as his gaze landed on it and then saw him note and discard any belief she'd electrocute him with the device. Even knowing what she was, he clearly felt himself to be exempt. After everything said and implied in the past ten minutes, he still believed himself untouchable. He took another step and spoke again, voice pitched low to create a sense of intimacy. She knew this, after all, she'd used the tactic countless times. *Can't con a con woman.* "Alace, I've wanted to meet you for so long."

She was ready, and when Regg lunged, she stepped to the side and back towards the door, leaving him to fall across the chair and to the floor. He came up with the gun, the thing she'd known was his target through the whole act. Staring into his eyes, she aimed the Taser as he lifted the pistol, and the air in the small room was filled with the glittering sound of electrical discharge as Regg roared.

***

Regg

Jesus, she did it.

His thoughts scattered as his body thrashed against the hard floor, but Regg held onto the idea that Alace, his Alace had pulled the trigger. The sharp ticks from the Taser fell away, silence except for a bass groaning he realized came from his throat. As the spasms rocketing through his muscles began to subside, he realized she was still standing. No blood, no holes in her beautiful face. Still breathing. He lifted and gripped hard, finger tugging at the lever and heard the empty click of the gun in his hand.

Fuck.

She'd set him up, leaving an unloaded gun available. He'd fallen for it, never really expecting she'd hit him with the weapon. *No coming back from this.* He shoved that idea aside, playing for time.

Jaw clenched, a burning pain from the contact points still resonating throughout his body, he swore. "Fuck, Alace, you fucking shot me."

"You shot at me." Her voice quavered, and he looked to see disbelief on her face. He'd watched enough video of her to know this emotion was real and raw. She'd crafted the scene, but hadn't really expected what happened.

"No, I didn't. I fell and you hit me with that damn thing." He let the useless gun fall from his grip. "Instinct, that's all." Propping up on one arm, he wiped the sweat from his face with his sleeve. "Jesus, that fucking hurt."

"You shot at me." Stronger now, with a tone of anger bleeding through. *Gotta control this.* "You didn't fall, you went for the gun." Her back straightened with a snap and she stared down at him, face a cold mask. "I wondered, you know. When I saw what you did with the others." He licked his lips, trying to decide what tactic to take next, when she floored him with the depth of her knowledge. *Fucking hell, she'd found everything.* She gave him names, not only of his dead hunters, those individuals who hadn't lived up to the Alace legend, but also of the men he'd used to deal with his discards. Let the information fall from her lips like ritual prayers, threading in locations and other information, ages, and things he didn't even know. Children's names, wives, and loved ones.

"What are you saying?" Attacking was his only option. He had to get her off balance, tilted out of control so when he came at her next, he could topple her easily. "Are you saying I wanted to kill you?" He laughed, pulling his legs up and twisting so he knelt on the floor, one hand propped on the overturned chair. "I fucking made you. Why would I want to kill my greatest creation?"

"So now you're Frankenstein?" He startled, her words making no sense, and he wondered for a moment if the current had scrambled his brains.

"I'm not the monster, Alace." He scoffed, watching her eyes narrow into green slits at his words. "You are."

There was a dead silence in the room, and her voice had taken on a tone of amusement when she finally responded. "Frankenstein was the scientist. The one who dabbled in human flesh for his own amusement." Her head tilted to the side, gaze pinning him to the floor as effectively as any shackles. "You're right, I'm a monster. Regg's monster." She leaned back, shoulders against the locked door as she blocked the only egress from this hellhole, and shook her head. "You're done, Regg. Give it up and I'll go away. Just tell me, monster to monster, that you'll lay everything down and leave me alone."

"Leave you alone?" He was surging to his feet when the room swung around him and his head bounced hard against the floor. Flashes of light hit the inside of his eyelids, and he wrestled his eyes open to see her standing over him, hands held at the ready to attack again. A flicker of fear trailed down his spine, curling his balls tight to his body. He hadn't even seen her move. *Jesus, she's a freak.*

"Yes, Regg. Leave me alone." She answered him like there'd been no interruption in their conversation. "That's all I want. Your word."

There was a reason Regg worked best from behind a keyboard, where it was easier to temper a response, where words could be edited and shaped to fit a function. Where it was acceptable to spend time molding phrases to fit the need, toning down knee-jerk reactions. In person, his filters frequently malfunctioned. That was the case right now, addled by being electrocuted and the fall, he didn't consider how Alace would take his discard of her demand.

"Fuck you. You think you've got the upper hand? What do you think will happen when people find out about you? What do you think will happen to your precious Eric when they learn all about *you*? I know too much to back down, honey. You want me to give it up? Fuck you, you give it up."

"You leave Eric out of this." The tremor in her voice should have been a clue, but Regg didn't notice, pushing past what he took as a sound of weakness.

Certain he'd won, Regg thought, *She'll come crawling back.* "I'll fuck with him in ways you can't even conceive. You think you're the only hunter I know? Fuck you. I know hundreds, and I'll have them working on this job before you even get home. Hope you kissed him goodbye before you rolled out, honey, because that'll be the last you see of him. Ashes and death, that'll be what rains down over you the rest of your life." He lifted his head and spat, seeing the spatter of blood as it hit near her shoes. "Ashes and death, and you'll be sorry. You're gonna be so sorry you crossed me, Alace."

"Leave him out, Regg. I'm telling you now, he's off limits."

"You think you can make the rules? You? Alace Sweets? You can't make me do shit." She brought her hand out from behind her, and Regg had a moment to recognize the silhouette of the gun. "What—"

CHAPTER TWENTY-ONE

Alace

One hand on the wheel, the other propping her head up with an elbow to the window, Alace steered the car away from Regg's subdivision. Keeping her face blocked from the known camera locations, she took the back way out through a gate propped open by the local lawn service. In the distance, seen through the reflection of her rearview mirror, a black column of smoke rose from the ground. No flames were visible yet, but they'd come. The smoke was growing visibly larger, and it marked the result of her final handiwork.

In the front pocket of her jeans, heated by the blood still coursing through her body, was a flattened slug. She'd dug the bloodstained metal out of the mess left behind.

Regg had made a critical mistake, one he hadn't recognized until it was entirely too late to save him.

He'd threatened Eric.

For once, she was glad the radio didn't work in this car. The enforced silence left her unable to divert her brain from what had happened.

Through the hours of driving, she turned the events over repeatedly in her mind, struggling with grief and rage. First the anger at finding out the depth of Regg's deceit, then the fear of knowing he'd actively recruited a man to have her killed.

As she'd dragged the body to his bedroom, top half bagged to contain the blood and brain matter she'd scooped up to stage the scene, she had systematically run through every moment of their encounter. Trying, even after it was set in stone, to see the point where she could have altered the outcome. The series of decisions that could have led to a different path.

Through her labors to first, place Regg's body so it looked like he'd been overcome by smoke, crushed by a dresser turned over in his distress, then on to the dismantling of the cameras she'd placed, undoing her work in every way, she'd tried to pick apart her actions as well as his, to no avail. There were simply no other outcomes she could see, not without altering Regg's intent. Into her bag had gone the hard drives, cameras, gun, Taser, and the paper documentation she'd taken from Regg's in-floor safe. Alace had spent precious time beginning the scramble and wipe sequence she'd already queued up on Regg's systems.

Killing Regg had always been an option, albeit an outside one, and Alace had planned for every possible outcome from today.

She had relocked the safe and then left Regg's workroom open as she tinkered with his vehicle. With the hood up and the car's grimy engine exposed, it had been the work of moments to damage the battery cables, creating the illusion of ill maintenance. She then had used a blade to scrape the insulation off a section of wiring harness, grounding it against the car's frame. The same blade created a small hole in a fuel line, positioned alongside the damaged wiring. She'd let it drip as she finished her work, gone outside to deal with the remaining cameras there. When she'd come back inside, the smell of gasoline had been strong, and she'd gathered up her bag and placed it just outside, where it would be easy to grab on her way back to her car.

Standing in his garage, she'd gone back over everything, ticking off a list in her head, ensuring she'd not forgotten anything that could potentially lead back to her. The time of death would be close enough to the house burning that it shouldn't be a problem, and she felt she'd done Regg's kids a favor by going that route. She could have staged it as a suicide, and with the breakdown of his marriage, it would have been believable. His kids would have had to live with that, though.

Lena's words echoed through her head, and Alace blinked. Maybe there was one last secret to untangle. Who was Lena's father, and how did Regg enter her life? Information was always good.

"Is it better to never know?" Alace's muttered question was whipped from her lips and out the window, rushing air through the car displacing the sounds with ease.

She'd stayed long enough after pushing the button on the car's remote start to see the flames licking along the garage floor under the vehicle, eagerly feasting on the fuel spilled there, crawling up the inside of the wheel well to chew along the wiring and tubing, breaking through and releasing even more caustic and flammable liquids.

The wording on a sign caught her attention as it flew past; Denver was only a couple of hours away.

What is Eric going to do?

That one question had been preying on her mind since she began making the trek home. *Is it still home?* Was she fooling herself about this feeling between them? They'd run hot together, and the connection was undeniable, but still she wondered if it could be sustainable. *He loves me.* Could that love withstand truly understanding what she did? The details as she'd laid out for him in the cabin? The story she was bringing home in her head?

Shut up, she told herself, *you're tired and it was a trying day.* Alace blinked, eyes stinging. *Trying. More like fucking devastating.*

She'd expected a lot of what she found, but some things were harder to swallow than others. She'd always known Regg was cold and calculating when it came to the work they did together. But seeing the look on his face made her question if she'd ever had a friend in him. *Was it wishful thinking? Me needing a stable connection, since every day of my life has been transient?* Here today, gone tomorrow. That's how she'd lived for so long, making a space for herself in Eric's life and house had been like sinking into a soft bed. Comfortable and supportive, something she didn't want to lose.

I won't lose him. He cares about me for me, not for what I can do. Certainty settled into her soul as she allowed herself to believe, finally. Eric was with her because of who she was. The damaged parts of her didn't frighten him. Breath clotted in her chest, she was overwhelmed for a moment with the knowledge. It could be storming all around them, embers falling from the sky as things fell apart and Eric would still love her. She knew he was waiting, and in her mind, she could imagine what he was doing, nearly see how he would be pacing his living room restlessly, eyes aimed to the windows as he watched for her to come home. *I'm on my way, honey.*

Alace lifted her chin, aiming the car towards Denver, foot heavier on the gas as she pushed the vehicle harder. For once, she didn't worry about drawing unneeded attention and found this reality freeing. She was just herself in this moment, and regardless what Regg had thought, she'd faithfully protected this identity through the years, which meant Alace Sweets was above reproach.

The only thing that mattered was going home. To Eric.

***

Eric

Forcing himself to patiently wait for Alace to come to him was one of the hardest things Eric had ever done. Every fiber of his being was shouting for him to rush outside and greet her, at the least to fling the door open and show her he was waiting. He knew from experience that sent the wrong message for the right reasons, highlighting his fears that one day she might choose not to return home. That he'd spent their time apart in dread. Those thoughts were gone, now.

He knew. She'd always come back to him.

So for Eric, waiting for her to finish the journey all the way home was his way of telling her he trusted her. He believed in them.

Her car door slammed, and a moment later, he heard the scraping of her key at the lock. "It's open," he called, his voice ragged and scratchy from disuse. The door swung open immediately, Alace silhouetted against the brilliance outside. Arms spread wide, he held his breath, blowing it out in a silent sigh as she ran to him.

A moment later, her arms were around his neck, fingers winding through his hair, and he felt the sharp stinging of her tug when she pulled his head down for a kiss. Eric gave in for a moment, let her control things for a breath, then two, and then he lifted her off her feet, arms around her waist and hips, bringing her up to meet his mouth as he crushed her lips with his.

She would always be his.

CHAPTER TWENTY-TWO

Alace

Bending at the waist, Alace yanked at the tank for the grill, lifting the empty unit from the enclosure and setting the full one in its place. She quickly manipulated the connections and turned on the controls, listening for a moment to hear the rush of gas escaping before turning it off. "Grill's ready," she called, knowing Eric would hear her through the open patio doors.

She was nervous. Uncharacteristically so. Today marked their six-month anniversary, and two weeks ago, Eric had announced it was past time for her to meet his friends. *Shoot me now.*

Trying to assuage her fears, he'd cuddled with her this morning, arms wrapped around and holding her close, his cock still buried inside her as he said, "You already know my mom, baby. We've done this all backwards. My buds are the easy part."

Their outings together hadn't been without drama. There had been random encounters with people who had known her as Querida. Alace rolled her eyes, turning the knob again and flicking the lighter with her thumb, watching as the gas burners were surrounded by blue flames. They'd known it would happen. She'd worked in the two places in town guaranteed to bring Eric into her path, after all, picked since both the bar and diner were popular places, which ensured a lot of the community had known her by sight, at least.

So Alace had to reinvent herself—again—but this time it was her real self she was inventing. Odd, but doable. She and Eric had spent hours in bed and on the couch coming up with possible scenarios. Undercover cop was out, not that it wasn't a cool idea, but mostly it was too easy to verify—or refute. So was an investigative reporter, since that one could lead people into places she'd rather they not go. After much debate, she'd settled on writing as a profession, at least one she could talk about. Using that, she could also play coy about a pen name, and no one would blink an eye.

A few of Eric's friends had even stumbled on them out for a drink or meal, so the crew coming today wouldn't be all new faces.

But all the important people in Eric's life would be here. His boss—who was, by the way, the district attorney for Douglas County—that man's wife, several college buddies, Eric's working cohort in the DA's office...and his best friend. Todd Worthson, who also happened to be a sitting judge, and the one person who knew what it had taken for Eric to find her. Todd had proven instrumental in the weeks and months after she'd first bugged out, when she was already on the job down in Alabama. Of everyone who would be invading—she had to keep reminding herself to not think of it that way, they were invited guests—their home, he was the biggest threat.

Todd Worthson could bring it all tumbling down around her ears.

She didn't think he would, but the fact remained he could.

Alace pulled in a breath and blew it out, closed the lid on the grill and turned towards the house in time to see Eric walking out, tongs in hand.

"Move over, woman. Grillin' is a man's work." He crowded her, getting close enough to brush his chest against her breasts before he bent his neck. She lifted to her toes, fingers digging into the sides of his waist as she kissed him. "Mmmm. Maybe don't move it. Maybe you need to stay right here." His lips caressed hers as he murmured, "Love you, baby."

He did. She never doubted it anymore. He'd proven her fears groundless, bringing her back to center, time and again.

"Love you more." She felt his lips move and knew by the crinkles at the corners of his beautiful eyes he was smiling down at her. Something she could see every day for the rest of her life and never tire of. "Now," she lifted that scant inch again and kissed him, "get to grillin', honey. Guests will be here soon."

"Hello, the house," she heard and froze in place, Eric chuckling at her reaction. Turning, she saw a man walk out, tall and broad, his carriage confident, stride long in jeans that fit him well. "Hey, man." He was pacing towards them, and Alace shifted to the side, going to give them some space, her attempts foiled when Eric's arm closed tight around her, pulling her close as he moved to meet their guest.

"Todd," Eric said, warmth in his voice. Alace examined his friend intently. Todd looked different from the official pictures she'd studied, more laidback, resembling the man in the photos Eric had from vacation trips together. He didn't quite present himself like a judge, with his too-long hair and easy smile. She realized he was staring back at her, corners of his mouth curling up into a boyish grin.

"Damn, E. She's gorgeous."

"Told you." Eric's arm gave her a squeeze. "No date?"

"Nope. She couldn't make it." Todd shrugged, tucking his hands deep into his pockets. "Story of my life, man."

Alace thoughtfully studied the two of them, watching as their conversation casually volleyed back and forth.

"Which one was this?" Eric led her away, and she glanced over her shoulder to see Todd following them towards the grill. She had no doubt Eric had arranged this, made it so the one person she was most nervous about meeting showed first, giving her time to settle down without a bigger audience. She relaxed into him and felt him press a kiss to the top of her head as she gave him her weight.

"That blonde from the corner store." Todd helpfully lifted the lid on the grill, as comfortable in Eric's backyard as if he hadn't stayed away for half a year at Eric's request. "Got a beer?"

Alace decided it was time to join the conversation, time to carve her space out of this friendship between the two men. "There's a full cooler in the house. I just need to add ice. I'll bring you one." Tipping her head up, she caught sight of Eric's smile and noted he looked even more at ease, lines of stress disappearing. *He was nervous about this, too*, she realized.

"Okay, baby." He gave her a squeeze and released her.

Alace was dumping a bag of ice into the opened cooler when she heard footsteps at the door and tipped her head up, freezing in place when she saw Todd. He studied her for a moment, and as he did so, his happy façade fell away, a tension flowing back into his features revealing to her the man who sat on a tall seat in ponderous robes. He stood there looking at her, and Alace felt his judgment was balancing on the edge, ready to go either way.

"I love him." She blurted this to a man she didn't know, but who meant the world to Eric.

"I know you do. He loves you, too." She nodded, but Todd wasn't done. "Can you keep him safe?"

That one question told her he knew much more than Eric had let on to her. Todd knew who she'd been, might even have an inkling of who she might need to be again. She was exploring ideas about how to put her unique skills to work in a better way, but those plans were still in their infancy, wishful thinking more than plans, if she were honest. Todd knew what she'd been might put his friend at risk, and she needed to reassure him without giving away things he might not already have guessed.

"I can." She didn't promise, didn't have to, her gut telling her confidence was the right path, and she saw the muscles in Todd's jaw relax a tiny amount. He looked at her for a long moment, gaze flicking back and forth across her face, and finally he nodded, accepting her statement at face value. She straightened, closing the lid on the cooler and shoved it an inch towards him. "Can you carry that for me?" Moving past the intense moment they'd shared, she needed Todd out of her space so she could breathe. For all she might appear carefree, fear still clotted her veins, making her heart race in her chest.

"Sure can." He hefted the container, bottles and cans shifting inside, clinking quietly against each other as they adjusted to find the best fit alongside their neighbors. "Eric said he'll be ready for the meat soon." She nodded, gaze still locked on his, knowing instinctively he wasn't done. "I like you, Alace. I like you for Eric. He was pretty intense for a while, and I think you know why. I'm damned glad he found you, and I'm even more glad you're here, now. He needed something, and it looks like you're it."

With that surprise pronouncement, Todd turned and stalked away while Alace stood and stared, mouth open, speechless for once.

***

Eric

"You're certain?" He pressured Todd for confirmation, wanting verification before he allowed himself to believe in his friend's words.

"Yeah, I'm sure. Not just redacted, but deleted, and where they couldn't be deleted, they're buried under a thousand pages of bullshit. She's vapor, man."

Todd had been working on erasing not just the traces of Eric's pursuit of Alace, those crumbs left behind when someone was searching and stirring up old information, but on the absolute clearing of the evidence that had led him to Alabama in the first place. It had been slow going, taking months longer than Eric wanted, but he'd known Todd was the only person he trusted to handle it.

No one else in his life knew the full breadth of what Eric had been willing to do to find Alace. Todd knew not only that, but everything. That had been a tense conversation, one filled with danger. If Todd had chosen the high road, Eric couldn't have stopped him. It would have cost Eric an open life with Alace, and he knew it. He also knew he needed to be honest with the one man who'd had his back through their entire lives. *Closer than brothers.*

No surprise when Todd chose the path of support, deciding to trust Eric's judgment, even as he'd been ruthless about his questioning. He'd demanded to know everything, and Eric gave it to him. It had taken time, but eventually knowing Alace's background, what had happened to her, and Eric's unfailing belief in what he'd found with her had been enough to convince Todd.

So when he'd approached him about this task, Eric had known it wouldn't be an issue. He was glad to know he'd been right.

"Thanks aren't enough." Eric reached out, gripping Todd's shoulder firmly, shaking him slightly. "I owe you."

Todd didn't respond, just flashed a grin that Eric found himself returning with profound relief.

All of that was now officially in the past, and he and Alace could move forwards.

He couldn't wait to see what the future brought them.

EPILOGUE

Nine years, eight months

Alace

Laying back on the poolside lounge that was arranged to give the best possible view of the ocean stretching out towards the horizon, Alace grinned at the constant babble of conversation that filled the background. Rough fingers found hers, and she didn't have to turn to know they belonged to her husband. He gave a squeeze, then laughed while he started a running commentary on what was happening in his mother's kitchen.

"Bebe's in heaven, beloved." Alace knew that to be true, Phoebe had confided as much to her yesterday when they'd arrived for a visit. Seeing her grandchildren always brought her an undeniable joy, so much it made Alace's throat clog with tears every time. "She's got both Lila and Tracey on stepstools helping her bake what appears to be a cake. This might be a failed endeavor. We'll have to wait and see. But I would argue there might be more batter on our children than in the bowl at this point." Eric's voice vibrated with humor. "She loves it, baby. I've never seen my mother this happy."

Alace twisted, looking over her shoulder at the scene unfolding before her. Tall, elegant Phoebe was bracketed on either side by a child, each with Eric's golden-brown hair, and though she couldn't tell from this distance, Alace knew their faces held his eyes, too. Eight-year-old Lila and her five-year-old little sister loved their grandmother to distraction, counting down the days between visits with all the intensity children brought to everyday life.

Movement to the side pulled her attention, and she turned, smiling as Eric's face grew near, closing her eyes when his lips brushed hers in a soft caress.

"God, I love you," she whispered when he pulled back, and got to see one of her favorite things happen as Eric's eyes lit from within. He bent back to her and kissed her again, this one hard and closed-mouthed, powerful. Possessive. As always. She grinned.

"I love you, too." His fingers squeezed again, then disappeared, the heat and pressure of his palm reappearing on her belly. "Are you ready to tell her the news yet?"

Alace shook her head, smiling at him. "Not yet. I want to hold off another couple of weeks." She heard her phone buzz once, then a second and third time, quick on the heels of the first.

Eric sighed and shook his head, tracing along her cheek with the tip of his nose. "You see to that. I'll go make sure my mother isn't promising the girls their own ponies." Horses had become Tracey's latest thing, with her profession declarations running the gamut from veterinarian to mounted police. She was always on the go, and the more fraught with danger the activity, the bigger her smile. Lila was their sensitive, quiet child, the one who seemed destined for a career in the arts. The stories she spun during quiet times were intricate and detailed, and Alace found herself wanting to capture them in some way. She rolled her eyes. *Since I'm a writer and all, you'd think I'd know how to do that.*

She shifted, put her feet on the cement apron surrounding the pool, and reached for her phone. She studied the alerts for a moment, then called to Eric as she stood, "I've got to get on the computer. I'll be as fast as I can."

He grunted, moving at her side towards the house, and she glanced up to see he was still smiling, focused on his mother with their children. "Lemme know if you need longer, baby."

Walking beside him, she leaned close, wrapping her arms around his waist and pressing her lips to his bicep. "Will do." Passing through the kitchen, she moved close to the girls and kissed the sides of their heads loudly. "Back in a jiffy, my babies."

In their bedroom, Alace retrieved her bag, taking out a laptop and battery. She assembled and booted the device up, waiting for it to cycle through the various checks she'd built into the operating system. Logging in took another series of keystrokes, with multiple factor authentication just to get into the computer, and then another series of cryptic connections to get to the system that had sent the alerts.

Scanning the messages, she found what she was looking for and took her time reading, then re-reading, flipping back and forth to review other data before she responded. Sending a series of texts, she informed the recipient of her take on the situation, giving an educated opinion on what should happen next.

Alace spent another thirty minutes checking in, looking through uploaded documents on a variety of cases she was currently managing. She then sorted additional nonurgent requests, prioritizing them to review in closer detail later tonight.

Alace had taken Regg's place.

Sort of.

Accepting a new role in the ecosystem of reprisals, she had garnered the respect of the community by cultivating hunters with an exceptional sense of honor, the only way she would consent to work with anyone. She still wasn't driven by the money, even if it was good. Half of all she earned went to charity, same as it always had. No, what got her blood rushing was the chance to set right things that had gone badly awry. Making a difference in the life of a victim, and along the way ensuring serial offenders lost any opportunity to continue their path of pain.

She'd never gone back out on a gig personally, having retired from that aspect entirely. But with Regg's contacts in hand, shifting her part to the one coordinating resources for a successful end had turned out to be unexpectedly rewarding. She knew Eric had worried. A lot. And he wasn't wrong in his concern. After spending so long going from challenge to challenge, with the wash of adrenaline a constant companion, Alace knew there would be no life in which she could be "normal." The biggest barrier was taking what she needed and mixing it with what was available, and doing it in a way that left her fulfilled while letting Eric get behind it without having to wrestle with his conscience every step of the way. His ethics weren't something she was willing to sacrifice, so she'd struggled until she finally found a balance that suited them both. Revenge wasn't only couched in final terms. Sometimes making them live with what they'd done was sweeter.

Writing was still her camouflage, covering a wide array of disappearances and odd occurrences. No one in town—save Todd, who she was convinced knew *everything*—had a clue that Douglas County was harboring the mastermind behind some of the most nationally-famous arrests of the past decade.

Within an hour, she was back in the kitchen, laughing aloud at the image of Eric standing next to his mother with cake batter smeared across his cheek and spoon in hand while their children ran laughing through the house.

Walking to him, Alace swiped a finger through the chocolate and tucked it into her mouth, savoring both the flavor and the heat that darkened his whiskey-brown eyes, thinking she could watch the hunger build on his face for at least seventeen lifetimes. *He is just so damned ...*

"Sweet."

~

THANK YOU FOR READING *Alace Sweets!*

ABOUT THE AUTHOR

Raised in the south, MariaLisa learned about the magic of books at an early age. Every summer, she would spend hours in the local library, devouring books of every genre. Self-described as a book-a-holic, she says "I've always loved to read, but then I discovered writing, and found I adored that, too. For reading...if nothing else is available, I've been known to read the back of the cereal box."

Also by MariaLisa deMora

Hard Focus

This is an intense page-turner, a gut-punch twist-filled story about a woman who has confidence in herself, believes she's a good judge of character, and has filled her life with people she can trust. She's right, but she's also very, very wrong. Readers will have a time of it trying to decide who to watch closest.

Where do you place your trust when your own instincts betray you?

Connie Rowe is a receptionist at a respected legal firm. She's a little bit sassy, a lotta bit happy, has good friends, and is adored by her neighbors.

Life is good.

She's got a boyfriend she enjoys spending time with. He can be a little intense, but he's got a lot going on in his own life, sorting out his young daughter and nightmare of an ex.

Life is grand.

"Trust your gut." That's what Connie's police officer father told her often, training his daughter to believe in herself through the years.

But … what happens when you can't? When your intuition lies?

What happens when things come into Hard Focus?

5-Star Reviews for Hard Focus

"Hard Focus is one very well-written tale. 5 stars is not enough for me."
~Tabitha

"What a powerful story. [deMora] kept me invested from the first word to the last."
~Jesse R

"[deMora] has a certain magical touch to writing her characters, that they become either your nemesis, your best friend, or your love interest. That is certainly portrayed in this spin around. Loved it, loved it, loved it."
~Sandy K

"I strongly recommend this book for both entertainment and to broaden your knowledge of certain laws that must be revisited."
~Words Turn Me On

"A intense page turner. Once you start, you can't put the book down."
~Tracey H

"A beautifully written, powerful read that I can't rate highly enough. This story will stay with me always."
~Gayle

"This book had twists I didn't see coming. Loved it!"

~Lori R

"Wow! I am in awe of deMora's skill in crafting this story."
~Kat W

"I keep sayin that there just aren't enough stars to give to some of Marialisa deMora's books...this one is no different!"
~deLane

"Where do I start with this one...I read this in 3 1/2 hours uninterrupted, I absolutely could NOT put it down. Very deep, keeps you guessing, what's gonna happen next, kind of book. I love how strong her characters are, especially the females!"
~Wendy I

"Sometimes I feel like MariaLisa deMora is the one I should be watching out for. I started reading her books because I'm addicted to MC Romance, but then she decides to change things up and I just follow her wherever she leads me like a Pied Piper. I never know what to expect, and sometimes I'm afraid to find out, but it's always an adventure."
~Rosa for iScream Books Blog

"A plot full of twists and turns, a story that's not quite what it seems, strong characterization, jaw dropping revelations... what more do you need from a book?"
~Manda M

"This book kept me turning the pages wondering what was going to happen. I am usually pretty good at guessing twists but not with this book. She totally surprised me and brought me out of my funk. 5 stars."
~Glenna M

"What an amazing story! Filled with a smidge of suspense, a dash of action and a heap of realism of our country's laws and how their vague application to victims can adversely affect its citizens and the people in their lives."
~Naughty Mom Story Time

ADDITIONAL SERIES AND BOOKS

Please note that books in a series frequently feature characters from additional books within that series. If series books are read out of order, readers will twig to spoilers for the other books, so going back to read the skipped titles won't have the same angsty reveals.

Rebel Wayfarers MC series:

Mica, #1
A Sweet & Merry Christmas, short story #1.5
Slate, #2
Bear, #3
Jase, #4
Gunny, #5
Mason, #6
Hoss, #7
Harddrive Holidays, short story #7.5
Duck, #8
Biker Chick Campout, short story #8.5
Watcher, #9
A Kiss to Keep You, novella #9.25
Gun Totin' Annie, short story #9.5
Secret Santa, short story #9.75
Bones, #10
Gunny's Pups, novella #10.25
Never Settle, short story #10.5
Not Even A Mouse, short story #10.75
Fury, #11
Christmas Doings, #11.25
Gypsy's Lady, #11.5
Cassie, #12
Road Runner's Ride, novella #12.5

Occupy Yourself band series:

> *Born Into Trouble*, #1
> *Grace In Motion*, #2 (TBD)
> *What They Say*, #3 (TBD)

Neither This, Nor That series:

> *This Is the Route Of Twisted Pain*, #1
> *Treading the Traitor's Path: Out Bad*, #2
> *Trapped by Fate on Reckless Roads*, #3 (TBD)

Other Books:

> *With My Whole Heart*
> *Alace Sweets*
> *Hard Focus*

More information available at mldemora.com.